2

The Girl from
Kingsland Market

The Girl from Kingsland Market

June Tate

Allison & Busby Limited
11 Wardour Mews
London W1F 8AN
allisonandbusby.com

First published in Great Britain by Allison & Busby in 2019.

A CIP catalogue record for this book is available from
the British Library.

First Edition

ISBN 978-0-7490-2488-8

Typeset in 11/16 pt Sabon LT Pro by
Allison & Busby Ltd.

The paper used for this Allison & Busby publication
has been produced from trees that have been legally sourced
from well-managed and credibly certified forests.

Printed and bound by
CPI Group (UK) Ltd, Croydon, CR0 4YY

*To Stefan and Mark Field
with love*

Chapter One

Southampton 1920

Phoebe Collins stood beside her fruit and vegetable stall in Kingsland Market, rubbing her cold hands together. Her mittens were not enough to totally keep out the sharp chill in the late November air, but she needed to have her fingers free to pick up her wares and serve her customers. She straightened the cabbages, polished the apples until the skins shone, moved the carrots around, picked out the few that were shrivelled and threw them into the basket beneath the stall. These, and other wasted bits, she would slip to the children who came scavenging at the end of the day to help feed their dirt-poor families.

This had been her father's stall for many years, and she'd helped to run it with him, but he'd lost his life in the Great War at the Battle of the Somme and she'd run it alone ever since. The war had been over for two years now, and times were hard. At nineteen, she'd had no other choice. She was good at selling and had managed to make a living – albeit a small one – ever since. Her mother took in washing to add to their income at the same time looking after her brother, Timothy, or Tim as they called him. He was ten and still at school, but on a Saturday, he'd come along and help her.

Kingsland Market was set up in a square, well lit from the surrounding streetlights, with many different stalls. Some were selling second-hand clothes, there was the Jones family with their pots and pans and kitchen equipment and Milly Coates with her home-made cakes and jams. On one stall Len Black, a cobbler, was at work with a boot over a last, hammering on a new set of soles, and there was Tony Jackson with his ironmongery. There were others with various goods and some selling fruit and vegetables too, but there was a camaraderie between them all. The banter could be quite saucy sometimes, but everybody was there to make a living.

Next to Phoebe's stall was Marjory Simmons, or Marj as she was known, a middle-aged woman of ample proportions and a heart as big as her body. She sold second-hand clothes, but they had to be in good condition and she was very adamant about that.

'Bloody cold today, girl, ain't it? Proper brass monkey weather. Thank the Lord it ain't raining. 'Ere, I've got a 'alf decent jumper that would fit you. You can 'ave it for a tanner.' She held it up for Phoebe to see. It was cream, made of heavy wool, with a polo neck. Phoebe looked at it and thought it was ideal for keeping out the winter weather. She handed over a sixpence and took it.

'Thanks, Marj, it's just what I need.' She put it to one side to wash and wear when it was dry.

At night Phoebe would take down the canvas top that covered her stall, then wheel it to a lock-up she'd rented on the edge of the market, where it would be secure until the following morning. Once a week, she'd go along to the wholesalers to buy her stock and barter ferociously about the prices.

She and her family lived in a two-up two-down council house in a tough area of the town. Not that it seemed that way to her, after all she'd lived there all her life so to her it was simply home. It wasn't that she was unaware of her surroundings. She knew that in the next street there was a brothel in a house rented by two girls, and she also knew to keep clear of the Stanley brothers who lived in the area and worked in the market. Their stall was full of second-hand goods bought from house sales. Lamps, furniture, china, bric-a-brac and a few antiques. Anything that would bring in a shilling or two. They were small-time villains, into anything illegal that would bring in money, but they were cunning, clever and ruthless. Always one step ahead of the law. Percy was the eldest at thirty. A dour-looking man who seldom smiled. He would look at you with a steely glare that was enough to chill your blood. His brother, Arthur, was twenty-three, reasonably good-looking with an eye for the ladies, but who had to do as he was told by his dictatorial brother.

Phoebe, aware that she was alone at night, carrying money after she closed, was prepared for all eventualities and always carried a long hatpin in the lapel of her coat, and hidden on her stall was a small cudgel, just in case of trouble.

It was Friday, pay day for those who were employed, and tomorrow was their busiest day, with families stocking up for the week ahead. Early every Saturday morning a butcher's horse-driven van would arrive and set up. Chickens and rabbits would hang from hooks at the open back of the van; on a long table in front would be displayed cuts of meat laid out ready for sale. Those who could afford it bought decent cuts, others would buy up scrag ends of mutton and bones to make a broth.

The upper classes would shop in the town centre, but Kingsland Market was where those who had little money or those looking for a bargain would do their buying.

'Mind your backs!' came a cry in a gruff male voice as Percy Stanley pushed a barrow through the middle of the market towards his stall. Sometimes the brothers would use a horse-driven vehicle when they had furniture to sell after going to a house clearance or sale. They would give the horse a nosebag to keep it quiet and would often have to clear up its mess with a shovel at the end of the day.

Every now and then the police would walk through the market, chatting to the stallholders and always stopping longer at the brothers' stall, which they searched for stolen goods. Percy would take delight in baiting them, knowing that there was nothing untoward for sale. Any stolen goods were well hidden elsewhere and trading for those was done very carefully at night, in different locations.

Whereas the police would exchange friendly banter with most of the traders, with the Stanley brothers their demeanour was quite different. They had no respect for these men, and it was a challenge among the men in the force to be the ones to eventually catch the brothers in their illegal deals and put them behind bars.

Percy was being his usual belligerent self as the constables looked through the goods on sale. 'Find anything dodgy, did you, then?'

One of the men looked at him with distaste. 'You'll end up behind bars one day, Percy. It will be my pleasure to see you locked away. Inside you may learn some manners and respect.'

Percy just laughed.

'Every villain makes a mistake one day, and on that day, I'll be just behind you!' snapped one of the policemen as he walked away.

Percy just muttered a few expletives as he watched the men leave.

Eventually it was time to close. Phoebe took down the canvas cover from its poles, laid it on top of her stall. She gave a bag of fruit and vegetables to a scruffy little lad who was looking longingly at the fruit and was hovering nearby, then she wheeled her cart away, locked up for the night and walked home.

Her mother, Mary was folding laundry when she opened the door and stepped into the room. The air felt damp from the washing and Phoebe put some wooden logs into the small grate of the range to dry out the room and made herself and her mother a cup of tea, pouring the boiling water from the kettle on the hob over the fire of the blackleaded stove. Tim was sitting at the table eating a bowl of hearty chicken and vegetable soup with a thick slice of bread and dripping.

Phoebe sat beside the fire, holding her frozen hands out to the warmth, rubbing them together to help the circulation. It was good to be inside after such a long cold day. She removed her high-buttoned boots and then her stockings, plus a pair of socks, pouring some of the hot water into a bowl, adding a little cold water, then putting her feet into the bowl. She sat back in the chair and sighed.

'I can't tell you just how good that feels. I've not been able to feel my feet all afternoon.'

'I know how you feel,' said her mother. 'No good me trying to dry the clothes in the backyard, they just freeze solid. The spring can't come soon enough for me. Get yourself some soup, that'll help warm you.'

Phoebe did so and sat at the table beside Tim. 'You going to give me a hand in the morning?'

He smiled at her. He loved being in the market. He was a good-looking boy and polite and the ladies loved him. Marj spoilt him whenever he was there, slipping him sweets. It gave the lad something to look forward to.

'Of course,' he said, 'make sure to wake me when you get up.'

'I will – you wrap up warm. I don't want you freezing to death!' She rubbed his tousled hair as she spoke. He was a good lad and Phoebe hoped he'd be able to find a decent job when he eventually left school. He was bright and, in her mind, being a market trader wasn't good enough for him. He was worth a better future.

'Best get off to bed, Tim. We have an early start in the morning. I'll not be long behind you.'

She and her mother shared a bed and Tim had the other room. There was no bathroom, so on a Sunday, when the market was closed, they would haul in the tin bath, fill it with water and take it in turns to bathe. The toilet was outside and on such cold days, no one was in a rush to use it, hanging on until the last moment. In the market they used public toilets, which were a deal more comfortable, housed in a brick building instead of a shed, which let in the cold.

Phoebe, once warm, sat down and ate; it had been a long day and she was hungry. She eventually rose from her chair. 'I'm tired so I'm off to bed, Mum. I'll buy some meat tomorrow for the weekend. If we make a stew, it'll last us a couple of days. Do you need anything else?'

'No, love, that'll do. I'll be up in a while after I've ironed these sheets.' She covered the kitchen table with a heavy cloth and put out two flat irons, placing one on top of the stove to heat up. 'I'll try not to disturb you.'

Phoebe chuckled. 'You'd have a job! I'm so tired I could sleep on a clothes line.' So saying, she went into the kitchen, swilled her face, cleaned her teeth, then made her way upstairs, undressed and climbed into bed, snuggled under the blankets, knowing that tomorrow would be a busy day.

Chapter Two

While Phoebe was sleeping, the Stanley brothers were inside a small garage on the outskirts of the town, checking the goods stacked against the walls. There were pieces of antique furniture, small statues, paintings and different artefacts of value that were a part of their stolen goods. Percy was ticking off various items on the list, looking pleased with himself as he did so.

'This lot should bring a pretty price,' he said to his brother.

'When are they being collected?' Arthur asked. 'We don't want them hanging around for much longer or the Old Bill will get wind of this place.'

'Len Taylor is coming down from the Smoke tomorrow night, around eight, so don't worry. This lot will be gone then. Will you stop your fretting! We don't use this place often and we're careful that we're not followed. I'm not stupid!'

Knowing his brother's hot temper, Arthur backed off. 'I know that. It's just that until we get rid of the stuff it's always a bit of a worry. That's all.'

Percy muttered to himself as he locked the doors. Outside were two bicycles the men used. They were less conspicuous than any other means of transport and easier to hide.

'Come on, let's go home. We'll leave the bikes there and then I'll buy you a beer before the pubs close.'

They eventually strolled to the Horse and Groom in East Street on the corner of Canal Walk, known as The Ditches. Not a salubrious part of town. It was here that the brasses plied their trade, where the dregs of the male population gathered. Villains met and illegal deals were done undercover. Drink-fuelled fights broke out with great regularity.

The brothers ordered two pints of bitter and sat in a corner away from other customers. No one bothered them. They kept very much to themselves. In their line of business, it didn't pay to become friends with outsiders. That way, no one could be bribed or threatened to give away any information about them. Apart from which, once crossed they were dangerous. In the past one or two chancers had tried to cheat them and had ended up floating in the docks. Nothing against the boys had ever been proven and so they were free to carry on with their way of life – so far.

At six o'clock the following morning, Phoebe was woken by the sound of the alarm. She reached out to shut it off before her mother was disturbed. Getting out of bed, she went into the other room and woke her brother.

'Get dressed, Tim. I'll get us some breakfast and put on a kettle for a wash, then we'll be on our way.'

When the boy came downstairs, Phoebe had raked the fire and thrown on some coal and wood to build the heat, made some porridge and was holding some bread up against the fire on a toasting fork.

Tim sat and ate his breakfast while his sister washed and then he did the same. After clearing the dishes, they left the house and headed for the market. It was dark as they walked and Phoebe carried a torch to use until they reached her lock-up. Other traders were doing the same but at this time in the morning they were all too busy to make much conversation except to say hello and grumble about the cold.

However, once they had settled on their patches, there was a buzz among the traders, especially the ladies, as there was a new trader on the square. A tall young man, well wrapped up against the weather with a scarf around his neck and a woollen hat pulled well down over his head, not revealing much of his face but enough to show his handsome features. His stall was selling men's clothes. Jackets, heavy-duty shirts in check, normal white shirts, vests, long johns, leather belts, bracers and socks. He smiled and greeted everyone with a cheery, 'Good morning', but that was all.

Marj sidled up to Phoebe. 'Bloody 'ell! I wish I was a few years younger, love. I'd soon 'ave 'im in my bed!' Her raucous laughter rang out over the square.

'Marj! Behave yourself,' chided Phoebe but she started laughing.

'You could do worse, love. You should get in there

while you can. A good-looking girl like you should 'ave no trouble.'

'I don't know who he is! Besides I'm happy as I am, thank you.'

Marj peered at her. 'Maybe so, but a good man beside you is a great comfort. A bit of love makes the world go round.' She glanced across at the newcomer. 'I didn't know there was a vacancy for a new stall. I wonder who 'e is?'

'No doubt we'll soon find out. You know what stallholders are like, they want to know who is on their patch. We don't need to worry, he's not selling the same goods as us.'

The Stanley brothers were curious too. Any stranger was looked upon with suspicion.

'Have you ever seen him before?' Percy asked his brother.

'No, never. Best keep an eye on him, I don't like strangers, they make me nervous.'

It was Tim who eventually spoke to the newcomer. During a lull, he amused himself by juggling with a couple of apples and dropped one which rolled towards the new stall. The stranger picked it up and handed it back to the boy.

'You won't be able to sell that now,' he said, 'it's bruised.' He nodded over to Phoebe. 'Your mother won't like that.'

Tim grinned. 'She's not my mother, she's my sister!'

'Oh my goodness, what a dreadful mistake! Please don't tell her, she would not be best pleased, I'm sure.'

'What's your name?' asked Tim.

'Ben, and you are?'

'Timothy, but everybody calls me Tim.'

The new trader held out his hand and shook Tim's. 'Happy to know you, Tim.'

Seeing her brother talking to the newcomer, Phoebe called to him to come back.

'Better go,' he said hearing his sister.

Ben leant forward. 'You won't drop me in it, will you? Your sister wouldn't be flattered to think I thought she was your mother.'

'No, I won't tell. Bye,' and he ran back to his stall.

'You mustn't bother the new man,' chided Phoebe.

'His name is Ben and he's really nice. He didn't mind at all, honestly.'

Phoebe looked over to the new stall. Ben smiled at her and held up his hand in greeting. Phoebe felt her cheeks flush, but she smiled back at him.

The day was busy as usual and Phoebe and Tim weighed the fruit and vegetables, putting them in brown paper bags before handing the goods to their customers, always with a cheery word. Tim was always polite, calling the ladies 'madam' and the men 'sir'. Sometimes, charmed by his manner, they would slip him a tip of a few pence, which he thanked them for and put into his pocket. Phoebe paid him a couple of shillings for helping out and this was on the understanding he didn't fritter it away. His tips were his to choose how they were spent.

At lunchtime, Phoebe sent her brother off to buy some fish and chips for their lunch, which they ate out of the paper between serving customers. It was a long day to be standing in the cold and a meal of some kind was a necessity.

Ben, the new stallholder, looked over and saw them eating. The look of longing didn't escape Phoebe and when they'd finished theirs, she sent Tim over to the man to ask if he wanted some as well.

'Oh Tim! You have been sent from heaven. I'm starving!' He fished in his pocket for some money and when Tim returned, he gave him sixpence for going, which delighted the boy.

'I can do this for you every Saturday if you like.'

The trader laughed. 'I can see you have an eye for business, young man. It's a deal.'

At the end of the day, the traders started to pack up their stalls, but Phoebe was having trouble undoing the canvas that covered hers. It had got twisted around the poles and she was struggling.

'Here, let me give you a hand, I'm taller than you.' Ben took the cover from her and soon untwisted it. He folded it neatly and handed it back to her.

'Thank you so much,' said Phoebe, 'it's never done that before. How was your first day on the market?'

He grinned broadly at her. 'I've no idea how you do this every day. My feet are killing me and I'm frozen to the bone.'

'You should buy a pair of the long johns you sell, and two pairs of socks help, the rest is practice. Are you here every day?'

'Yes I am, so I'll take your advice.'

'Bring sandwiches is another piece of advice. If your stomach's full it helps keep out the cold.'

'Thanks, I'll remember. See you tomorrow!'

Marj sidled over. 'Oh love, you've made a good start there.'

'I haven't started anything, Marjory!'

'No need to get stroppy, girl. I know you are, because it's the only time you call me by my full name.'

Phoebe just laughed. 'Then behave!'

As she and her brother wheeled the stall away for the night, Tim said, 'That Ben really is nice, Phoebe.'

'Now don't you start too! Come on, get a move on so we can get home in the warm.'

'I wonder where he keeps his stall?' the boy added as an afterthought.

Ben had a lock-up just outside the market square. Having secured the door, he made his way to a small cafe for a sandwich and a mug of tea, then he strolled to The Grapes pub on Oxford Street and ordered a pint of bitter. Wandering over to a table, he sat and started reading the local paper he'd picked up on his way. It was early in the evening and the bar was almost empty, but before long the door opened and another workman entered. Ordering a pint of beer, he paid for it, then walked over to where Ben was sitting and joined him.

'So, how was your first day at work?'

With a grimace Ben told him. 'How these traders do that every day, I don't know. I nearly froze my balls off!'

His companion laughed. 'Better get used to it, my friend, you could be there for some considerable time. It's one of the joys of working undercover. Anything interesting happen?'

'No, it was busy, being Saturday, but nothing untoward.' He smiled slowly. 'The best thing about today was a lovely girl on a fruit and veg stall who saved my life by letting her little brother go and buy me some fish and chips. I was starving.'

'Now, you behave yourself, don't let a pretty face stop you from doing your job.'

Ben pretended to look outraged. 'Excuse me! Are you suggesting I'm not up to it?'

'No. Just a warning – but on the other hand it might be to your advantage to further this friendship. If she's a regular she might be a source of information. Nothing gets by among the traders. They always keep tabs on each other.'

Ben frowned. 'I'll give it a day or two and see. I need to tread carefully. I don't want to give any cause for suspicion or the whole thing will be a waste of time.' He drank up. 'I need to go and soak in a hot bath to get my circulation working again.' Picking up his paper, he left the bar and waited for a tram to take him home.

Home was a very comfortable flat over a shoe shop in Bedford Place. He took off his coat, went to the bathroom and ran a bath, throwing in some bath salts before he stripped off the rest of his clothes and stepped into the hot water. Laying back he let out a deep sigh, wondering just how long he was going to have to man his stall in the freezing cold.

When he'd dried himself, he sorted out the clothes for the morning. He remembered Phoebe's advice and had taken a pair of long johns home with him. He laid them out with a long-sleeved vest, a jumper, then a thicker one and two pairs of socks, thinking to himself he'd look two sizes larger in the morning with all this clobber, but he had to shut out the cold, that much he'd learnt today. He cooked some eggs and bacon and after eating, he set the alarm, climbed into bed and fell asleep.

* * *

Phoebe walked home with Tim. As they passed the street next to hers, she saw a queue of men waiting outside the house rented by the two prostitutes. Tim also saw them.

'What are they waiting in the cold for, Phoebe, it isn't a shop?'

She hurried him along. 'I've no idea,' she lied.

For once there was no washing hanging about as they entered the house, but the aroma of cooking filled the air.

'Oh, Mum, that smells good.'

'I'm making a stew from a bit of ham on the bone. Did you bring any veg with you?'

'Yes,' said Phoebe, taking out some onions, a cabbage and a cauliflower from a bag beside her. 'I bought some cheese to make a sauce for the cauliflower too. That and the stewing steak I bought today should see us through for a bit. When it's gone, I'll buy a chicken to roast. We had a good day, so it'll be a nice treat.'

'There's a new man in the market, Mum,' Tim chipped in. 'He's ever so nice. He gave me sixpence for getting him some fish and chips. He even helped Phoebe undo the canvas over the stall when it got tangled.'

Mary looked over at her daughter. 'Is that right?'

'Yes, don't know who he is, but he's very polite. I was pleased of the help. I think he's new to trading as he said he didn't know how we did the job every day.'

'Young, is he?'

'Now don't you start! It's bad enough with Marj teasing me about him.'

Her mother just smiled and stirred the pot on the stove. She'd like to see her daughter settled with a nice young man, she thought, as she added some salt and dumplings to the meal. It would be nice for her to have someone to care for her, look after her. Phoebe had taken over her husband's position since his death, which was a godsend, but she did have a life of her own, after all.

As they sat down to their meal, Phoebe looked at her mother. 'How about going to the cinema tomorrow afternoon? You'd like that, wouldn't you, Tim?'

His eyes lit up. 'Can we go and see the *Keystone Cops*? It's on at the Gaiety. They're so funny, they make me roar with laughter.'

'All right with you, Mum?' she asked.

'Yes, I could do with a good laugh.' So, it was decided.

The next afternoon, they queued for a short time to get into the cinema and sat ready for the film. The pianist arrived and took his seat in front of and to the side of the screen and as the credits rolled he started to play. As with all silent films, the pianist contributed to the excitement by interpreting the motion on the screen, playing stirring music as the Keystone Cops hurtled around on a fire engine that was out of control, with the cops hanging from it, clinging on to a ladder for dear life. All three of them were crying with laughter as they watched the mad antics. The second film was just as hilarious, and they left in a state of exhaustion.

Mary clutched at her stomach as they reached the street. 'Oh, my poor tummy is aching with laughter,' she complained.

Tim was grinning broadly. 'That was so much fun, but it's a wonder they don't get hurt.'

'Maybe they do,' declared Phoebe, 'but they wouldn't show it. They certainly are clever, though.'

They wandered home, thoroughly entertained.

'Right, young Timothy,' said his mother. 'Go and get your stuff ready for school in the morning. I don't want a mad rush because you've forgotten something. I've got a busy day ahead of me.' But she was only chivvying him along. Young as he was, Tim had learnt to be organised because Phoebe always left early, and he'd learnt how to cope for himself.

Every Monday morning, Phoebe would walk to the wholesalers and restock her stall. She was a favourite with the sellers who knew her story and admired the girl for taking over her father's stall. They also knew that she would argue fiercely with them about the price of the goods. It took guts to do this, but she stood up to them all.

'I'm not paying that price!' she retorted to the man trying to sell her cabbages. 'I could get them cheaper in the market.'

'Oh, Phoebe, you'll be the death of me,' he complained before reducing his price. 'I've got a family to keep, you know!'

'Oh come on, Archie. Don't give me that old flannel, I know you bury all your money in a tin in the garden,' she laughed. 'Now what about some onions?'

A little later she walked away, pleased with her wares, which would be delivered to her that afternoon.

Monday was always quiet after the weekend and she took this time to clear the stall, moving the vegetables into boxes to allow her to wash the stall down. She prided herself on the cleanliness and the goods she sold, knowing that some of the other stallholders weren't so thorough. It paid in the long run, as the customers could see the difference and would come to her for their goods.

She saw Ben arrive and smiled across at him. She was pleased to see that his things were laid out in a pristine fashion, so he obviously took a pride in his work. She was curious as to how he became a trader. He was well spoken and not as rough and ready as many of the other men who worked the market.

Ben wandered over to her when he was set up. 'Good morning! How are you today? I can see you're having a good clean up – now I know why your stall looks so inviting to the customers.'

'Well I wouldn't like to buy my food from a dirty stall, would you?'

'Certainly not. I took your advice, by the way, and I've several layers on today.'

She smiled at him. 'You'll get used to it in time. What made you do this work? You obviously aren't used to it?'

He hesitated for a moment. 'I was out of a job, so I thought I'd give it a try.'

'What did you do before then?'

He was saved from answering as a customer stopped at his stall and he left to serve them. As he didn't return, she never did find out.

Marj wandered over. ''Ow's your new friend, then?'

'He's not my friend, Marj. He's new to this and I was asking him about his previous job, but he had to go.'

Her friend looked across at Ben. 'Not the usual sort to be a trader, I would 'ave thought. Interesting.'

The Stanley brothers were of the same mind.

'Go and have a chat to the new trader and do a bit of digging. He's not your usual type. See what you can find out,' Percy told his brother.

Arthur wandered over to the stall and looked through the stock. 'These warm shirts look good. Decent price too.' He looked at Ben. 'Been trading long, have you?'

'No, this is my first time. It takes some getting used to, standing about in the cold.'

'What on earth made you choose this way of life, if you don't mind me asking?'

'I moved down here from Gloucester and the only work on offer was in the docks and I didn't fancy that, so I thought I'd give this a try. How about you? Have you always been a trader?'

'Yeah. Me and me brother have done it all our lives. Buying and selling's in our blood. Well, best get back.'

'Well?' asked Percy.

'He came down here from Gloucester looking for work. Didn't fancy the docks so here he is. Seems harmless enough.'

But Percy wasn't convinced. 'Maybe so, but we'll keep an eye on him.'

'Well at least Len Taylor will clear the stuff tonight, so we'll be as clean as a whistle for the time being.'

'We'll take a break until around Christmas. People get careless then, rushing around getting ready for the festive season.'

'Ha! Be like a holiday,' laughed Arthur. But his brother was not amused.

Chapter Three

It was mid December and the market looked very festive. The stalls were decorated with tinsel and baubles. Lanterns were hung in each stall with lit candles inside and someone had brought an old phonograph and some records and was playing Christmas carols. Tony, who sold saucepans among his goods, used two lids to play like cymbals until he was told to stop because it was too loud. He did so after much fussing, instead he picked up a bunch of mistletoe and visited all the females on their stands, lingering at Marj's, but it was all done with good humour.

Phoebe had bundles of holly and mistletoe for sale beside her stall and half a dozen Christmas trees. She and Tim – when he was there – used to sing along to the carols. Phoebe had a sweet pure voice, which was much appreciated by the other traders who would join in with gusto. At this time more than any other, there was an air of jollity in the market, filled with the Christmas spirit – apart from the Stanley brothers, who had just strewn a few strands of tinsel on their stall, so as not to look different, but it hadn't been done with any cheer and it showed.

Ben wandered over to Phoebe's stall. 'Doesn't the older Stanley brother ever smile?' he asked.

'I don't think his mouth knows how,' she retorted. 'To be honest, he scares me a bit.'

'Why? Have you had any trouble with him?' he asked quickly.

'No, never, but he's got a cruel face and when he looks at you it makes me go cold.'

'Yes, I can see what you mean. He's a mean man with a mean face. Just keep clear of him is my advice.'

'Oh, don't you worry, I do. I was wondering,' she said, 'if you could get one of your warm jackets in Tim's size, if it isn't too expensive. I'd like to give him one for Christmas. He's almost grown out of his.'

'I'll see what I can do,' Ben said. 'Give me a call when you close, I'll help you move the trees again.'

She thanked him profusely. Ever since she'd had them delivered, Ben had helped put them away, which had saved her time and energy. To thank him she'd sometimes bring him a large piece of her mother's bread pudding, which he devoured eagerly.

Marj watched their growing friendship with interest, but these days didn't tease her friend, hoping that the nice young man might come to be important to the young girl of whom she was so fond.

* * *

As Christmas Eve approached, young Tim's excitement grew. Like most children, the thought of opening presents on Christmas morning was something to look forward to, but for many a child whose parents were too poor, it was mostly a disappointment. Some of these children were the ones that hovered around the market stalls at closing time, hoping to glean anything that was free. With this in mind, Phoebe always had a stash of sweets to hand out on Christmas Eve and any spare fruit and vegetables.

Ben watched as she quietly handed round such bounty to children wearing worn clothes and scuffed shoes. He noticed how she did so, quietly and unobtrusively, so as to leave the children with some dignity. It was endearing to watch. He too added to this with warm gloves and scarves from his stall. He had also managed to purchase a jacket in Tim's size, which Phoebe had hidden away until Christmas morning.

Towards closing time, Phoebe looked at what remained on her stall. All the Christmas trees had sold, and she had one at home to be decorated that evening. There was no holly left but just one small sprig of mistletoe. The rest had gone.

It had been such a busy day. Seeing how tired Tim was, she'd sent him home early, telling him to start decorating the tree, knowing how he loved to do this. She gave him a bag of apples, oranges and some mixed nuts she'd ordered for the Christmas period only, to take with him and she would add another of vegetables with her to go with the chicken on Christmas Day, which she'd purchased the day before.

Ben put his stall away, then returned to help Phoebe with hers. He wheeled the cart and she carried the canvas cover. Inside the shed, Ben put the stall down and seeing the sprig of mistletoe, he picked it up and as Phoebe walked in behind him, he held the sprig over their heads and kissed her gently on the lips.

'Happy Christmas, Phoebe!'

She was so surprised she didn't know what to say for a minute. Then she stuttered, 'You too, Ben.'

As she locked up she asked him, 'Where are you spending the holiday?'

'With some friends. It should be a lot of fun. See you in a couple of days. Have a good time.'

The Stanley brothers put their stall away and took some fish and chips home to have with a couple of bottles of beer. They had a long night ahead of them, so they made themselves comfortable in a couple of armchairs to grab a few hours' sleep.

In the very early hours of the morning, the Stanley brothers got out their bicycles and rode away towards the more palatial part of the town where the houses were bigger and set back in a private garden. They hid the bikes in a hedge; and creeping along, chose a house that was in darkness. They crept round to the back door. Using a jemmy, Percy proceeded to break into the premises as quietly as possible. Using torches, they crept into the house, picking up anything that was small and expensive. Going into the living room, they ignored the presents under the tree and opened cupboards and drawers, removing pieces of silverware, putting them into a sack each one was carrying.

Then slowly moving upstairs, they quietly opened a bedroom door. In the bed, the owners of the house were asleep as the brothers quietly opened drawers, removing any jewellery they saw before going back downstairs and out of the house, moving onto the next one, doing the same. After the third house, they found their bicycles and rode away.

Once back in their own home, they tipped out the contents of the sacks and studied their haul, eyes glittering with anticipation at the cash they would pocket from their ill-gotten gains.

'We were bloody lucky that no one woke up,' Arthur remarked.

'Not at all. That's why I picked tonight. The adults would have been so tired with all the preparations for the day ahead, they would have been exhausted. Merry Christmas!' He held up a gold necklace and a string of pearls. 'These will bring a decent price, with these rings.' The diamonds from a couple of rings sparkled in the light.

'With a bit of luck with so much going on today, no one will discover anything missing. Maybe it will even go unnoticed for longer. Nevertheless, I'll take some of it and catch a train after Boxing Day up to London. I'll call Charlie and arrange a meet. The sooner these are passed on the better. I'm going to get my head down for a few hours.'

'Me too,' said Arthur. 'I'm bloody knackered!'

On Christmas morning, Tim woke and rushed downstairs to see what was in his stocking. Phoebe was up already, and the room was warm. She grinned at her brother.

'Didn't think it would be long before you were up.' She handed him a stocking to open. 'Here, you can open this now, but we'll wait for Mum before we open the presents under the tree.'

He took it from her and started to take out the contents. There were sticks of barley sugar. A pair of gloves and a scarf, a pen knife and a toy car, plus an orange, an apple and a small bar of chocolate. The lad was thrilled.

Mary soon joined them and they sat down to breakfast. Phoebe had cooked bacon and eggs and had toasted some bread, which they ate with marmalade. It was a veritable feast. Normally their breakfast fare was simply a bowl of porridge and mug of tea. When they had finished, Phoebe replenished their mugs with fresh tea and then she went over to the tree.

'This is for you, Mum.' Phoebe handed Mary a package and watched her open it. Inside was a warm shawl in deep maroon. Mary was delighted and placed it around her shoulders, thanking her daughter profusely.

Phoebe then handed Tim a large parcel tied with ribbon. 'This is yours.'

His eyes bright with anticipation, he tore at the wrapping and let out a cry of delight and surprise when he saw the warm jacket. 'Oh, Phoebe, thank you, it's lovely!' He immediately put it on over his pyjamas, did up the buttons and buried his hands deep within the pockets.

'This will keep me warm, it's so thick.' He flung his arms around her neck. 'Thank you.'

She was delighted that it fitted him with enough room for him to grow a little. 'Ben managed to get it for me,' she told him.

Tim beamed. 'I'll thank him next time I see him,' he said.

'There's this too,' she said, pushing her way behind the tree to retrieve a large hoop that had been hidden from sight. 'You'll need to find a stick to help you bowl it along. I'll probably find one in the market for you.'

Mary rose to her feet and retrieved a parcel, handing it to Phoebe. 'This is for you.'

Inside was a hand-knitted woollen hat in bright red and a pair of warm mittens with a scarf to match.

'Oh, Mum, whenever did you find the time to make all this?'

Laughing, Mary said, 'While I waited for the laundry to dry!' Then she gave a parcel to Tim.

Inside was a hand-knitted jumper in dark green. 'That should keep you nice and warm, son.'

After clearing away, the three of them sat preparing the vegetables to go with the chicken. They peeled the potatoes, the carrots and the parsnips, cut off the outer leaves of the sprouts and Mary prepared a batter for a Yorkshire pudding. Then they put a Christmas pudding on to steam. Once that had been done, they all changed out of their nightclothes.

As Mary laid the table, she wished with all her heart that Edward, her late husband, could have been here to share their happiness. He'd been a good husband and father and she missed him still. He would have been so proud of his daughter and the way she'd taken over the stall, and of young Tim, who had such a lovely nature, but she knew that she was better off than many other widows and she was grateful for that.

* * *

After the Christmas dinner, the dishes were cleared away, and still wearing the party hats from the crackers, the two women settled down, one on the settee, the other in an armchair, and fell asleep. Tim was at the table playing with his new car. The house was at peace.

The day after Boxing Day, Percy Stanley was in a backstreet in the East End of London, tucked away in the back room of a shop, his stolen loot being appraised by another villain, Charlie Blackmore. Blackmore made his living from buying stolen goods and selling them on. His pawnbroker shop sold everything that had a price and was a front for his unscrupulous dealings. The police were aware of this, but he was a devious man and so far had stayed out of trouble. He and Percy were arguing about the prices he was offering.

'You're a fucking con man, Charlie! Do you think I'm bloody stupid or something? Those pearls are worth more than that, *and* that diamond ring!'

Charlie wasn't bothered. He knew that Percy had to get rid of his stuff quickly and he knew that he was the only fence he trusted.

'Take it or leave it, that's my final offer.' He sat back, smoking his cigar.

Percy walked up and down cursing loudly, but he knew he had no choice. 'Another ten quid and you've got a deal.'

Charlie just raised an eyebrow and stared at him.

Eyes narrowed, Percy stared back at him and waited, but as Charlie didn't say a word, Percy finally had to concede.

'You're a bloody robber. Every time I come to you, you take me for a ride.'

'You could always try someone else, my friend.' He

smiled softly. Then, taking a wad of notes out of his pocket, he peeled off the amount he needed and handed it over.

Percy grabbed at it and put it in his inside pocket, muttering beneath his breath as he did so. 'You'll be wanting a pint of my blood next!' he snapped, then he walked to the door and left.

Charlie Blackmore chuckled to himself. This gear he'd just bought was worth a nice little earner for him, and what's more, he disliked Percy Stanley intensely and it gave him great pleasure to see him squirm. Any other punter he would have been prepared to offer a little more, but not Stanley. Let him crawl!

Percy sat on the train back to Southampton, still fuming. He knew he'd been cheated and that stuck in his craw. In his home town he was feared, but in that back room with that bloody shyster, he was nobody! That was hard to stomach. He'd have to find another outlet in the future. He scowled as someone getting off at the next station wished him a happy Christmas.

'Stuff Christmas!' he yelled back at the man and slumped back in his seat.

When he arrived in Southampton, he made for the nearest pub. Walking up to the bar he slammed some money down on the counter. 'A large Scotch and don't you dare mention Christmas, understand?'

The barmaid just looked at him, thinking what a miserable old bugger he was. 'Suits me,' she said and served him his drink. He took the glass and sat down, wracking his brains as to who else he could find to move the rest of his stuff in the future.

He eventually walked home without finding an answer. He'd have to make some discreet enquiries over the next few weeks. Not in Southampton, but he had a few contacts elsewhere. He'd get his head down, have a good sleep and decide tomorrow.

Chapter Four

The new year began and Christmas was long forgotten. The weather was not quite as cold on some days, which pleased the traders in the market, but they all longed for the spring. January and February were dull and dark months and there was always an air of depression around this time.

In Ireland there were troubles with the IRA and there was talk of more troops being sent over.

'Everybody 'as enough trouble without those bastards killing people,' Marj grumbled one morning. 'Look about you! Everyone 'as a long face. It's that time of the year and I 'ates it!'

'Never mind, Marj, it won't be long now. We'll soon be able to take off a couple of layers of clothes. I'm sick of being bundled up, I have to say.'

'Makes no difference to me, love. Ain't nobody going to look at me, not at my age.' She gave a wicked grin. 'Mind you, I've 'ad me moments in the past.'

Phoebe looked at her friend with affection. 'I bet you were a handful.'

Marj burst out laughing. 'That's a poor choice of words love.'

Ben wandered over. 'It's good to hear somebody laughing. It's so quiet today and look at all the glum faces around you. Apart from you two lovely ladies, of course.'

'Ooh, you with your silver tongue,' Marj joshed. 'Flattery gets you everything young man, so you take care. I might forget myself!'

He was laughing now. 'You are a cheeky woman, but you know that. I don't know what's got into the older Stanley brother. He's been like a bear with a sore head ever since we came back. I've even heard him snap at his customers. That's not good for business. Any idea why?'

'Perhaps Father Christmas forgot to call on him,' Phoebe joked.

'I doubt he ever did, if the truth was known.' He walked back to his stall.

Ever since he'd been cheated by Charlie Blackmore in London, Percy had been unhappy with his lot. He'd tried to find someone else to buy his goods but without success. However, a few weeks later, he'd arranged to sell a few pieces of jewellery to a villain who was coming to see him from Bournemouth. He wasn't too happy about this arrangement, as the two men had crossed swords a couple of years earlier, but wanting to get away from his contact in London, he thought he'd have a chat and see if he could do business with him. He was going to meet him at his lock-up later that night when the market would be empty.

Phoebe and her family had long finished their evening meal. Tim was fast asleep and her mother had gone to bed early. Raking the ashes, Phoebe made up the fire for the night, closing the damper down so the fire would only burn slowly, keeping the house warm for the morning. She made herself a cup of tea and went over the goods on her stall in her mind, making notes of the vegetables and fruit that would soon need replenishing. She'd meant to do it before closing but had a last-minute rush and hadn't had time.

Ben had gone home by the time she was ready to put her stall away and she was the last in the market to leave. She suddenly sat up. She'd been in such a rush, she didn't remember locking the door behind her! If it was left open all night, there was a strong possibility her goods would be stolen. Quickly putting on her boots and coat, she let herself out of the house quietly and rushed out.

The streets were quiet. The pubs were shut and houses were in darkness as she made her way. It was a bit eerie and although she was used to these streets and had lived around them all her life, as she walked, she felt uneasy. But when eventually she didn't pass a soul, she gave herself a good talking to.

'Pull yourself together, you stupid girl. There's no one around, so relax for goodness' sake!' But soon after she entered the market, she was surprised to hear raised voices and she stopped to listen.

'You thieving bastard! Think you can put one over on me, do you? Well, better men have tried and failed.' She recognised the voice of Percy Stanley coming from inside his lock-up a few doors down. Then she heard another male voice, one she didn't recognise, but whoever it was, was equally as angry.

'Don't give me that crap, Percy. I know you of old. Why come to me, anyway? Has old Blackmore given you your walking ticket, is that it?'

Percy was enraged. 'Who do you think you're talking to?'

The other man gave a harsh laugh. 'Look at you! Pumped up with your own importance. You're a nobody but you won't admit it. You're strictly small-time. I only came up out of curiosity to see what you had to sell.'

There was another angry exchange, the sound of things falling. The noise of a scrap. Cries of anger and pain. Phoebe was about to flee, but the two men tumbled out of the building exchanging blows. She moved back into the darkness but then just behind her she saw cardboard boxes piled high and rubbish to be cleared in the morning. She quickly hid behind it, crouching down, making herself as small as possible, but through a gap she could see what was going on.

The two men fought fiercely, swapping punches, swearing at each other until Percy, being the stronger of the two, had his opponent on the ground, holding him by his throat.

'Small-time, am I?' He squeezed even tighter. The other man was fighting for breath, trying to break free. Then with one almighty heave, he managed to push Percy away and scramble to his feet, but as he turned towards his opponent, Phoebe was horrified to see Percy Stanley take a knife from his pocket and plunge it into his chest. She covered her mouth to smother her gasp of horror as she saw the look of surprise on the victim's face just before he sank to his knees and lay still.

She didn't dare breathe.

Percy examined the body, then stood, just staring at his victim for what seemed an age, cursing quietly. Then, picking up the body, he carried it inside. To Phoebe, still in hiding, not daring to move, it seemed an eternity before anything happened. Then to her surprise, the trader walked out alone, locked the door and started to walk away in the opposite direction.

She suddenly had cramp in her leg and moved slightly. One of the boxes tumbled. Percy stopped and turned. Phoebe was paralysed with fear. Would he kill her too? But at that moment a cat leapt down from the roof above her and landed with a squawk. Percy walked on.

The girl was too scared to move until she was sure the trader was well out of sight, only then did she dare stand up – and was violently sick. Her legs were trembling and she staggered before regaining her balance. The only thought in her head was to get to the safety of her house and she hurried away in the opposite direction, her heart pounding until she had to stop for breath, before carrying on, her key ready in her hand.

At last she was home. Opening the door and locking it after herself, she slipped the bolt across for added safety, went into the kitchen for some water to drink, then cupped her hand beneath the still running water and splashed her face with it. She stood, clinging to the kitchen sink to try and gather her wits, before going back into the front room and collapsing in a chair.

She had just witnessed a murder! She could hardly believe it and went over every detail in her mind. That man must have been dead or Percy wouldn't have locked up and left him. What would he do now? He couldn't leave the body there to be seen when he opened up in the morning. Should she go to the police? What if she did and they went to the brothers' lock-up and found it empty? The brothers would have it in for her and her family! No, she couldn't put them in jeopardy. She'd keep quiet and see what happened in the morning, not tell anybody what she'd seen. After all, she alone was witness to what happened and Percy didn't know she was there, so she'd be safe . . . wouldn't she?

While Phoebe was trying to find a solution to her problem, Percy Stanley was doing the same. As he entered his house, his brother looked up, and seeing the blood on the front of Percy's coat and shirt, leapt to his feet.

'Jesus Christ! What happened to you, are you hurt?'

Percy pushed him aside as he took off his coat. 'No, I'm not, but that bloody shyster, Frank Clarke from Bournemouth is!'

Arthur paled. 'What have you done?'

'I killed the bugger.'

'You what? Are you bloody mad?'

Percy glared at his brother. 'I didn't mean to. We got into an argument, then it came to blows and before I realised it, we were outside the lock-up. I had the bleeder on the ground by the throat, I was just going to teach him a lesson, but he threw me off, got to his feet and came at me, so I had no choice but to use my knife.'

Arthur was shocked. 'Where is he now?'

'In the lock-up, there was nowhere else to put him at the time.'

His brother was livid. 'In the lock-up! That'll be great when we open up in the morning, what will happen then? The police will be called, that's what, and you'll end up swinging from a bleedin' rope!'

'Don't be ridiculous! We've got to get rid of the body and clean up the blood tonight. That's why I came home, I need you to help me, I can't do it alone.'

'How the hell can we hide a body? For Christ's sake, Percy, it's not a sack of potatoes!'

'I've put him on the spare barrow in the lock-up. We'll cover him with old sacks and wheel him to the churchyard and leave him there, then we'll have to go back to the market and swill the ground inside and out to get rid of the blood.'

'What if someone sees us wheeling the barrow?'

'What, at this time of night? Everyone's in bed, the streets are empty. I didn't see anybody when I met Clarke. Come on, we don't have time to waste. Get your coat.'

The two men hurried to the market, collected the body, covered it with sacks and headed for the cemetery. Arthur was looking around all the time in case anyone was about but, as predicted, the streets were empty and before long they reached the entrance to the graveyard of the church. Percy pushed the barrow well inside, then, in the middle of several gravestones, he stopped. Alongside the cemetery was an unkempt hedge with overhanging branches.

Percy pushed the barrow over to the hedge. 'Here, give me a hand to lift him off. We'll leave him here behind the branches where he can't be seen. With a bit of luck, no one will find him for ages.'

Arthur removed the sacks and grabbed the corpse by the shoulders, but as he looked down at the face, he shuddered as he saw the open eyes vacantly staring at him. He felt the bile rise in his stomach and swallowed quickly. They lay the body down, hiding it as best they could, then hurried away, back to the market.

With the use of a hosepipe and a lot of vigorous brushing with a stiff broom and some sand to soak up the blood, they obliterated any signs of the fight and the struggle that had ensued inside and out of the lock-up and returned home, exhausted.

Arthur slumped into a chair and lit a cigarette. 'I want to know what on earth made you two fight? After all, the bloke was only coming up here to look at some jewellery.'

Percy glowered. 'He called me a nobody. Said I was small-time!'

His brother looked at him in astonishment. 'You killed him for that? What's the matter with you? For that you could end up with a death sentence and I could go to prison for years for helping you. All because of your bloody pride!'

'Nobody calls me small-time and gets away with it!'

Arthur, incensed by the triviality that had led to such a serious conclusion, was seething. 'Well, you're no crime lord, are you? Let's face it we *are* small-time, that's why we have to deal with the likes of Blackmore, unlike the big London villains. You've put my life on the line for nothing!'

Percy grabbed him by his shirt and put his face close to his brother, eyes blazing. 'Are you looking for trouble too?'

'What are you going to do, knife me as well? How would you explain that . . . brother?'

Percy pushed him in the chest, then let go. 'Just watch your mouth, that's all.'

Arthur gave a soft smile. 'You are the one who needs to be careful. You need me and don't you forget it!' He got to his feet, pushed past his brother and went upstairs to bed.

Chapter Five

Phoebe climbed out of bed and dressed. She'd hardly slept during the night, unable to get the horrendous vision of the scene in the market out of her head. She was terrified of seeing Percy Stanley, knowing what he'd done, and realised she would have to try and behave normally. To do otherwise could raise his suspicions and that would be disastrous. She wondered what would happen when they opened their lock-up where the body had been hidden, but to her surprise, when they opened the door, there was only their stall inside.

In the market, the traders were setting out their stalls and Ben looked across at Phoebe. She was very quiet, hardly saying a word. This was unusual – she usually wished him a good morning and chatted away to Marj, but not today. She looked very pale and he wondered if she was unwell. When his stall was ready, he wandered over to her.

'Morning, Phoebe. Are you all right?'

She turned quickly and answered with a startled look. 'Yes, I'm fine, why do you ask?'

'You're very quiet and you're not your usual cheery self, I wondered if perhaps you were unwell, that's all.'

He noted the look of relief as she smiled at him. 'I didn't sleep well last night, that's all. You all right?'

'Yes, fine. Oh, best go, I have a customer.'

But as the day wore on, he watched her. Something was bothering her. She was full of nervous energy, dressing her stall, then changing it. She was on the go all the time, which was so unlike her. Normally, once the stall was set up, she relaxed between customers, sometimes making a list of stock that was running short, but today she couldn't keep still.

Phoebe was unaware of Ben's scrutiny, she just wanted to keep busy, make the day pass quickly. She hadn't looked across at the Stanley brothers' stall, unwilling to look at the man she'd seen murder another in cold blood. She picked up a basket of apples to replenish those she'd sold when a voice came from behind her.

'Mind your backs!'

Recognising Percy's voice, she dropped the lot. Percy walked on, pushing a wheelbarrow, but Ben came rushing over to help her. 'You'll have to check these aren't bruised, but I think you've got away with it,' he said scrutinising those he retrieved. He noticed Phoebe's hands were trembling as she took them from him, but he didn't comment.

She thanked him. 'The man made me jump, I didn't realise he was there,' she explained.

Marj sauntered over. 'You all right, love, only you're like a scalded cat this morning?'

Phoebe managed to smile at her friend. 'Didn't get much sleep last night, that's all. It's put me out of sorts.'

In the afternoon a couple of constables walked through the market, stopping at various stalls, chatting to the traders as was their habit. Phoebe froze as they stopped for a chat, stuffing her hands into her coat pocket to stop them from trembling.

'Afternoon, Miss Phoebe. Everything all right?'

'Yes, thank you, but if you could find a few more customers I'd be better!'

'Wish I could, love, not many about today.' They moved off.

Arthur Stanley saw the policemen and sidled up to his brother. 'Be very careful what you say, you hear? One wrong word could put us in the shit, so watch it!'

As the men headed towards them, Percy took a deep breath and started unpacking a few articles and putting them on the stall, keeping his gaze on the wrappings.

The policemen picked up one or two pieces and examined them before putting them back. Percy ignored them.

'Lost your tongue, Stanley? You've usually got a mouthful of abuse when we call,' remarked one.

Arthur held his breath as his brother looked up and glared at the constable.

'I'm fussy who I talk to and you are not worth me wasting my time.'

The constable snapped back at him. 'My sentiments too, but sometimes in our line of duty, we have no choice, which is why I have to speak to the likes of you. Keep out of trouble or I'll have you – that's all I've got to say.'

The brothers watched the two men walk away with great relief. Arthur took out a handkerchief and wiped the sweat from his brow, then lit a cigarette and drew heavily on the nicotine to calm his nerves.

Ben stood behind his stall deep in thought. Something was going on here today, but he couldn't put his finger on it. Phoebe was on pins, the Stanley brothers were edgy. What on earth did one thing have to do with the other? As far as he could see, neither had any connection. Phoebe never had anything to do with the two men – quite the opposite, she kept well away from them. From Percy, in particular, yet today, when he'd taken her by surprise, she seemed scared. He stood trying to make sense of it all.

At the end of what seemed a very long day, Phoebe packed up her stall. She couldn't wait to leave the market. Her nerves were frayed and she knew she'd have to pull herself together in the days to come or she'd be a nervous wreck. Ben offered to help her, but she smiled and said she was fine, there wasn't a heavy load to push and she could manage.

He didn't argue, just watched her. Never before had Phoebe been in such a rush to leave, he noted. Normally she took her time, made doubly sure that the canvas cover on poles was not damaging the fruit as she lay it on top of her stall, but not tonight. She was in too much of a hurry to leave. He was concerned. He liked the girl and hoped that, after all, it was a lack of sleep that had made her unlike herself today. But he didn't really believe that and that worried him even more.

As he started packing up his stall, he watched the Stanley brothers. Percy wore his usual belligerent expression, but Arthur was muttering to him and the older brother turned and snapped back at him. They continued exchanging angry words as they walked to their lock-up.

Ben put his stall away, then walked back into the now empty market and wandered over to the door of the Stanleys' place. He tried the door but it was firmly locked. He turned but stopped and looked at the ground. It felt different beneath his shoes. He lifted his foot and peered at the soles. Running his finger along one of them, he gazed at the sediment on his finger, rubbing it. It felt like sand. How strange. Kneeling down, he studied the ground. There was nothing untoward to see. It was scrupulously clean. But as he studied it more carefully, he realised that only outside the lock-up and the ground leading to it was that clean. He shrugged. Maybe they'd spilt something and had cleaned up after. He stood up and walked away.

Phoebe took a deep breath before entering her house. She *must* behave naturally or her mother would immediately notice any change in her. She opened the door and stepped inside.

'Hello, Mum. God, I could kill a hot cup of tea.' She walked over to her brother. 'Have a good day at school, Tim?'

He grimaced. 'We had mental arithmetic today. I hate it.'

'But you're good with figures. Look how you manage giving change on a Saturday in the market!'

'It's the teacher I don't like. It's that Miss Giles. She's such a misery.'

'Ah well, you can't like everybody in this world.' She

removed her coat and sat to drink the cup of tea her mother handed her.

'Like you don't like that Percy Stanley,' Tim said, just as she took a sip.

Phoebe spluttered her tea all down her dress at the mention of the name.

'Phoebe!' yelled her mother, who rushed over with a tea cloth to wipe her dry.

'Sorry, Mum. It's hotter than I thought,' she said quickly as way of an excuse.

Three weeks had passed and everything had settled down. Phoebe was once again her normal self, having pushed her bad memories into the back of her mind during the day, at least, and struggling with a feeling of guilt at keeping quiet about what she'd witnessed. The two brothers had relaxed as each week passed and no news of a body being found had surfaced.

There had been brighter days, although still cold, and the sight of the sun cheered everyone except Ben, who was becoming restless. He had been sent to keep an eye on the brothers, but days passed and the reasons for him being at the market were diminishing. Before long he'd be moved. He stood looking about him. He couldn't honestly say he'd enjoyed his stint as a trader, but looking across at Phoebe he smiled. The time here hadn't been entirely wasted and he'd miss seeing her every day. He couldn't let that happen, he decided, and walked over to her when she didn't have a customer.

'Would you like to save me from myself, dear lady?'

She looked at him with a puzzled expression. 'Pardon?'

'Oh, Phoebe, I'm so fed up with the winter and I have a

fit of the blues. If you would allow me to take you out to dinner, it would save me. What do you say?'

She laughed quietly. 'I wondered what on earth you were on about.'

'Say you'll come out with me, it would give me so much pleasure. How about later this evening?'

'Tonight?'

'Are you busy? Don't say you are. My mother always said, "Don't put off until tomorrow what you can do today." So I'm being a good son following her advice.'

Seeing his smiling face, she thought it's just what she needed at this moment. 'All right, young man, we can't disappoint your mother. What time?'

He was delighted. 'How about seven o'clock? If you tell me where you live, I'll call for you.'

She wrote the address on a piece of paper and handed it to him.

He took it, read it, put it in his pocket and walked away whistling.

Marj sidled over and with a nudge in Phoebe's ribs she said quietly, 'Oh my Lord! I wondered when 'e would get round to it.'

'What do you mean?'

'Taking you out, of course! Didn't notice 'im 'elping anyone else in the market when it was time to go 'ome. Only you!'

'Oh Marj! You're an incurable romantic. It's only dinner.'

'No, love, it's only the beginning and don't you go and mess it up! 'E's the perfect man for you, mark my words!' She walked away, humming quietly, 'If You Were the Only Girl in the World.'

* * *

When Phoebe told her mother she was going out to dinner with Ben, Mary was delighted. Tim had often spoken to her about the new trader for whom he bought fish and chips each Saturday, and this evening she'd get to meet him. While her daughter was changing, she brushed her hair, tidied herself and the living room, hoping to create a good impression for all their sakes. They may not have much money, but she still had standards.

Phoebe was looking forward to her evening. Over the few months that she and Ben had worked together, he'd been a good friend, helping her put her stall away at night, chatting to her at odd times during the day, and she found him easy to talk to. Not that she knew very much about him, really. Perhaps this evening she'd get to know him better.

A few minutes before seven o'clock there was a knock on the door. Tim rushed to open it and invited Ben inside. He was carrying a bunch of flowers, which he handed to Mary after he was introduced to her.

'These are for you, Mrs Collins.'

She was delighted and surprised. 'Thank you. It's been a very long time since a man has given me flowers.'

'It's my pleasure. How are you, Tim?'

The boy beamed at him. 'Fine, thanks. I'll see you on Saturday, as usual.'

Ben turned to Phoebe. 'You look very nice, if I may say so. Are you ready?'

'Yes, I am.' She kissed her mother and patted Tim on the head. 'Don't forget your homework!'

'It's nearly finished,' he protested.

As they got to the door, Ben looked at Mary. 'Nice to

meet you, Mrs Collins. I hope I see you again sometime.'

'You are always welcome,' she replied with a smile.

Once outside, Phoebe tucked her arm through Ben's. 'That was lovely of you to give my mother flowers.'

'Not at all. I'm delighted she was so pleased. Now let's get a tram and head for the restaurant. I don't know about you, but I'm starving.'

'You're always starving, it seems to me,' she teased.

'Well, I'm a growing lad!'

Phoebe laughed. Ben was just over six feet tall. 'Good Lord, if you grow much more, I'll need a pair of steps to be able to talk to you!'

'No need – for you, I'll bend down. Ah, here's the tram.'

They alighted in Above Bar Street where Ben took her to a small but elegant restaurant that had recently opened. Phoebe had heard good reports about it and was thrilled to realise they were to eat there.

The waiter took her coat and they settled to choose from the menu. The choice of dishes was somewhat overwhelming and seeing her dismay, Ben asked, 'Would you like me to order for you?'

'Yes, that would be nice, thank you.'

'Is there anything you don't like to eat, like fish? If so, you had better tell me now.'

'No, I love all food, so carry on.' She sat back and looked around the room. It was nicely decorated in soft colours. There were only one or two tables occupied and Phoebe suspected that it was still early for some to dine. But after a full day's work, she was hungry – like her escort, who had just handed the menu back to the waiter. Soon, the waiter returned with a bottle of white wine.

Ben tasted a little the waiter poured into his glass and nodded to him to continue. Phoebe watched Ben with interest. It was obvious to her that he was used to the service in a restaurant and was familiar with a wine list. Now she was even more curious to learn about him.

Chapter Six

They started with a small portion of smoked salmon, served on a bed of mixed salad, with a twist of lemon on top. Phoebe didn't know when she'd seen anything more appetising. This was followed by roast lamb and a selection of vegetables with roast potatoes.

'I hope you don't mind,' Ben said, 'but I do miss my Sunday roast. We always had it at home.'

'Where is home?' Phoebe waited, hoping to glean more of her companion's background.

'Gloucester, in the Cotswolds, a beautiful part of the country. Have you ever been there?'

She shook her head. 'I've never had the opportunity to leave Southampton. I took over the stall when Dad died in the war, so I was tied, really.'

He gazed across the table at her. How sad, he thought.

This lovely girl, whose future had been mapped out for her. Now she was head of the family and working hard to maintain a living wage to keep them. He was filled with admiration for her.

'It's tough for one so young, to have the responsibilities that you have, but you're doing a good job. Your father would be proud of you.'

Phoebe fought to control the emotions building inside her. She'd so loved her father. They had worked together in the market since she was fifteen and she missed him more than she ever told her family, knowing that they too still felt their loss in their own way. Tim, maybe less so. He'd only been six when his father had left for the front and for a child that young, as the years pass, the memory fades. Now four years on since he'd seen his father, he spoke of him less often.

Answering Ben, she said, 'I'd like to think so. It's my mother I feel so sorry for, left a widow, like so many others. What about your father, Ben? Did he have to go to war as well?'

'He did, but he was one of the lucky ones, he came home. He doesn't talk about it, though, and so I never question him. I assume he wants to forget those dreadful days.' He paused. 'I think we should forget them too! We're here to enjoy ourselves.'

'I am enjoying myself,' she said. 'It's been a very long time since I've been out to dinner and to such a lovely place. What do you do in the evenings after the market?'

'Go home. Sometimes I go to the pub for a drink or after I've cooked something to eat, I might go to the cinema.'

'You can cook?' She grinned at him. 'You sound truly sufficient unto yourself, as the saying goes.'

'O Lord! That sounds so boring.'

'Oh, you're not boring, Ben. Far from it! It's been nice having you to chat to at work and I'm so grateful for your help at times. Are you now settled in your spot?'

What could he say, knowing that soon he may be moved. 'I'll see how it goes. I'm getting used to working in the open. I'm toughening up at last!'

The waiter arrived and removed their empty plates.

'I do hope you like the dessert I've chosen,' he said. 'It's a favourite of mine.'

Phoebe stared at the plate in front of her when the waiter served her. Her eyes lit up when she saw the chocolate mousse, served with ice cream.

'Oh, Ben! How very decadent.'

'Tuck in,' he said, delighted with her obvious enjoyment of his choice.

After they sat drinking coffee. Phoebe looked at Ben and said, 'I can't tell you how lovely that meal was. Thank you for inviting me.'

He beamed at her. 'It was my pleasure, but it's still early. When we've finished the coffee, we could go somewhere for a drink, if you like, to round the evening off before I deliver you to your door.'

'That would be nice.'

Ben paid the bill and they walked arm in arm to the Red Lion on the high street. They sat at the table with their drinks and when Phoebe said she'd never been there before he told her the history of the place.

'This is one of the oldest inns in the country. I think it dates back to the twelfth century.' He pointed out the minstrels' gallery. 'I believe it was used as a courtroom for trials of the nobles who plotted against Henry the Fifth.'

'Really? I had no idea.' Looking around, she could imagine folk of bygone days in their clothes sitting there listening to such trials. She suddenly shivered. Would she one day be sitting at a trial for murder?

Sensing her change of mood, Ben asked, 'What is it? You shivered, are you cold?'

'No, I was just thinking of how awful that must have been for those on trial, that's all.'

He placed an arm around her shoulders. 'That was then, Phoebe. Besides, you're with me, so you'd be safe.'

'Would you be my knight in shining armour, then?'

'Not likely! Can you imagine how uncomfortable that would be? No, I'd be wearing a curled wig and an embroidered coat with a sword at my side.'

She started to laugh. 'You in a wig! Now that would be ridiculous!'

'Doesn't sound like me at all, really. I'm so pleased we don't live in those times.'

'I think Marj might have enjoyed it,' she said. 'Can you imagine?'

'Oh my, she would have caused havoc!' They both started laughing at the very idea.

They only had the one drink, knowing that they'd have to be up early in the morning. Ben walked Phoebe home and at her door he took her into his arms. 'Thank you for this evening, I really enjoyed it.'

Looking up into his eyes, she said, 'So did I, it was such a treat, Ben. Thank you.'

'We'll have to do it again – that's if you'd like to?'

'Yes, I would like to.'

'Good. I'll see you in the morning.' He bent his head and kissed her soundly. 'Goodnight, Phoebe.'

'Goodnight. See you tomorrow.'

He waited until she'd opened the door and then he left with a wave and a smile.

Phoebe removed her coat and sat in the chair by the fire. Ben had kissed her and she'd liked it. Marj would be delighted, she thought, and chuckled. She went over the evening in her mind and realised that, but for knowing where he lived and his father had survived the war, she was no nearer to learning much about Ben . . . other than she really liked him. Well, she would see him in the morning and no doubt her friend would give her the third degree, wanting to know every detail of their evening.

However, in the morning when she arrived at the market, it was buzzing with gossip. As she wheeled her stall in place, Phoebe turned to Marj, who was already set up.

'What's going on? What have I missed?'

Marj sidled over and quietly said, 'There's been a murder. They've found a body in the church graveyard. Been there some time, it seems.'

Phoebe froze, and without thinking looked over towards the stall of the Stanley brothers. Percy Stanley happened to look up at the same time and saw her gaze. His eyes narrowed as he noted how scared she looked before she turned away.

'You all right, love?' asked Marj. 'Only you've suddenly gone so pale. Not sickening for summat, are you girl?'

'No, no. It was just a shock, that's all. Who is it, do they know?'

'Not yet, they only came across it this morning when the gravediggers arrived to dig another grave for a funeral tomorrow. Terrible shock, it was. Poor buggers.' She went to turn away and stopped. 'I forgot! 'Ow was your date last night with young Ben?'

Happy to change the subject, Phoebe smiled. 'It was lovely. He took me out to dinner, then we went to the Red Lion for a drink before he walked me home.'

Marj sidled up to her. 'Did he kiss you goodnight?' she whispered. Then seeing the sudden flush of Phoebe's cheeks, she cackled. 'Lucky girl.' She looked around. 'Where is Ben? 'E ain't here yet. Not like 'im to be late.'

Ben had been summoned early to police headquarters and told about the murder.

'We believe it's the body of Frank Clarke, a fence from Bournemouth. A letter addressed to him was found in one of his pockets. The body has decomposed, of course, but the bitterly cold weather has preserved it somewhat. We're just waiting for confirmation. It's possible he came up to Southampton to see the Stanley brothers – but that's only supposition at this point.'

'Have you any idea when he died?'

'Not yet. We're waiting for a report from the pathologist. But keep a close watch on the brothers in the market. Percy already has a record for grievous bodily harm in the past.'

Ben left and headed for his lock-up. He thought back to the night when he'd checked the brothers' lock-up and found the sand on the soles of his shoes. It didn't make any sense then, but it could be important if Clarke had been at the market for a meet. He'd have to wait to see if the timing was right. He'd made a note of his findings along with his reports on the brothers.

Phoebe was relieved when she saw Ben eventually arrive and hurried over to him.

'Are you all right? It's not like you to be late. You're usually here before me, I was worried.'

'Oh, thank you, Phoebe, I had an emergency dental appointment. That's all,' he lied. 'How are you this morning?'

'You won't have heard, but there's been a murder. A body was found in the churchyard early this morning.'

He feigned surprise. 'Really? How dreadful. Who was it, does anyone know?'

'No, other than it was male.'

He saw her drawn expression. 'Now don't you worry yourself about it, Phoebe. Sadly these things happen, not too often, thankfully.' He placed a comforting hand on her shoulder. 'It's nothing for you to worry about.'

How she longed to tell him the whole story, but she dare not. It was a secret she had to keep. 'You're right, of course. It's just something that's too close to home, that's all.' She walked back to her stall.

Percy Stanley was unsettled. Yes, Clarke's body had been found, that had to happen at some time, but why had the girl on the fruit and veg stall looked so scared when he caught her looking at him? It didn't make sense. He realised that she was wary of him, but she wasn't the only one in the market to be so. It suited him to have people fear him. Everyone here knew he'd served a short term in prison for GBH, which made them careful around him, but the look on the girl's face was more than that. He couldn't understand it and that was a worry. He didn't like uncertainties, not in his line of business.

Chapter Seven

Percy Stanley spent the day watching Phoebe. He was decidedly edgy. He was aware that after that first glance, which had bothered him, the girl had kept her back to his stall so she wasn't able to see him. That too was unusual. In the market you're too busy serving to bother where you stand, but she was making a determined effort to block him. Why would she do that? And at this particular time? It had been late in the evening when he'd met Clarke, the market had been deserted. She wasn't there – no one was around, only that bloody cat that had startled him. He'd stopped and looked back, but the place was empty. He shook his head, it didn't make sense. Eventually he dismissed it, putting it down to nerves. He had no doubt the Old Bill would come round asking questions at some time, and they would certainly question him and his brother, he was sure of that. Well, let them! No one had seen them remove the body and then deposit it in the churchyard, so there was no proof. The sacks that had covered Clarke had been burnt, so there was absolutely nothing to tie them to the incident.

Phoebe was only too happy to leave that evening as everyone was discussing the murder, but when she arrived home her mother had also heard the news and started talking about it.

Phoebe stopped her in midsentence. 'Can we change the subject, Mum? It's all I've heard all day long and I really don't want to hear any more.'

Mary stared at her daughter. It was unlike Phoebe to be so snappy. 'All right, love, if you say so.'

Phoebe was immediately contrite. 'Sorry, I didn't mean to bite your head off, but I'm fed up hearing about it and what's more I'm cold and tired.'

'You sit by the fire, love, and get warm. I'll brew us a fresh pot of tea.'

As she did so, Mary was thinking how fortunate they were to have the stall. Without it, and the income that Phoebe brought home, they would be in dire straits, yet she felt guilty that her daughter was being denied a better life, going out, meeting other young people instead of working so hard to feed and house them. What *she* earned from taking in washing certainly wasn't enough on its own. Perhaps this new bloke in the market would be the one for Phoebe, but if he was – what then? How would she and Tim survive? He was only ten, not old enough to find a job. She pushed such thoughts to the back of her mind as she poured Phoebe a cup of tea and one for herself.

'How was your evening, love? I was in bed when you got home. Did you have a good time?'

Thankful for a change of subject, Phoebe told her mother about the food and the new restaurant, then the history of the Red Lion.

Mary smiled. 'I knew about that. Your dad and I used to go there for a drink on pay day before we had you kids.'

Looking at her mother, Phoebe's gaze softened. 'You really miss him, don't you?'

With a wan smile Mary answered, 'Every minute of every day. He was a good man as you know, working with him as you did.' She paused. 'You remember him, but young Tim's memory fades as he grows up. That makes me sad. But maybe it's for the best.'

'Where is Tim?' Phoebe asked, suddenly realising her brother wasn't there.

'He's gone to play with the lad a couple of doors down. He'd done his homework, so I let him go. He'll be back soon.'

At that very moment, Tim came rushing through the door.

'There's been a murder! They found a body in the churchyard.'

His mother tried to shush him, but he was too excited to notice.

'Imagine that. It must have been a shock for the men who found him. I bet they were scared. I would have been.'

'Enough, Tim!' Phoebe turned to him. 'This isn't the kind of conversation I want after a long day's work.'

'But Phoebe—'

'I said enough! Now wash your hands ready for supper.'

Mary followed him into the kitchen, and putting her

arm around him she whispered, 'She's tired, love, and all they've talked about in the market is the murder and she's had enough. All right?'

He just nodded, washed his hands and went back and sat at the table, ready to eat.

Phoebe wasn't the only one to be on edge. Arthur Stanley was sitting alone in his local, silently cursing his brother. His temper had put them both in danger. Percy could end up with a death sentence and he could spend years in prison, his life wasted for nothing. The police were bound to come round to question them if they discovered the identity of the victim. He wasn't worried, he'd just deny everything, but Percy was so hot-headed and if he lost his temper, he might give the game away. He ordered another drink.

Days passed. Clarke's brother had posted him missing and after finding a letter with his name on it in his pocket, his brother was informed and asked to come to Southampton to identify the body. It was a gruesome thing to have to do after so long, but Jimmy Clarke recognised the watch and ring that had been removed.

The police interviewed Jimmy afterwards.

'Have you any idea as to why he would come up to Southampton?' he was asked.

'I had a drink with him the night before he went missing. He said he was coming to see a customer, someone he'd dealt with years before. I gathered that whoever it was, was not anyone he had a lot of time for.'

'Did he mention this person's name?'

Shaking his head Jimmy said, 'No, and I didn't ask. I

wasn't really interested. Me and my brother don't work together. I'm a carpenter. I mend furniture, make doors and tables, all legit! We live in different worlds and look where he's ended up! Now I'll have to arrange a funeral.'

When Ben read the medical report, he checked with his notes and realised the night he'd gone to the brothers' lock-up could possibly be around the time of the murder. He mentioned it to Detective Inspector Jack Bentley, who was in charge of the case.

'It all seemed a bit strange at the time. I couldn't understand the use of sand. If you spill something, a bucket of water is usually sufficient to clean up, but I'm wondering now if it has any significance? Sand would soak up any blood before it was washed away.'

The detective turned to his colleague. 'Bet you ten to one he came to see Percy Stanley. There were three houses robbed on Christmas Eve and some jewellery was among the missing items. It was a professional job, no fingerprints. Maybe Clarke came to buy the goods and they met at the lock-up. If there was a fight and Clarke was killed, there would be a considerable amount of blood to clean up. Maybe that's where the sand was used. Then they dumped him in the churchyard!'

'We could get a search warrant for the Stanleys' house and take a look,' his colleague suggested.

'We could indeed. Mind you, he's probably stashed the stuff away by now, but if we search the house, it might just rattle his cage and he may decide to move it. He's under observation in the market, so if we don't find anything at the house, we've got tabs on him if he goes to collect something. Chances are it will unsettle him if he had anything to do with the crime. That's when villains make mistakes.' He rose to his feet. 'Come along, let's get on with it.'

That evening, as the brothers sat down to eat, there was a loud banging on the front door. Percy opened it to be confronted by the detective inspector and several policemen.

Waving the warrant, Bentley pushed his way in. 'I've a search warrant to go over your house.' Turning to two of the officers, he sent them upstairs and the rest started to open up cupboard doors and pull out drawers, spilling the contents on the floor.

Arthur sat at the table watching them, holding his breath as his brother protested.

'I hope you're going to put all that back,' he complained, pointing to the mess on the floor. He was ignored. He sat at the table and lit a cigarette. 'I've no idea what you're looking for, gents, but you're wasting your time.' His brother kicked him under the table and frowned at him.

The police were thorough in their search but found nothing.

Percy sneered at them. 'Didn't I tell you?'

Bentley glared at him. 'Think you're clever, don't you? It's only a matter of time!' He walked out of the house followed by the others. Turning to one of the men, he said, 'He's moved the stuff, now he'll be watched even closer because he'll want rid of the goods if he's tied to the murder. We just have to be patient.'

Inside the house, Arthur let out a sigh of relief. 'Thank God that's over. Now what?'

'I'll have to get rid of the stuff we took. I can't risk trying to sell it now. It's the only thing that could tie us into Clarke.

We'll just have to bide our time. Pity, it's worth a bomb!'

'Jesus! Never mind the money, it could put both of us away and you at the end of the hangman's noose.'

'Will you shut your mouth! I'm not going down for murder, no way. I just need time to think.'

'Where have you hidden the spoils?'

'Best you don't know, then you can't tell anyone.'

With a look of astonishment Arthur snapped back at him. 'What do you mean? If I was to tell someone, I'd be sent to prison too, and I can assure you that no one is going to put me behind bars.'

'Well I've just removed the temptation.' He glared at his brother. 'I don't trust anybody, not even you.'

Arthur just stared at him, lost for words.

Chapter Eight

As the weeks passed, the thoughts of the murder had begun to fade from most people's minds. Life continued in the market. Phoebe and the Stanley brothers were the only people still living with the memory. She tried to shut the violent scene from her mind and continue her daily routine. Every day she saw the man who had committed it and she was still nervous around him, but she did her best to hide her feelings.

Percy Stanley had been very clever. He was certain that the police would keep a watch on him after searching his house and had left the stolen goods where he'd hidden them. In time, the police chief said they couldn't afford the extra men to watch him any longer, and Ben was informed that he alone was to keep an eye on the man. Until now, the routine for Percy Stanley and his brother was to leave the market at the end of the day, go for a pint at their local pub and then go home.

The one thing that helped Ben during this tedious task was his time spent with Phoebe. He'd continued to take her out and their friendship grew. They would go to the cinema, for a drink, an occasional meal, and on a Sunday sometimes he'd be invited to Phoebe's home, where Mary would cook them a roast dinner.

Marj was delighted. To her mind, Ben was a cut above the local lads and just the person she would like to see Phoebe settle down with. She said as much one day as they supped a cup of tea together on the stall.

'So, darlin', 'ow's the great romance going?'

Phoebe laughed. 'It's not a romance, Marj, we're just good friends, that's all.'

'No, love, you couldn't be more wrong. I see the way 'e looks at you, 'e may not have let on yet, but I recon 'e 'as real feelings for you. You wait and see!'

Phoebe wandered back to her stall. She really liked Ben and knew that *her* feelings towards him were deepening, but apart from a kiss and a cuddle, he'd not said anything to make her think there was anything permanent between them. Besides, if there were, what on earth was she to do? Her work in the market was keeping her family. There was no way she could give it up – get married, have a home of her own. She wasn't disappointed – that was the way it was. She knew that when her father had died, it made her the breadwinner. Her mother and Tim were her life, she was responsible for them. They relied on her, she couldn't leave them to fend for themselves.

She was not alone in her dilemma. Ben too was in a

quandary. He'd fallen in love with Phoebe, but hadn't been able to tell her the real reason he was working in the market. It upset him to think he had to have secrets from her, but it was his job and to share the news with her would blow his cover. Apart from this, he realised how the Collins family relied on her for their upkeep. As it happened, at the moment he had no choice but to carry on as he was, but he didn't enjoy the subterfuge.

Phoebe was coping with her conscience. It seemed to her that all interest in the murder had also died. She was the only witness. Her evidence could put Percy Stanley away where he deserved to be. Whoever the victim was, villain or not, he didn't deserve such a death and Stanley shouldn't be allowed to get away scot-free. He'd already served a prison sentence for GBH. He was a dangerous man, who, if allowed to wander freely, could possibly kill again. But although she felt strongly about the right and wrongs of the situation, she didn't have the courage to inform the police. After all, she had no proof of what she saw. It would be her word against his.

At last spring had arrived. The parks were full of daffodils in bloom, the wild cherry trees in blossom and the spirits of the townsfolk were lifted. It was Phoebe's turn to tease her good friend Marj. Tony Jackson, the man who ran the stall selling hardware, had been paying attention to her. He'd taken her out for a drink a couple of times and when he wasn't busy in the market, he'd wander over for a chat.

Phoebe sidled over to her friend when Tony had left one morning.

'You know what they say, Marj? In spring a young man's fancy turns to thoughts of love! I reckon Tony has fallen for you.'

Marj blushed like a schoolgirl. 'Don't be so bloody daft! In any case, Tony is 'ardly a young man any more. 'E's fifty, for God's sake.'

'Snow on the roof doesn't mean there's no fire in the grate,' said Phoebe, quoting another old saying. 'Wouldn't you like a bit of company in your old age? Someone to cuddle into on a cold night? You're always telling me that love makes the world go round – or are you all mouth and no trousers?'

'You been reading a book of quotes by any chance?' her friend retorted.

'No, but I hate the thought of you living the rest of your life alone.' She grinned broadly. 'You could still give a man a run for his money, I'm sure.'

There was a wicked twinkle in Marj's eye when she answered. 'That I could!'

'Well, what are you waiting for?' Phoebe walked away, leaving her friend to think about her advice.

Phoebe was really fond of Marj. When her father died and she took over the stall next to her, the woman had watched over her. Helped her with various rules and regulations of the market. Given her tips about looking after her stall, about the things that sold well. She owed Marj a great deal and longed to see her taken care of by someone who was kind and caring. Tony Jackson was both.

She said as much to Ben as he helped her put her stall away that evening.

He helped her lock up and after putting an arm around her said, 'You are a romantic at heart, Phoebe.'

'There's nothing wrong with that, Ben! Just because Marj and Tony are no longer young, it doesn't mean they have no feelings any more.'

'Oh, I quite agree, you only have to see my parents together to know that. They are still head over heels for each other. Come on, I'll walk you home.'

When they arrived, Phoebe invited Ben in for a cup of tea. She was surprised not to see her mother in the kitchen, only Tim, who was filling the kettle.

'Where's Mum?'

'She's in bed, she said she wasn't feeling well.'

Phoebe ran up the stairs to find Mary swaddled in bedclothes, shivering and complaining about the cold.

Phoebe put her hand on her mother's forehead, it was burning. 'How long have you felt like this?' she asked.

'Since yesterday, but I had some laundry to finish. Then, when I'd delivered it, I came to bed. My breathing's bad and I have pains in my chest.'

Phoebe found a couple more blankets and tucked her mother in, then went downstairs and sent Tim for the doctor and made a cup of tea for her mother.

'What is it?' asked Ben.

'She's not well, she says she's cold but she's burning up. I'm really worried.'

Ben made her sit down after she'd helped her mother drink a little of the warm beverage. 'I'll wait with you for the doctor. Try not to worry.'

The doctor duly arrived and examined Mrs Collins.

Then he told Phoebe he was going to call an ambulance as he thought her mother may have pneumonia.

'The sooner we get her to the hospital, the better.'

When the ambulance arrived, Ben offered to stay with Tim until she came home.

'Don't worry about Tim. I'll be here until you return, however long that may be. I won't leave the boy.'

Phoebe climbed into the ambulance and waved to Ben and Tim who stood watching. She noticed how Ben had a comforting arm around her brother's shoulders and knew he was in safe hands.

Mary was quickly taken into a ward and examined by the doctor. He gave instructions to the matron, then he came into the waiting room to see Phoebe.

He came straight to the point.

'Your mother has pneumonia. I'm putting her on oxygen to help her breathing. Her temperature is very high, and we must try to bring that down.'

'Is she going to recover, Doctor?'

'The next twenty-four hours will be crucial. We'll do our very best for her.'

'Can I see her?'

'Yes. Sit with her for a while, if you wish. Don't worry if she seems a little confused, that's normal under the circumstances. I advise you to go home after and get some sleep. Come back in the morning. We'll have a clearer picture then.'

A nurse took Phoebe into the ward and to the bed where Mary lay. She closed the curtains around the bed and left her alone with her mother.

Phoebe gazed at the prostrate figure beneath the bedclothes, eyes closed, a mask over her face, an oxygen cylinder beside the bed. She took her mother's hand in hers, fighting back the tears. She spoke softly.

'My goodness me, Mum! I can't leave you alone for five minutes and you're in trouble. The doctor is nice, love, he's going to try and get your temperature down, and then you'll feel better.'

There was no answer.

'When the warmer weather comes, we'll take a picnic one Sunday and go to the beach. Tim will love that. Perhaps we'll ask Ben to come too.'

She sat for another hour, stroking her mother's hand, talking softly, then she stood up, kissed her mother on the forehead and said, 'I have to go now, Mum. Ben is looking after Tim and he'll be worried wondering how you are. I'll come back in the morning. I do love you, Mum. You get well, you hear?'

Her mind in turmoil, Phoebe hardly remembered getting home, but as she let herself into the house and saw Ben, who rose to his feet as she stepped into the room, she burst into tears.

Gathering her into his arms, Ben just held her close until she had recovered enough to tell him and Tim what had happened. She tried to play down the seriousness of the situation so as not to frighten her young brother, but Ben saw what she was doing and once Tim had gone to bed, he asked her for the true situation.

'Mum's very ill, her temperature is high and she's on oxygen to help her breathe. I'm scared Ben, really scared. I'm to go back in the morning.'

'Right,' he said. 'If it's all right with you, I'll camp out on the settee with a couple of blankets, give Tim his breakfast, see him off to school and if you want me to, I'll come to the hospital and sit with you.'

'But what about your stall?'

'This is far more important. Now, what have you in the house to eat, you must have something. Tim and I had some stew that was on the hob, there's a little left – try and eat just a bit of it.'

She made to protest but he was adamant. 'You need to keep up your strength. Now, just sit down and I'll cut you a slice of bread and butter to go with it.'

Too weary to argue, Phoebe did as she was told. She was relieved to have someone to take control as she was incapable of thoughts, other than those of her mother.

Once she'd eaten, she found a couple of blankets for Ben, who stoked up the fire and kissed her goodnight. 'Try and get some sleep. I'll be here if you need me.'

Phoebe slept fitfully for a while, then sank into a deep sleep, waking suddenly just after seven o'clock. She quickly dressed and made her way to the kitchen, where she saw Ben and Tim sitting eating porridge and toast.

'Good morning! Sit and have a cup of tea while I make you some breakfast,' Ben said. 'Did you get any sleep?'

'Eventually. You all right, Tim?'

He smiled at her. 'Ben can cook! He made the porridge and toasted the bread by the fire. How about that!'

Phoebe grinned. 'He's an unusual man, I'll grant you.'

'My dad cooks,' Ben said proudly. 'He makes a terrific roast dinner. He and my mum taught me. Mum said if I was leaving home, I needed to know how to feed myself properly.' He kept the conversation light for Tim's sake until it was time for the lad to go to school.

Ben offered to walk him there, but the boy refused politely. At the front door, he hesitated. 'Give Mum my love, Phoebe. Tell her I miss her.'

She got to her feet and hugged her brother. 'That I will. Now off you go and be a good boy. See you later.'

Just after nine o'clock, Ben and Phoebe took a tram to the hospital and checked in at the reception. They were told to go to the ward where the nurse would see them. But as they arrived they were greeted by the doctor, who took them into an empty side room.

'Sit down, Miss Collins.'

Phoebe's heart sank at his serious tone. She felt Ben take her hand.

'I am so sorry, my dear, but your mother passed away an hour ago. We did all we could for her, but she slipped quietly away.'

Phoebe let out a cry of anguish. Ben put an arm round her shoulders.

The tears came slowly, it was too much to take in. Her mother gone – and so quickly.

'Can I see her?'

'But of course.' He looked at Ben and said, 'Perhaps you could come with the young lady?'

Ben nodded and they stood up and followed the doctor. He opened the door to a side room and let them enter alone.

Phoebe walked over to the bed and looked at her mother. She leant forward and kissed her forehead. 'Oh,

Mum, what will we do without you?' She sat on the chair beside the bed and placed her hand over her mother's and cried softly.

Ben stood beside her, his hand on her shoulder, and let her release the grief that overwhelmed her.

A while later, Ben left the room saying he wouldn't be long. He spoke to the doctor and arranged for the body to be taken to the hospital morgue until a funeral could be arranged, thus saving Phoebe more anguish, and returned to her side.

Eventually she stood up. 'It's time to go. I have arrangements to make.'

'First, we'll go home, give ourselves time to think. It's all been so sudden that it's hard to accept.' He caught her firmly by her shoulders and stared into her eyes. 'You do not have to handle this alone, Phoebe. I'll be here with you until it's over.'

She leant against him. 'Oh, thank you, you have no idea how that makes me feel.'

'Come along, let's get a tram and at home we can at last gather our thoughts and make a list of what's to be done.'

Chapter Nine

The two of them sat at the table, drinking cups of strong tea. Phoebe was still in shock from the sudden loss of her mother.

'I'll have to tell Tim when he comes home. There's no point in going to the school, it wouldn't make a bit of difference to Mum. It's best he's in his own home to get such news.' She turned to Ben. 'That poor boy, he's now an orphan – and so am I. But he's so young. He adored his mother, he'll be devastated.'

'Of course he will, but life can be harsh, Phoebe. We just have to face up to it when it happens. He has you . . . and me. He's not alone in this.'

With tears brimming her eyes, Phoebe gazed at him. 'I don't know what I'd do without you, Ben, but you must go back to work, this isn't your family and you'll be losing money.'

'Now you listen to me, young lady! I told you, you wouldn't have to face this alone and I meant every word. A few days off the market isn't going to break me. We have a funeral to organise, Tim to look after, then we can go back to work. It's probably a good thing to do. Keeping busy is the best answer. It doesn't give you so much time to think. Now let's get some food on the go for when Tim comes home.'

Between them they chopped vegetables and a little meat that was in the larder and made a hearty soup. Phoebe changed the bed linen and put it in the copper in the outhouse to boil, hung the pillows on the line to freshen. She sat on the bare empty bed she'd shared with her mother and wept. Never again would Mary share this room with her. Never again would they lay and chat about the day's happenings. Never again would she walk into the house and see Mary ironing the laundry she took in to swell their coffers. Never again! She lay on the bed and sobbed for the woman she loved.

Downstairs, Ben could hear her anguish, but he left her to her grief, knowing she had to get it out of her system before she could move on. He longed to comfort her, but he let her be.

Eventually Phoebe came downstairs, her pretty face swollen with weeping. She washed her face and saw to the laundry and laid the table, waiting for her brother to return, dreading the moment.

Tim opened the door and stepped into the living room, shutting the door behind him. Turning, he saw Ben stirring a pot on the stove, then he saw Phoebe and knew by the expression on her face that something was wrong.

Phoebe walked over to him and gently led him to the settee. Taking his hands in hers she spoke softly. 'I need you to be brave, Tim, as I've some sad news to tell you.'

The boy's eyes widened with concern. 'It's about Mum, isn't it? Is she all right?'

Taking a deep breath she said, 'Mum passed away this morning, Tim. Sadly the doctors couldn't bring her temperature down. She's with Dad now.'

'She's dead?'

Phoebe, unable to speak, nodded.

'Oh, Phoebe, I'll never see her again,' and he burst into tears.

Phoebe held him close and let him cry.

Ben looked over at the pair and was saddened to see the boy's distress over the loss of his mother. He was a good lad whose world had suddenly collapsed. It was a lot to take in. He walked over to the boy and gave him a handkerchief.

Knowing he was in a state of shock, he encouraged Tim to come and sit by the fire to keep warm. He placed a shawl of Phoebe's around his shoulders, knowing that shock can chill a body. He made a cup of tea and put a splash of brandy in it and gave it to Tim, then made another one for Phoebe. He always carried a flask of brandy with him to keep out the cold, and today it filled a need more than on most days.

Eventually, Ben served up the soup and cut some bread and they sat around the table, not really wanting to eat, but nevertheless finding a comfort from it.

As Phoebe cleared away the dishes, Ben turned to the boy. 'Tomorrow, Tim, I'm taking Phoebe to book your mother's funeral. Do you want to come with us or go to school?'

'I'll come with you please, Ben. I couldn't face school.'

'That's fine. I'll get a message to your teacher explaining your absence. A couple of days away won't do any harm, but after that we all have to get back to work and you to school. You understand, don't you? This isn't disrespecting your mother, it's just a fact of life. We all have to work to keep the money coming in to pay the bills.'

'Yes, I know, it's all right.' The boy looked at him. 'I'm so glad you're here, Ben. Phoebe needs you.'

'She needs you too, Tim. We men have to be strong for the women in the family. You'll help me, won't you?'

The boy sat up and straightening his shoulders said, 'Yes of course I will. Mum would want that.'

'Good lad. I knew I could rely on you. Tomorrow after breakfast we'll go and make the necessary arrangements.'

The next morning, the three of them went to the funeral directors, showed the man the death certificate they'd been given and booked a date for the funeral, a week hence. Phoebe handed over the money to cover the cost. It had taken almost all of their savings.

Ben suggested they went for a walk and then stopped for a hot drink and some cake on the way home. He couldn't think of anything else to do to break the spell of despair that was hanging over them.

They settled in a small cafe and all drank hot chocolate and ate sponge cake.

Ben turned to Phoebe. 'I think that tomorrow we should return to the market. Tim, you can help Phoebe until the funeral. You have to work to make up the money that's been paid out today. You understand this, don't you?'

The boy nodded. 'I'll work hard, you'll see.'

'Is there anything else I can do, Phoebe, before I go back to my flat? I have to have a bath and get a change of clothes and I have things to do. If that's all right with you?'

'Oh, Ben, of course you must go. You have been such a help. I don't know what we would have done without your support, but Tim and I will be fine. I'll see you in the morning at the market.'

Leaving the cafe, Ben kissed Phoebe goodbye and went to Tim's school, where he spoke to the headmaster to explain the boy's absence. The man was most understanding and agreed to let Tim stay away until after the funeral.

'He's only ten; he needs time to get used to the idea. Working with his sister for a few days will do him good. Please give my condolences to Miss Collins.'

From there Ben reported to his superior at the police station, explaining there had been a death in the family, not explaining whose family.

It was decided that Ben should continue in the market for another month. If by then the Stanley brothers hadn't tried to move the stolen goods, the case would be put aside, but left open.

On his way home, Ben wondered how he would explain to Phoebe his eventual departure. Would he be free to tell her the truth or would he continue to have to lie to her? Well, he'd sort that out when the time came. Right now, he needed to soak in a bath and get some clean clothes. Sleeping on the settee was not conducive to clean living.

Phoebe and Tim decided to walk along the pier before going home. It was nice to be out in the fresh air. They walked hand in hand, looking through the slats to the water below and then bought some sandwiches to eat. Sitting, looking out over the water.

'Will Mum go to heaven?' Tim suddenly asked.

'Yes, love. She'll be with Dad now. He'll be glad of her company, because he must have missed her.'

Tim pondered over this for a moment. 'Yes, I hadn't thought of that. I'm glad she's not wandering in a strange place on her own. I wouldn't like that.'

Phoebe smiled to herself and wondered at the innocence of children.

'You'll have to help me to sort through the goods on the stall tomorrow. We must make sure to move anything that looks stale. We have to keep up our good reputation.'

'When I leave school, I'll work full-time to help you.'

'That's very kind of you, Tim, but by then you might want to do something else. We'll wait and see. Now, let's get home. We need to get ready for tomorrow. I'll fill the bath for you later and have one myself, so we'll be ready for the customers.'

'Marj will wonder where you've been,' he said. 'I like her, she's kind. She gives me chocolate.'

Phoebe was looking forward to seeing her friend. Marj had always been there for her from the very beginning and she needed the warmth of her friendship now more than ever.

In a strange way, Phoebe was looking forward to returning to the market. It was a feeling of normality she needed at the moment, and she worried about her young brother. They both were grieving over their loss and being busy would be their saving grace.

* * *

The following morning, Phoebe and Tim arrived at the market, opened the shed and wheeled out the stall. They pushed it over to its patch and saw that Marj was already setting up. She hurried over to them.

'Oh, Timmy, Phoebe, I 'eard about your mother. I'm so very sorry.' She gathered them both into her arms. 'Is there anything I can do, anything you need?'

'No thanks,' said Phoebe. 'Ben has been with me ever since we found mother so sick. He even waited with me in the hospital and helped me arrange the funeral.'

'Ah, God bless that boy! I knew he was a good'un!'

She looked at Tim and held his chin gently. 'You are the man of the house now, young Tim. You have to look after your sister.'

'We look after each other, don't we, Tim?'

'Yes, we do. Dad's looking after Mum up in heaven and I'll look after Phoebe down here.'

Marj couldn't speak for a moment so moved was she by his words.

'And I'll keep an eye on you both!' she declared. 'Oh look, there's Ben.'

They turned to see Ben putting his stall in place. He walked over, put an arm around Phoebe, kissed her on the cheek and smiled at Tim.

'Everything all right here?'

'Looks bloody marvellous to me, laddie!' Marj was grinning broadly. 'Well, best get set up if we're to make any money today.'

Phoebe and Tim went through the fruit and vegetables on the stall, making sure the goods were still fresh.

During the day, other stallholders came over to give

their condolences, which was kind but Phoebe was relieved when it was over and they could get on and work.

Ben treated them to fish and chips midday, which gave Tim something to do. The boy was quiet but worked hard when they were busy. Closing time eventually arrived and they packed up ready for home.

Ben came over to see they were all right. 'I'm sorry I can't come back to the house with you, I have to meet someone to talk business.'

'We'll be fine,' Phoebe said. 'We've had a busy day and, to be honest, we're so tired I think an early night is on the cards for both of us.'

He kissed her goodbye and left them to go home.

Ben was keeping watch on the Stanley brothers in the hope that they may decide to move the stolen jewellery. Every night he kept out of sight and saw them go into their local as was their habit before going home. But after waiting for a couple of hours, it was apparent they were home for the night, Ben made his way back to his flat, frustrated that the case in question didn't appear to be progressing.

Percy Stanley, though, was thinking that, as things had quietened down, he could possibly retrieve the stuff he'd stolen. But who would buy it? Without a buyer, he didn't want his ill-gotten goods in the house, just in case the police called. No way was he going back up to the Smoke to trade with Charlie Blackmore, who would pay him a pittance. His only other way was to visit second-hand shops in other towns and sell the jewellery piece by piece. He had no choice. Perhaps next week.

Chapter Ten

It was the day of the funeral. Ben arrived early to be with Phoebe and Tim when the hearse arrived. He took one look at the grief on Tim's face and walked over to him. Placing a firm hand on the boy's shoulder he said, 'Take a deep breath, lad, we are the men here and we have to be strong. OK?'

Tim nodded and walked to the door.

Outside stood the hearse. Phoebe, Tim and Ben stood behind it and were joined by near neighbours as the hearse moved off. Soon Marj and Tony Jackson joined the mourners as they made the sad journey to the church. Unable to look at the coffin, Phoebe kept her gaze upon the ground as she walked.

Once inside the church, Ben sat between Phoebe and Tim, with Marj and Tony behind, along with the neighbours and friends of Mary.

Phoebe went through the service automatically, turning the pages of the hymn book as was required. Her mind devoid of feeling – almost in a trance. She scarcely heard the words the vicar spoke from the pulpit, but as the congregation stood for the final hymn, it all became real and her tears flowed. Ben put an arm around her shoulders and held her close as they made their way to the interment.

'Ashes to ashes, dust to dust.' The vicar's voice carried in the quiet air.

Eventually, Phoebe took Tim's hand and stepped up to the grave and each of them picked up a handful of earth, threw it on the coffin below. It was only then that Tim's tears flowed. Holding him tightly, Phoebe walked back and stood cuddling him as the other mourners took their turn. At last it was over.

Phoebe looked at the small collection of wreaths waiting to be laid and was grateful to those who had sent them. The mourners followed Phoebe and Tim back to the house. She'd made sandwiches and cakes the previous day, wrapping the sandwiches in damp tea cloths to keep them fresh. Ben made pots of tea and helped where he could.

Marj had her arm around Tim. 'I'm so proud of you, lad, and so would your mother 'ave been, the way you stood today at 'er funeral. A young man, not a boy.'

He looked pleased. 'Thanks, Marj. Ben said we had to be the men of the house.'

'You were all of that, my love. You know, don't you, that we are mates me and you, and if ever you're worried and want a chat, but not with your sister, you come to me. All right?'

He smiled. 'Thanks, Marj.'

She hugged him. 'Now, go and eat. A growing boy like you needs to feed 'imself.'

Tony Jackson had been listening to the conversation. 'That was kind of you, Marj. You have a big heart.'

'I love those two!' she declared. 'They 'ave 'ad a 'ard life and now it won't be any easier.'

'That Phoebe is a strong young woman, she'll cope.'

'Yes, and now she has Ben. I always hoped they would get together. Tim would have a father figure in his life too. A boy needs that.'

After everyone had left, the three of them washed up and cleared away. Then they collapsed in chairs now the ordeal was over.

Ben spoke. 'I know we're all shattered so I booked us a table at a restaurant in Oxford Street. It isn't far to walk and I'm sure Phoebe doesn't feel like cooking.'

She looked at him with surprise. 'Oh, Ben, how thoughtful – and you're right. To cook a meal would be one task too much today.'

'What do you think, Tim? Are you for it?'

The sadness reflected in the boy's eyes changed to one of excitement. 'Oh yes, that would be great.'

Settled at the table in the restaurant a while later, they tucked into roast chicken and all the trimmings. After such a traumatic day, they were all hungry now that they'd relaxed.

'I thought the funeral went well,' Ben said. 'It was so nice to see that Marj and Tony had closed their stalls to come and pay their respects.'

'There were some lovely flowers,' Tim said. 'Mum loved flowers.'

'I expect there'll be plenty where she is,' said Phoebe.

He stopped eating for a moment. 'Will she forget us now she's with Dad?'

Ben looked at the boy. 'Never! Both your mum and dad will be watching over you both. You won't forget them, so why would they forget you?'

Tim shrugged. 'I don't know, it was just a thought, that's all.'

'Tomorrow you have to go back to school, Tim,' said Phoebe gently. 'I expect your friends will ask about Mum. You must expect that, but in time they'll forget and you'll be back to normal. We all have to get back to normal, she would want that.'

'Leave some room for some ice cream, Tim,' said Ben with a grin.

The boy's eyes widened. 'Ice cream! I love ice cream.'

'I know, we'll all have some, then we have to go home and go to bed, ready for the morning.' Ben turned to Phoebe. 'Will you be all right tonight?'

She smiled at him. 'I'll be fine, but thanks for being with us through everything. I can't tell you how much it helped us both.'

'Oh, you won't get rid of me that easily, Phoebe. I intend to be around for quite some time.'

She saw the look of affection reflected in his eyes and wondered exactly what he meant by that. The future had never been mentioned between them. Was he to be her future? She knew that's what she wanted, but how serious was this man she'd grown to love?

* * *

Ben walked them home and saw them safely in the house. He kissed Phoebe goodnight.

'I'll see you in the market.' Turning to Tim, he said, 'I hope school goes well. I'll see you soon.' Then he left.

'I like Ben,' said Tim as he undressed in front of the fire. 'He's a nice man.'

'Yes, he is,' Phoebe said as she helped him. 'Now, off to bed, I'll call you in the morning.' She gave him a quick hug. 'I love you, Tim.'

He hugged her back. 'I love you too. I'm going to take good care of you, you'll see.'

She felt a lump rise in her throat. 'I'm sure you will. Now, off you go.'

Once she was alone, Phoebe sat in front of the fire staring into the flickering embers. Well, her mother was laid to rest and she was alone to look after her brother, be responsible for him as he grew into a man. 'I'll do my best, Mum, I promise,' she whispered. She let the silent tears flow. The house seemed so empty without her mother's presence. It was still so hard to accept that she wouldn't be in this kitchen again when she came home. But now the funeral was over, life had to go on. She alone was the breadwinner now. There was rent to be paid as well as household bills, and Tim seemed to grow daily, which meant new clothes and shoes. Taking a deep breath, she got to her feet, saw to the fire and went to bed.

Chapter Eleven

Percy Stanley had decided to try and sell the rest of his ill-gotten gains. It bothered him that he still had them, and he'd decided to go to Salisbury and try and sell some pieces to one of the jewellers in the town. He was unknown there and felt safe in trying to get rid of some of it. He didn't mention his plan to his brother. The less he knew the better.

That evening, after closing the stall, going for a pint as was their habit, he grabbed a sandwich and made an excuse to leave the house.

Ben had secreted himself in the doorway of an empty house along the road where he had a clear view of the brothers' front door. Surprised to see Percy emerge on his own and look around furtively before walking off, Ben wondered if he was about to retrieve the stolen goods. He followed him discreetly, glad of the fact that tonight there was no moon and the streets were dark. But where was he headed?

He was surprised to see Percy enter a public toilet and emerge shortly after, clutching a package, then walking off, looking around to make sure he hadn't been seen. Ben followed at a distance, making use of the dark to cover his existence. Eventually, after a roundabout route, Percy returned to the house. Ben waited for a while but eventually decided the man was home for the night. He walked back to the toilets and entered. There were the usual urinals and two private cubicles. He entered one and looked around. He looked at the cistern and lifted the lid, but it was empty, so he moved to the next one. The lid of the seat was wet as was the lid of the cistern. He could only assume that this was where the goods were hidden. He shook his head at the audacity of the man. The chance he took that the toilet would continue to flow so no one would have to look inside the cistern. The stuff must have been in a waterproof cover.

Although it was late, Ben went to the police station to report, but the detective in charge of the case had gone home hours ago. The desk sergeant told him, 'I'll leave my report to be read first thing. Go home, laddie, there's nothing more you can do tonight.'

Ben walked home, frustrated, certain that a search would uncover the stolen goods, but unable to do anything about it. He went to bed a very disgruntled man.

Early the next morning, Ben was surprised to see Arthur Stanley open up the stall on his own. When he was set up, he wandered over to Stanley and casually said, 'Strange to see you on your own. Is your brother ill?'

'No, he's off on business, that's all.'

'Oh, that's good news. Will he be back in time to help you pack up?'

'Probably. He said he was only going to Salisbury, that's all.'

'Let's hope we have a busy day, it makes the day pass that much quicker. Well, best get back.' Ben had seen the two police who usually inspected the market arrive. They made their way round the stalls, chatting to the stallholders, but lingered at Ben's, picking up various items while talking quietly.

'The house was empty when the men called earlier. Where is Percy Stanley?'

'Salisbury, I'm told. The house should have been searched last night!' He held up a shirt for inspection.

The officers strolled over to another stall and eventually approached Arthur. 'On your own today, then?'

With a glare he answered, 'You've got eyes, ain't ya?'

'No need for that tone of voice, young man, I asked a polite question. It's so unusual not to see you both together, that's all.'

Arthur just stared at them and they walked away.

Ben was certain that Percy was off trying to sell the pieces of jewellery and was still annoyed. Had they searched the house last night, he felt sure they would have found the goods, but at least they knew where to look. No doubt they'd be on the phone to the local police in Salisbury with the information.

Having arrived early, Percy wasted no time in visiting the first jeweller who bought second-hand goods. He entered the shop.

An elderly man greeted him from behind the counter. 'Good morning, sir. Can I help you?'

Percy put on an act that would have graced any stage. He looked upset and spoke softly. 'My old aunt died last month and left me a couple of her rings. Now, I'm not married and I don't have anyone to give them to and I wondered if you would be interested in buying them?'

'Let me take a look,' said the jeweller.

Percy handed them over and the man looked somewhat surprised when he saw the quality of the jewels. He studied them through his eyeglass.

While he did so, Percy gave him his tale of woe. 'My aunt married above her class. Her old man had money and we were happy for her, but what would I do with these? The cash would be a help with bills and a new pair of shoes. Maybe a new shirt.'

The jeweller put down his eyeglass. 'These rings are quality.'

Percy feigned surprise. 'Really? Well I thought they looked nice, but what would I know?'

'You're a lucky man, Mr . . . ?'

'James. Harry James.'

The jeweller took another look, then he thought for a moment. Percy held his breath.

'I can offer you three hundred pounds for the two.'

Percy was delighted, knowing that old Blackmore in London would have halved the price. 'Thanks, that's wonderful. You've no idea what that money will do for me.' He pocketed the cash and left the shop.

He took himself off to a small cafe and had breakfast followed by a cup of coffee, hardly able to cover his delight. He'd try the string of pearls next, but in a shop further away.

Here he gave the same sad story. 'Someone told me they were real.'

'Oh yes, sir. Your aunt was a lucky lady, these are certainly real.'

Percy emerged from the shop with another small wad of money and a big smile. Oh yes, he thought. Mr Harry James is a very lucky fellow.

Percy Stanley was having a great day, but back in Southampton, young Tim Collins was not. Children can be heartless and the questions that were asked of him during playtime were hard to handle.

A small crowd of boys surrounded him.

'So you ain't got no mother no more?' asked one.

'No, she died.'

'So who is going to cook your meals and do the washing, then?'

'My sister, Phoebe.'

'Did you see her die?'

'What was it like?'

'Is she buried so the worms get to eat her body, then?'

This was too much for the boy and he lashed out, hitting the lad. Then he rushed into school in tears, cannoning into the headmaster, who, seeing his distress, took him into his study.

'Sit down, Tim.' He poured a glass of water and gave it to him with a handkerchief. Then he waited for the boy to recover.

'Children can be cruel, Tim. Especially those who don't know what it is to lose a mother. You mustn't mind them, they don't understand.'

'One said she was buried so the worms can eat her body!' Tim blurted out.

'Now that was unkind, but we two know that your mother isn't in that coffin. She's in heaven with your father. Our bodies are what we use down here on earth. In heaven it's different. We start again. Your parents will be young and without pain. Being happy together, looking down on the family, watching over them. She would have been cross with the boy that upset you.'

Tim looked up at the headmaster. 'I hit him, sir.'

'Oh dear, but I'm not surprised, I would probably have done the same in your shoes.'

'You would?'

With a wry smile, the man nodded. 'But you can't go round thumping everyone who says stupid things.'

'No, sir.'

'Give it a couple of days, lad. They'll soon forget. Now, I've got to blow the whistle for the end of playtime, so I suggest you return to your class.' He watched the boy walk away, sad for him having to learn such a hard lesson so early in life, but knowing it would probably be the first of many as he grew into a man.

Chapter Twelve

Percy Stanley caught a train back to Southampton in time to help his brother shut down the stall for the day. Ben watched him as he arrived and saw how pleased he looked, surmising that the trip had been a success. Which indeed it had been. Before leaving Salisbury, Percy had offloaded all his remaining pieces of jewellery and now felt secure. The police hadn't a chance now of putting him in the frame for the burglaries and therefore the murder of Frank Clarke, who might well have been to see him to purchase such goods. Now there was nothing to tie him into the man. But his confidence was disturbed before leaving the market that night.

Ben had closed early, wanting to report Percy's return to his superiors and Phoebe was putting away her stall, when one of her displays slipped off the barrow, spilling out of the doorway. Percy was passing at the time and picked up some of the fruit and stepped inside Phoebe's shed to hand them over. Phoebe didn't hear him and turned to be faced by the man she'd seen murdering a stranger. She screamed with fright.

Percy glared at her. 'I was only trying to help,' he snapped, but he paused when he saw the look of sheer terror on her face. His eyes narrowed as he moved closer to her. She stepped back from him and he could see she was shaking.

'What's the matter, girlie?' He stared hard at her. 'Why are you looking so scared?'

'You made me jump, that's all.' But her voice trembled as she spoke.

'You sure that's the only reason? Why are you shaking? Think I'm going to harm you in some way, is that it?' He grabbed her by the wrist.

Phoebe snatched her hand away and pulled herself together. 'No, of course not! You shouldn't creep up on me like that, it gave me a fright!' She took the fruit from him. 'Thanks.'

He watched her replace the goods, but her hands were shaking as she did so. He walked away, puzzled by her extreme reaction.

When he'd gone, Phoebe leant against the wall and slowly slid down it until she was sitting on the ground, still shaking. Never had she been so frightened in all her life! Now Percy Stanley was aware that she was scared of him and she'd seen the expression on his face as he'd questioned her. He'd been surprised at her reaction – rightly so, as he was unaware of the fact that she'd witnessed the murder.

But what if he eventually realised the reason – what then? But as she sat there, she argued with herself, there was no way he could discover the truth. He hadn't been aware of her presence. But as she finally locked up, she was a worried woman.

As Percy sat in the pub having a pint of beer with his brother, he couldn't get out of his mind the look of terror on the face of that girl from the fruit and veg stall. He knew that his reputation made some of the stallholders wary of him and that his presence sometimes made them uncomfortable. That he was used to, but tonight was very different and he couldn't put a finger on the reason behind her fear. It bothered him.

Phoebe arrived home and started to get her and Tim's supper. Her own worries were forgotten as Tim told her about his day and the teasing he had suffered from the schoolboys in the playground, but she was heartened when he told her of how the headmaster had taken him to his study and talked to him.

'He was right, Tim. It will be as Mum used to say – a seven-day wonder. It will pass, just try to ignore it, then they'll get tired of teasing you. One day the same thing will happen to one of them and only then will they truly understand.'

Tears filled his eyes. 'I miss her so much, Phoebe.'

She went over to him and held him close. 'So do I, love, every day, but we must be brave and carry on. It's what she would expect. She is with us all the time, Tim, here in our hearts.' She held her hand over his. 'She never will be far away.' Taking a deep breath, she said, 'We'll try and do something nice on Sunday. We need a treat. Perhaps we could take the ferry over to the Isle of Wight. That would be nice – a good sea breeze will blow the cobwebs away. What do you say?'

He cheered up immediately. 'Can we take a picnic and sit on the beach?'

'What a great idea. I'll buy some bread rolls on Saturday.'

'Perhaps Ben would like to come too,' he suggested.

'You can ask him on Saturday when you help me with the stall.'

Ben had readily agreed when Tim approached him. 'What a great idea! I could do with a day out away from work.' He wandered over to Phoebe. 'Thanks, I'd love to come with you tomorrow. Do you want me to bring anything?'

'No, I'll pack a picnic. The water will be too cold to swim, so we'll just sit on the beach.'

'I'll bring an old rug,' he offered. 'Which ferry had you in mind?'

'There's one that leaves just after ten o'clock. We can have a walk round Cowes first and look at the shops.'

Grinning, Ben said, 'You women and your shops! But Cowes is a quaint place. We'll stop and have a coffee before we settle on the beach. I'm really looking forward to it.'

Percy Stanley stood watching them chatting. The girl looked relaxed and normal, he thought, but then she looked up and caught him staring and the smile on her face disappeared and she looked away quickly.

Ben noticed the change in her. 'What's the matter? You suddenly looked worried, is something wrong?'

'It's that older Stanley brother,' she said quietly. 'He scares me for some reason. I feel uncomfortable around him.'

'He has that effect on most people, Phoebe. He's an unsavoury character. He hasn't bothered you, has he?'

She shook her head. 'No, but the other evening as I was putting my stall away, some of my goods fell off. He picked them up and walked into the shed. I didn't hear him and turned round and there he was. He gave me such a fright, I'm afraid I screamed.'

'If he gives you any trouble, any at all, you come to me. Understand?'

She gave a wan smile. 'Thanks, I'll do that.'

'I'll help you and Tim close up tonight before I move my stuff, all right?'

She nodded, but Ben could see she was really disturbed.

'You never have to worry about anything, Phoebe, because I'll always be around.' He gave her a brief kiss and walked back to his stall. He did notice during the rest of the day that Percy seemed to watch her every move. *Now why would he be so interested?* he wondered.

Marj walked over to Phoebe. 'I couldn't 'elp overhearing your plans for a trip to the Isle of Wight.' She looked slyly at her young friend. 'Things getting serious, then?'

'Not that I'm aware of. Ben's been a rock during Mum's death and the funeral, and he's been great with Tim, but nothing's been said about any future.'

'Give it time, love, 'e'll tell you when 'e's ready.'

'What about you and Tony, then?' Phoebe asked, eyes twinkling with mischief.

'Oh, we're chugging along nicely, thanks, and that's all

I'm saying!' She walked back, her throaty laugh lingering in the air.

Yes, she was enjoying her new relationship with Tony, mused Marj as she stood behind her stall. He was a nice chap. Kind, considerate. They'd been out for the occasional drink, a film or two, a meal now and again. She realised she was getting used to having him around. It was comforting, she admitted to herself. They had enjoyed a kiss and a cuddle, but that was as far as it went. She knew that she'd only have to give him a little encouragement for it to go further, but if she did, she mused, she'd be getting into a serious relationship and she wasn't at all sure she was ready to commit to that. Did she want a man around permanently? Was another marriage something to be considered? She enjoyed her freedom; did she want to have to look after a man again? Cook his meals, do his washing? No, she didn't! A lover, maybe? Now that was more like it. All the enjoyment and none of the domesticity. But was Tony the sort of man who would agree to that? She wasn't at all sure. He had old-fashioned values; he might be shocked at such a suggestion. She giggled to herself as she thought about it. She quite liked the idea of being a 'scarlet woman'.

On Sunday, Phoebe, Ben and Tim caught the ferry to the Isle of Wight. They sat outside on the deck chatting while Tim wandered around exploring. Phoebe told Ben about her brother's experience in the playground and how upset he'd been and how kind the headmaster was to the boy.

'It's a lot for him to handle,' Ben agreed. 'But children are surprisingly resilient. It's just a shame he hasn't a father to help him get over such a loss, but he's got us, Phoebe. He's not alone.' He put his arm round her.

She leant against him, her head against his shoulder. 'I don't know how I would have coped without you, Ben. I'll always be grateful to you.'

He didn't answer. Knowing that he'd fallen in love with Phoebe he was faced with a predicament. If he wanted to further their relationship, to have a future together, he'd have to be honest with her. She'd have to know who he really was, what his work entailed and at the moment it wasn't possible. This subterfuge didn't sit well with him, but he didn't have a choice. Once his duty in the market was over, then he'd be free to tell her the truth.

The ferry arrived in Cowes and they wandered around the quaint streets, looking in the shops, bought ice creams, had a coffee, then made their way to the beach, laid out the rug and settled in the sun. It wasn't warm enough to wear swimsuits, but they were able to sit comfortably without coats.

Having bought a bucket and a spade, Ben helped Tim build a splendid castle with a moat and a drawbridge using a piece of wood found in the sand.

Phoebe watched the two of them together, as they constructed their castle, concentrating, working together, laughing when things went wrong, thrilled with the end result. Ben was so good with Tim. A father figure was just what her brother needed, but if Ben left the market, how Tim would miss him – as would she. She quickly brushed the thought aside. Today they'd enjoy all being together.

The police enquiries at all the second-hand jewellery shops in Salisbury had paid off. The diamond rings and the string of pearls had been found. The jewellers had given a description of Harry James and it was obvious that Percy Stanley was the seller, which was verified when mug shots of him had been shown to the unfortunate buyers who had to return the goods, and on Monday morning, a warrant had been issued for Percy's arrest.

The market wasn't particularly busy on a Monday morning. The stallholders would clean their stalls and make a list of goods that had to be bought to replace that which had been sold the previous week, therefore it was with some interest that the sudden arrival of a police van and several uniformed police stopped everyone from working.

Phoebe and Marj stood together as they converged on the brothers' stall.

Arthur paled as they stood in front of him. Percy stood straight and just glared at them.

Holding up a piece of paper, a police sergeant walked behind the stall, looked at Percy and spoke. 'I am a police officer and I have a warrant for your arrest, Percy Stanley.' He produced a pair of handcuffs. 'Arms behind you and don't give me any trouble, I'm not in the mood!'

'Arrested on what charge?' Percy demanded.

'Burglary and selling stolen goods, for starters.'

'I don't know what the bleedin' hell you're talking about!'

'They all say that. Now . . . hands!' The constable put on the cuffs and read him his rights.

Arthur watched in silence as Percy was led away and glared at his brother as if to warn him to remain silent.

There was a sudden buzz around among the vendors.

Ben looked across at Arthur, who was standing with a stunned expression.

Arthur was now a worried man. If his brother had been found as the seller of the stolen jewellery, how much longer would it be before the murder would also be pinned on him, and if that happened it would mean a term of imprisonment for him too. The thought terrified him. For all his pretence of being big and tough like his brother, inside he was a weak man. He'd seen the inside of a prison and the men who inhabited such a place when he used to visit his brother. He'd heard the stories of what can happen inside, how dangerous a place it could be, and he was scared.

No one else was sorry to see Percy taken away, except perhaps Phoebe. In one way she was glad she wouldn't have to see him every day, but what if the police found out that he was guilty of the murder of the person found in the churchyard. What if it was suspected, but she was the only one who could prove it was him . . . what then?

Marj broke into her thoughts. 'Bloody good job that bastard's gone. I never felt comfortable when 'e was around. A villain of the worst kind, 'im! Cruel bugger! You only 'ad to look at 'is eyes to know 'e didn't have a scrap of compassion. Doubt that 'e even knew what it was.' She looked across at Arthur. 'I 'ope he shoves off, an' all. Without 'is brother around to look after 'im, 'e'll be bloody useless. Full of 'ot air, not got a brave bone in 'is body!'

Ben wandered over. 'Well, it's all going on today! Any idea what it's about?'

'The coppers say burglary and selling stolen goods,' Marj told him.

* * *

At police headquarters, Percy Stanley was in an identity parade. In a side room were the unfortunate men who'd purchased the jewels. They were to be sent in, one by one with an officer, and told to walk down the line, look carefully at each man and if they recognised anyone, to tap him on the shoulder and walk away.

Both of the men picked out Percy Stanley.

Chapter Thirteen

In an interview room, Percy sat at a table with two detectives sitting opposite. A look of defiance on his face, he stared at them but inside he was shaking. He knew he was in trouble as soon as he'd been picked out in the identity parade, but no way was he going to show the coppers how he felt. He leant casually back in his chair and waited.

One of the detectives had a list of the stolen jewellery in front of him with a few items ticked off. He ran his pencil down the list and circled the ones that were still missing. He looked up.

'Now don't waste police time by denying you took these items, Stanley.' He shoved the list across the table for Percy to see. 'You've been recognised as the seller of these goods, but I want to know where the missing pieces are. The ones that are circled.'

Percy gave a cursory glance at the list. 'I have no idea. They ain't nothing to do with me.'

The detective glared at him. 'But you don't deny selling the pieces that are ticked off the list?'

There was no point in denial, he knew that. 'No, I don't deny it.'

'Strange, then, you have no knowledge of the others as they were stolen at the same time.'

Percy just shrugged. 'Nothing to do with me.'

'Perhaps you were going to sell them to Frank Clarke.'

'Who?' asked Percy.

'Don't give me that old bullshit, Stanley! Clarke lives in Bournemouth, you and Clarke have done business in the past, but you had a falling-out, I hear, so don't take me for a fool.'

'Oh him! I ain't seen the man in years. So what's he got to do with anything?'

'Don't pretend you hadn't heard that he was murdered and his body left in the cemetery.'

'I heard about it, of course I did, but I didn't know who it was.'

'What a load of cobblers! I'll tell you what I think. I think he came to buy your stuff and you had another falling-out and you knifed him.'

Percy pretended to be outraged. 'You ain't pinning that on me! Yes, all right, I'll cough to the burglary and selling the other stuff, but not murder!'

The detective sat back and stared at his prisoner. He smiled softly. 'I've waited for this day for a long time. Every villain makes a mistake at some time and you have made yours. I'll prove that you killed Clarke if it's the last thing I do!'

Percy just glared at him. 'I'm innocent, I tell you, but carry on, enjoy yourself, but you have to prove it and as I didn't do it, you haven't a chance in hell!'

'We'll see,' said the detective. He looked at the constable on the door. 'Take him back to his cell.' He picked up his papers and left the room.

As he walked back to his office he turned to his colleague. 'He did it, I'm sure. I'd like to see him swing on the end of a rope. Now we have to prove it and that may take some time. Tomorrow we'll bring in the brother. We'll give him twenty-four hours to sweat, then we'll question him.'

Arthur was indeed sweating. After the police had taken his brother away, he shut up the stall. He couldn't bear to be the topic of conversation with all the other traders staring at him, yelling caustic comments. It was obvious the stuff that Percy had sold in Salisbury had been traced and that his brother had been identified or the police wouldn't have arrested him but . . . would they be able to tie Percy into the murder? If they did, he too was looking at a stretch in prison.

Ben watched him as he packed his stall and saw how nervous he was. He was the weak link in the enquiry, he felt sure. Now that Percy had been arrested, perhaps his stint in the market would soon be over and at last he'd return to normal duties and be able to tell Phoebe everything.

Later at police headquarters there was a briefing to go over the daily events and the arrest of Percy came up, then the murder of Clarke. The detective in charge had a large board with a picture of Clarke and Percy, along with a list of stolen goods.

Reading the board, Ben suddenly remembered the night he'd walked to the brothers' lock-up and found sand on the ground where it was obvious the entrance had been cleaned. He checked his notebook. It was after the robbery but before the body had been found. He mentioned it to the man in charge.

'Maybe that's where Clarke met with the prisoner. Perhaps they had a row and that's where the murder took place. He'd have to clear it up and move the body before the next morning.'

'It was very late that night when I was there and noticed the sand on my shoe. I thought it strange but had no reason to think anything untoward had occurred,' Ben said.

'We'll send forensics round tomorrow, but too much time has passed really to find any clues. However, if we're right, it might put the fear of God up young Arthur! We'll do it before we get him in for questioning. I'll get a search warrant for his lock-up. We'll go in the morning.'

Arthur had decided to carry on as usual. His brother had been arrested for burglary but he was still a free man. If he continued to work, he hoped it would show he had nothing to worry about. He was therefore surprised to see a forensic team with a search warrant waiting outside the lock-up when he arrived.

'What do you want to look inside for?' he demanded.

'I have a warrant, so just stand aside, if you please,' he was told.

The men removed the cart and thoroughly searched the ground inside, taking samples from the floor. Then they looked over the stall itself and started removing all the goods on display, to Arthur's annoyance.

'You buggers be careful! I have to sell those items to the public. You mark any and I'll be making a claim against the police for damaged goods!'

He was ignored. Then, when the team had finished, they packed up their gear and walked out.

Arthur was furious. 'Hey! Aren't you going to pick up this stuff and put it back on the stall?'

They ignored him and left.

Cursing loudly, he picked up the items, searching for any dirt marks and replaced them. Eventually, he wheeled the stall over to his pitch, aware of the stares from the other sellers, which he ignored. But Ben, who was watching him carefully, noted his nervousness despite his show of bravado. He wondered how he'd hold out when being questioned later that day.

It was just before closing time when a constable arrived and walked over to Arthur.

'I've been sent to escort you to the station for questioning. I'll wait until you put away the stall.' He saw that Arthur was about to argue. 'If you refuse, I'll take you there in handcuffs. Your choice!'

Arthur locked up his stall, trying to show he didn't care. But inside he was quaking. What would they ask him? Would they mention the murder? He, of course, would deny everything. Even being part of the burglary, knowing his brother wouldn't have dropped him in it by saying he was involved. It was a rule they lived by if one of them was ever caught for breaking the law.

He was taken into an interview room and left there, sitting at a table.

'Let him sit and worry,' said Detective Inspector Jack Bentley, who was in charge of the case. 'He's not as strong as his brother. He'll be wetting his trousers by the time we get to him.'

The longer he waited, the more nervous Arthur became. He longed for a cigarette to calm his frayed nerves. His mouth was dry and he needed a glass of water, but no one came.

After half an hour Bentley entered the room with another detective and a constable, the latter taking up a place by the door as the other two sat at the table opposite Arthur.

'About bloody time!' Arthur declared. 'Can I have a glass of water?'

Bentley nodded to the constable, who left the room and returned with a glass of water, which he placed before Arthur who drank it greedily.

'Where did your brother meet Frank Clarke? Was it at the lock-up?'

The sudden question took Arthur by surprise. 'What?'

'You heard me,' snapped Bentley. 'Where did your brother meet Clarke?'

'Who the hell is Clarke?' Arthur had quickly recovered.

Bentley frowned. 'Don't play dumb with me, son. Clarke came up to buy the stuff your brother nicked in the robberies of the three houses he burgled.'

'I don't know nothing about that or this Clarke fellow.'

Bentley sat back in his chair, silent for a while, just looking at the man opposite him, noting the beads of sweat forming on his forehead.

'I believe that you helped him. He didn't break into those houses alone, I'm certain of that.' He leant forward and spoke softly. 'Now I understand you feel you have to stand by your brother and that's admirable of you, but in this case it's pure stupidity. You are a young man with his whole life before him. Your brother is a full-time criminal – you know that – and what's more, he will be sent down at least for stealing and eventually for murder. Maybe you had a hand in that too! He'll take you with him if you insist on lying.' He paused and looked young Arthur up and down. 'You're a good-looking young man; they'll love you in prison. You'll have some big strapping bloke come up to you and offer to protect you from the others. Of course, there will be a price to pay for his protection.' He saw Arthur pale. 'If you reject him, then he'll spend his time making trouble for you, making you pay for his losing face in front of the others. You won't last five minutes!'

Arthur gathered his senses and glared at the detective. 'I have nothing to do with any burglary and I've no knowledge of any man called Clarke!'

Bentley gathered his papers and stood up. 'You obviously need to take time to think about this. I'll give you that time as I loathe to see anyone throw away his future.' He looked at the constable at the door. 'Take him to a cell, I'll see him later.'

As he walked past the cells, Arthur was talking loudly in the hope that his brother who was in one of them would hear him.

'I don't know why I'm here. I don't know nothing about any burglary, or a man called Clarke!'

The constable opened a cell and pushed Arthur inside.

'You best be quiet, Stanley, or you'll be in trouble!' He shut the door and locked it.

But just along the corridor, Percy sat in his cell and smiled. He'd heard the message his brother had sent. Good to know he was denying everything. All he had to do was to continue that way.

But as Arthur sat in the empty cell with its stark walls, the one bed with just a blanket and a pail beside the bed, his bravado quickly subsided. This is what it would be like in prison, shut away day after day. This could be his life all because his brother was belittled by a remark from Frank Clarke! His only consolation at the moment was that the murder had to be proved and, as yet, there was no proof.

Chapter Fourteen

After further questioning, the police had no choice but to let Arthur go. They didn't have any evidence to hold him and he vehemently denied all knowledge of the burglary and the murder. Ben had been told to maintain his place in the market and keep an eye on young Arthur. Which meant that Ben had no choice but to still keep his real occupation hidden from Phoebe.

It became common knowledge among the traders that the older brother was under suspicion of the murder, which unsettled young Phoebe. She was torn, not knowing what to do, still filled with guilt at withholding evidence, yet she kept silent. But she became quiet and withdrawn.

Ben was worried about her and one evening when they went for a walk, he led her to a bench in the park and putting an arm around her asked, 'What is troubling you, Phoebe?'

She looked startled. 'What do you mean?'

'Ever since Percy Stanley was taken away, you've been subdued. Evidently you have something on your mind. What is it? How can I help?'

She gazed at him, longing to share her concerns, but this was her secret and one she couldn't share, not even with Ben whom she trusted more than anyone.

'I'm fine, honestly. I'm still trying to get over the loss of my mother. I worry that I have Tim to take care of. It's a great responsibility.'

He could understand that – after all, she was only a young woman. It hadn't been that long since her mother had died, she was obviously still grieving.

He pulled her closer. 'You'll be fine. Your mother and father would be proud of you. Your business is steady; you have a good head on your shoulders. You'll manage. It takes time to get over the loss of your mother, but eventually you'll learn to live with it. We all have to face such difficulties – it's life, I'm afraid. It isn't always easy.'

'But what if I was ill and couldn't work. What then?'

'Now stop that! You're worrying about unnecessary things. You're a fit young woman. Don't give yourself a problem that isn't there.'

She gave a wry smile. 'You're right, of course, I'm just feeling a bit low, that's all.'

'You're allowed. Come on, I'll take you for a quick drink, that'll cheer you up, then we'll go and collect Tim from his friend's house. We'll buy pie and chips on the way home.'

The change did her good, and when she saw Tim's delight at the food, her spirit lightened.

* * *

124

Life went on and Percy, languishing in prison awaiting his trial, was soon forgotten and so no one made any further snide remarks about him to his brother.

Arthur, now more relaxed, was beginning to enjoy his freedom. No Percy to bully him and run their lives. The police hadn't bothered with him again and he began to enjoy life. He went out in the evenings to the pub, flirted with various women, and even took one home for a night of sex. Life was good.

Ben, who was keeping a watch on him, wrote all this in his notebook. One evening, when Arthur had been in the pub for a couple of hours, Ben wandered in, ordered a pint of beer and pretended to be surprised to see Arthur sitting alone. He wandered over and sat beside him.

'Hello. Nice to sit quietly with a beer after a busy day, isn't it?'

'Yeah,' he replied. 'We work bloody hard out in the open in all kinds of weather. We earn a break.'

Ben noticed that Arthur's speech was slightly slurred, which didn't surprise him. He'd waited for a couple of hours in the hope that the young man would be relaxed and maybe a little loose-mouthed, if led in the right direction.

He looked at Arthur. 'It must be nice for you to be able to please yourself as to what you do and when.'

'What do you mean?'

'Well, it seemed to me that your brother tended to run your life. I always thought it must be difficult for a young man like you to be told what to do all the time. I felt it was a bit unfair, to tell you the truth.'

Arthur looked at him with a somewhat glassy stare but pleased by the unexpected show of sympathy. 'Yes, Percy did like to have his own way.' He took a long swig of his beer, then chuckled. 'Now I pleases myself.' He leant forward. 'I took a girl home the other night. Couldn't do that before.'

Grinning, Ben said, 'Good for you. Every man should sew his wild oats before settling down. Let me get you another beer.'

As the evening wore on, Arthur continued to chat. 'Percy never treated me with any respect, he doesn't respect anyone. He thinks he's the big I am! Well he isn't now. He's locked up in a cell and I'm free. He respects me now.'

'Oh, and why now?'

Arthur tapped the side of his nose. 'He needs me. For the first time in his life, he needs his little brother.'

'Oh, and why is that?'

'I know stuff, that's all I'm saying. I'm keeping schtum. For once in our relationship, I hold all the cards, so he has to respect me.'

Ben didn't press him further, but finished his beer then got to his feet. 'I'm off to get something to eat before I go to bed. See you in the morning.'

When he arrived home, Ben wrote up his notes about the conversation. It was obvious to him that, indeed, Arthur did hold all the cards and if only he was made to talk, he could give the police the information they needed. But how could they bring this about? However, he had made an inroad this evening, and if he continued to befriend Arthur, perhaps he could lead him into a false security and catch him out.

* * *

The following morning, Arthur was late setting up his stall. Ben walked over to him and with a smile said, 'How's your hangover?'

Arthur pulled a face. 'My head's killing me. I should have gone home when you did.'

Ben laughed. 'You should always eat when you're on a bender. That'll teach you.'

Arthur grinned. 'I'll remember.'

Walking back to his stall, Ben was pleased. He felt that he'd taken an important step in making Arthur think he was someone who was friendly towards him, unlike anyone else in the market, and whatever Arthur said, he must feel alone at times without Percy.

Phoebe had seen the exchange between the two men and was unsettled by it. Why was Ben being so friendly to Arthur Stanley? It didn't make any sense. The two brothers had been like pariahs, yet there was Ben chatting away and laughing.

Marj too had seen the exchange between the men and she wandered over to Phoebe. 'Your boyfriend chooses strange friends,' she said with great sarcasm.

'He isn't my boyfriend but, yes, it does seem a bit strange. Still, Ben is nice to most people.'

'The brothers ain't most people!' retorted her friend.

'It's not our business,' Phoebe said.

Marj wandered back to her stall, muttering beneath her breath.

That evening, Ben reported to his boss about meeting Arthur in the pub and it was decided that he try and strike up a friendship in the hopes that the young man would let slip some vital information, rather than have him back for further questioning.

It was Friday and the market had been busy. The traders started to pack up for the day. As Arthur was about to wheel his stall away, Ben stopped him.

'Don't know about you but I'm parched. Fancy a pint?'

Arthur looked pleased, 'Good idea. I'll wait for you to close up.'

The two men eventually walked to the nearest pub, ordered two pints of bitter, and sat down, easing themselves into comfortable chairs.

Ben stretched his legs. 'God! I'm glad that day's over. Pleased to be busy, of course, but I really need this.' He lifted his pint glass. 'Cheers!'

Arthur reciprocated. 'Cheers.'

'So, what have you been doing with yourself?' Ben asked.

'Not much to be honest. I'm looking forward to Sunday to have a rest.'

'I expect it takes some getting used to, being on your own now. Although your brother was not the easiest person to live with, I'm sure you miss having someone in the house.'

Arthur grimaced. 'Strange, isn't it? In one way I'm happy to be able to please myself, but you're right, at times the house feels empty.'

Laughing, Ben made a suggestion. 'Perhaps you should find a wife and settle down?'

Arthur looked bemused. 'Nah! I'm far too young to tie myself to one woman. As they say, why buy a book when you can go to a library! I like variety. For once I'm free to take a girl home if I want to.'

'Well, you're a good-looking bloke; you shouldn't have any trouble there.'

Arthur looked pleased at the compliment. 'What about you, Ben? Have you got a woman? I notice you are friendly with that girl Phoebe.'

'Yes, we're friends. She lost her mother recently, as you know. I just like to be on hand to help her if she needs it.'

'That's clever. Then when you're ready, you make your move. Smart, very smart.'

Ben ignored the remark and changed the subject.

'Have you been to see your brother? I'm sure he's anxious for a visitor. It can't be a load of laughs to be shut away in a cell.'

With a scowl Arthur said, 'You'd think so, wouldn't you? I caught a train to Winchester one Sunday a couple of weeks ago. Took some fags and soap and sweets, but all I got was a balling out. Why hadn't I been before? Had the takings on the stall dropped now that he wasn't running things? As if I wasn't capable. To tell you the truth, I nearly got up and walked out! No thanks for coming, no thanks for the goods I took.'

'How ungrateful! He's treating you like a child.' Ben could see Arthur was feeling resentful and began to feed this thread. 'You are more than capable of working alone. I've seen you. He ought to show you some respect for carrying on after he put you in this position.'

'Well he had better respect me. He forgets he owes me. He bloody needs me, and he'd better remember that. If he pushes me too far, he'll rue the day.'

'And why's that?'

'I hold his future in my hands, that's all I'll say.'

'That sounds serious. What do you mean?'

But Arthur just shook his head. 'It's for me to know.'

It was obvious that Arthur wouldn't say any more so Ben finished his drink. 'I've got to go, I'm afraid. Thanks for the company. I'll see you in the morning.' Then added, 'Don't forget to eat or you'll be in no fit state to work tomorrow and you know how busy we are on a Saturday.'

Arthur grinned at him. 'You're not my mother, you know!'

'Thank the Lord for that! See you tomorrow.'

As he walked home, Ben was wracking his brains wondering how he could get Arthur to be more explicit about what hold he had over his brother. He was certain it was about the murder or he wouldn't have mentioned Percy's future. There had been no evidence in the lock-up so the police still had nothing to prove the men had anything to do with Clarke's demise. But Arthur was beginning to trust him. It would take time, but if he could get him really drunk one night, then perhaps he'd let slip something really important. That's what he decided to do.

Phoebe watched the daily interchange between Ben and Arthur and it unsettled her. One evening, when she and Ben went out for a walk, she questioned him about it.

'Why have you got so pally with Arthur Stanley? I thought you couldn't stand the brothers.'

'I feel a bit sorry for the bloke, to be honest. Let's face it, he isn't the brightest of men. His brother ran his life and now he seems a bit lost. That's all.'

'I wouldn't trust him with my cat if I had one!'

Ben laughed at her retort. 'If I was a woman, I would probably feel the same. It's just that I hate to see him trying to cope alone.' He could see she wasn't convinced but she didn't say any more and he dropped the subject.

Chapter Fifteen

Young Tim was feeling chipper these days as he'd become friendly with Laura, a daughter of recent new stallholders, selling haberdashery goods. Cottons, silks for embroidery, cloth and offcuts. She was about the same age as him and only recently on a Saturday she'd joined her family. Consequently, they both helped out in the market, but in quiet moments, they played together and at lunchtime, they sat on one of the benches to eat their fish and chips.

Phoebe watched them and was pleased. Laura seemed a nice child and she was thrilled to see her young brother happily chatting away. He had school friends, of course, but it gave him something to look forward to at the weekend, other than helping her on the stall. She still worried that he didn't have a father. A boy needs a man as a role model, she felt.

Someone with whom a lad could kick a ball and talk about male interests. Ben was good with him and she was grateful for that, especially as Tim so enjoyed his company.

Marj too had watched them and said to Phoebe how nice it was to see the children together, but knowing how her friend worried about Tim not having a father to guide him added, 'Now, if you and Ben were to get married, that boy's life would be perfect!'

Phoebe looked at her in surprise. 'Marj! Ben and I are just good friends. Will you stop it.'

But the woman wouldn't be silenced. 'You know, I'm surprised 'e 'asn't tried to make your relationship more permanent. That young man is in love with you, Phoebe, but something is stopping 'im from telling you. I just wonder what, that's all.'

Phoebe didn't answer for, truth to tell, she'd wondered the same thing. Ben had made various comments, like he'd always be around to take care of her, but that was as far as he'd gone. She sensed he wanted to say more but when he'd not done so, she'd been confused. But then his sudden friendliness with Arthur Stanley also confused her. A customer arrived and stopped her train of thought.

Tim and Laura were happily tucking into their fish and chips. 'I love having this wrapped in newspaper and eating with my fingers,' she said. 'It always seems to taste better.'

'My mum always used to say that.' A sudden expression of sadness didn't escape Laura.

'You must miss your parents.'

Tim was slow in answering, giving her remark some thought.

'I miss Mum every day, but sometimes I can't remember what Dad looked like or how his voice sounded and that's *awful* . . . he was my father!' His voice broke with emotion.

'But didn't he die in the war?'

Tim nodded. 'He was away for a long time, but he didn't come home when the war was over – there wasn't even a funeral.' He blinked away his tears. 'But he's with Mum now, so that's nice. They'll keep each other company. Phoebe says in heaven they'll both be young again and without pain.'

Laura paused. 'Do you think they'll be playing harps like sometimes you see pictures of angels doing?'

Tim grinned. 'I can't imagine my mum playing one. She used to sing out of tune. We used to tease her about it!'

'When I die, I want to float about from cloud to cloud,' she said, waving her arms up in the air. 'Meeting people as I float by. But I definitely won't be selling cottons and materials!'

'I wonder if they cook in heaven?'

Laura looked appalled. 'They've got to cook or how will I get my fish and chips?'

Further conversation was interrupted when Laura's mother called her and they both returned to their stalls.

There were no such innocent thoughts inside the head of Percy Stanley after the lunch break, as he walked round the exercise yard in Winchester Prison. He was still an angry man. His belligerent attitude had upset several of the other inmates and once or twice it nearly came to blows. He sat down on a low wall and lit a cigarette. Another prisoner walked over to him holding out an unlit Woodbine.

'Gotta match, mate?'

'I ain't your mate. Piss off!'

The convict looked at him, anger flushing his cheeks. 'You miserable bastard!' Then he leant forward and with a mighty shove, sent Percy backwards off the wall and walked away leaving him to scramble to his feet. Furious at being caught out, he hurled abuse at the retreating figure, then brushed himself down, searching for the dog-end. Cigarettes were precious commodities in prison.

Several of the inmates had witnessed his downfall and had laughed derisively, which didn't help his frame of mind. A bell rang and the men eventually filed back into the prison and to their designated areas. Some to return to their cells, others to clean the floors and other designated chores, some to scrub out the toilets, and Percy to the laundry room.

It was hot and damp inside the laundry. There the bedding and other items that were washable were put in various machines. Steam from the machines filled the air and as Percy walked past one of these, two of the inmates bumped into him deliberately, sending him tumbling against the side of the vat. He put out a hand to save himself and screamed as the heat scorched his flesh.

A warden rushed over and shoved his hand in a nearby bucket of cold water. 'You should be more careful, Stanley,' he snapped.

'It wasn't my fault, I was pushed!' he yelled.

'Now there's a surprise! That'll teach you to stop being so bloody-minded. It doesn't work in prison. Come along, off to the hospital and get this seen to.'

As he was escorted out of the laundry room, Percy saw several men grinning at him and he knew who the culprits were.

If he expected any sympathy from the prison doctor, he was disappointed. The medic had been a prison doctor for too long. Most of his patients had been injured through payback from other prisoners with a grudge to settle. Only a small minority were genuine patients. As Percy started to complain the doctor silenced him.

'I'm not interested in your sob story, Stanley, just tell me what happened.' He examined the burn. 'This will take some time to heal. I'll keep you in for a while to make sure there are no complications and we'll see how it goes.'

'Is that it?' Percy asked angrily.

'Yes, it is, and if you decide to become difficult, I'll send you back to your cell and you can sit it out on your own. My ward – my rules!' He instructed a nurse about which dressing to apply and walked away.

Percy winced and moaned with the pain as the nurse applied the sterile dressings. She was as gentle as she could be but knew that this was going to take some time to heal.

All the time his hand was being attended, Percy, in between the cries of pain, was burning with hatred for those who'd caused this and deep down swore his revenge. He was led to a bed, given a pair of pyjamas and left to get settled. He ignored the man next to him who smiled in greeting, and lay down, propping up the pillows with his one good hand. His injured hand felt as if it was on fire and the pain made him tired. Eventually he dropped off to sleep.

* * *

The next few days in the hospital, Percy, despite the pain he suffered, was enjoying the new regime. It was relatively peaceful in the ward. The meals came in on a trolley. At night it was quiet as opposed to the nightly voices ranting from those shut up in cells. Warders yelling at the convicts to keep quiet. Here he didn't have to watch his back from those he'd upset. It was like being on holiday, apart from the daily change of dressing to his hand. Although he didn't admit to it, when he saw the damage to his flesh, he was worried as to how it would ever heal. He wasn't able to flex his fingers without a great deal of pain and he was afraid he'd lose the use of them. For the moment, the doctor was unable to give him any reassurance.

'We will just have to wait and see. My main concern is that it might become infected and then as the skin heals it shrinks and tightens, making it difficult to move your fingers . . . you will have to learn to be patient!'

Fortunately, it was Percy's left hand, so he was able to write to his brother, tell him what had happened and ask him to visit. Then he added a list of things he required.

Arthur confided all this to Ben after he'd received the letter.

'He said he was pushed by a couple of blokes and his hand is badly burnt.' He looked worried. 'He's in the prison hospital, so I guess it must be bad. I'm going tomorrow. It means closing the stall for the day, but I don't have a choice.'

'Oh, I'm sorry to hear that, but of course you have to go. He must be in a lot of pain and he'll be glad of your company.'

'That'll be a first!' Arthur grumbled. 'But maybe this time he'll be in a better frame of mind.'

'Try not to worry.'

'Thanks, mate.' Arthur smiled at Ben. 'That's kind of you.'

Ben walked back to his stall. 'Mate!' That pleased him. It showed that Arthur was beginning to trust him. Perhaps he could get him to do so even more – enough to confide in him. That would take time, but the end result would be worth it.

Chapter Sixteen

Arthur arrived at the prison and was eventually escorted to the hospital after the usual formalities of being searched and the goods he'd taken in removed for inspection. The warder unlocked the door to the ward and let him through. There were only three patients, so he saw Percy immediately and walked over to his bed, where his brother was sitting, legs over the side, staring at the door with anticipation of a visitor.

'All right, Percy?'

'No, I'm not bloody all right!' He held up his bandaged hand. 'How could I be all right, you idiot!'

Arthur sighed. Nothing had changed. 'How's the hand?'

'Bloody painful! They had to give me a morphine injection last night.' For a moment he looked worried. 'I'm beginning to wonder how long before it heals and if I'll have the whole use of my fingers after.'

'What do you mean?'

'It's difficult to flex them at the moment, and when the flesh does heal, I'm wondering if they'll be the same as normal. Thank God it's my left hand.'

'What does the doctor say?'

'I'll have to wait and see.'

Looking around, Arthur smiled. 'Well, at least this is better than being cooped up in a cell. It's quiet and peaceful. Spacious, clean.'

Percy reluctantly agreed. 'At night it's a blessing. No yelling and shouting. I haven't slept so well since I was sent here. Warders don't harass you. There's one on guard outside, but that's all.' He paused for a moment. 'It makes you wonder how difficult it would be to break out of here.'

Arthur looked horrified. 'Have you lost your bloody mind? Your case hasn't come up in court yet. Imagine trying to break out and getting caught? You'd be here for bloody years!'

'I'm going down for a time, anyway. The police have an open and shut case. If I could get out, I could disappear altogether, at least I'd be free.'

'Yeah! Looking over your shoulder for the rest of your life!'

Percy changed the subject. 'How's business? I hope you're running the stall properly?'

'Don't you talk to me like a child! I'm doing very well on my own. I don't need you breathing down my neck every minute telling me what to do.' Arthur's frustration burst forth. 'You think you know everything and I'm useless, well *look* at you! At least one of us knows how to stay out of trouble.'

Percy was livid. 'Who do you think you're talking to? Without me behind you, you'd be *nothing*!'

Arthur smirked at him. 'The very fact that you thought you were so special could put you at the end of a rope. You should remember that . . . *brother*! And if you really want to know, I'm living the life of Riley on my own, pleasing myself. Going out with women! I don't need you. So get off my back!'

He got to his feet and walked to the door and asked to be let out.

To have his brother answer him back was so unusual, that for a moment Percy was speechless, but he managed to yell abuse at Arthur as he was let out of the door.

The nurse came over. 'Stop that yelling, Stanley!' she snapped. 'You are disturbing the other patients.'

'Who do you think you're talking to, Nurse? No one tells me what to do!'

She ignored him, but when it came time to change his bandage, she was less gentle and he flinched with the pain. When she'd finished she just looked at him. She didn't have to say a word. He understood her message.

The following morning, Ben set up his stall, then walked over to Arthur. 'How was your brother?'

'Bloody-minded as usual. Apparently, his hand is badly burnt, but apart from that the hospital isn't a bad place to be. It's quiet and peaceful, with only one guard at the door. You wouldn't believe what Percy said to me.'

Suddenly curious, Ben said, 'I can't imagine.'

'He was only wondering how easy it might be to escape. Stupid bastard! I told him he was out of his bloody mind.'

He grinned broadly. 'Then I gave him a piece of *my* mind.'

'You did?' This came as a complete surprise after seeing Percy and Arthur together, with Arthur being very much the underdog.

'Well, I'm sick of him belittling me, wondering if I'm capable of running the stall alone. In fact, I told him what a great time I was having being alone. I even told him about the women!'

Ben started to laugh. 'My goodness, I bet he didn't like that.'

Arthur stood tall, bristling with his own importance. 'I didn't give him the chance to comment. I told him to get off my back and then I walked out!' He started to laugh. 'He was so surprised he was speechless for a minute. Mind you, he started yelling at me as I left, but I didn't care. I'm free, he's locked up. Why should I worry?'

'Why, indeed!' Ben agreed, 'Good for you!' He walked back to his own stall smiling to himself. The more that Arthur began to believe his brother wasn't important, the less likely he'd feel obliged to him. That must be to my advantage, he thought. But he'd pass on the message that Percy harboured ideas of escape.

On Saturday, during a lull in business, young Tim was sitting alone on some steps eating his fish and chips, looking decidedly miserable. Ben walked over and sat beside him.

'Where's your girlfriend today, then, Tim?'

The young boy blushed. 'She's not my girlfriend, we're just friends, that's all and she's off staying with her grandmother for the weekend.'

'Oh, I see. I thought you'd been stood up. So, what are you going to do tomorrow?'

The boy shrugged. 'Don't know. I thought I would be kicking a football about with my friends in the street, but they are going out too.'

'Oh, that's a shame.'

The boy picked up a chip and chewed on it, lost in thought. 'Sometimes their dad played with us. If my dad was still alive, I could play with him.'

For once Ben was at a loss for words.

'Do you like Phoebe, Ben?'

With a startled look Ben said, 'Of course I do. She's a lovely girl.'

'Well, why don't you ask her to marry you, then you could be my dad?' Tim gazed up at him, waiting for an answer.

Ben took a deep breath as he tried desperately to gather his thoughts. 'Well, young Tim, marriage is not something you take lightly; after all, you commit yourself to someone for life. There's more to marriage than liking somebody a lot.'

'She's a good cook,' the boy offered. 'You wouldn't go hungry.'

Ben tried to hide a smile. 'I know that, I've tasted her cooking.'

'She keeps the house clean and washes and irons my clothes.' He waited for a response.

Ben chuckled. 'I'm not looking for a housekeeper, Tim. When I feel the time is right, then I'll make a decision about marriage with some lucky lady who'll be happy to have me.' He ruffled the boy's hair, got to his feet and walked back to his stall, smiling.

It wasn't as if the idea hadn't crossed his mind. He was in love with Phoebe and he had thought seriously about being married to her and being a stepfather to Tim, but he wasn't sure how she was going to react when eventually he was able to tell her the truth about his real occupation. Would she understand that he couldn't take her into his confidence? Would she understand that he had no choice? Or would she be hurt and think he couldn't trust her? In any case, he was still on the job, so any decision would have to wait. But he felt for the boy. He suddenly had an idea and walked over to Tim.

'There's a cricket match on tomorrow afternoon. How would you like to go to that?'

The boy looked delighted. 'Thanks. I don't know anything about cricket, though.'

'I'll explain the rules as they play. Run over and ask Phoebe if it's all right with her.' He watched the animated conversation between brother and sister. Phoebe looked over and nodded. Tim held up two thumbs, jumping up and down with glee.

'I'll collect you at half past one,' he called.

It was a warm sunny day as Ben and Tim took their seats at the cricket ground. The young boy was so thrilled to be there and fidgeted in his seat, turning around and surveying his surroundings.

'This is just a match between two counties. Hampshire against Sussex,' Ben told him. He then explained about the stumps, the cricket pitch itself and what the aim of the batsmen was. They both sat up as the teams came onto the field to applause from the substantial crowd.

As the match progressed, Ben was explaining what was happening and then the scoreboard, which was a mystery to Tim, who didn't know how the figures changed until Ben told him about the man who was working them. At the tea break, they enjoyed sandwiches, cake and a cup of tea.

As they settled, Ben asked Tim what he thought of the match.

'Well . . . it's a bit slow compared to football, but when that man scored a six, I got really excited. I thought he was going to be run out!'

Laughing, Ben said, 'There you go, you've already learnt the language of the game with the batsman being run out!' The boy looked pleased.

Arthur Stanley was also feeling pleased with himself. Last night he'd picked up a woman whom he'd taken to his house and who had stayed overnight. This was a first for him. Normally any woman he'd taken home for sex had left soon after, but this one had lingered and then to his surprise agreed to stay over. He had watched her undress with great relish and when she climbed into bed beside him and he'd felt the warmth of her naked flesh against his, he was beside himself with joy.

Running her hands over his biceps she whispered in his ear. 'Oh Arthur, I love being with a real man.' She slowly slid her fingers to his chest, then slowly she moved them lower, stroking him gently. He let out a moan.

'Do you like that, Arthur?'

Unable to speak he just nodded.

'This is so much better than a quick fumble on the sofa, don't you think?' Her hand slipped even lower. 'Oh, Arthur, you naughty boy! Now, darling, use a bit of self-control because I want to enjoy this too.' She quickly mounted him and guided him inside her.

Arthur was lost in a sea of sexual delight as the girl rode him, slowly at first, then she quickened her pace. 'Oh my God!' he cried. He then laid back, breathless, beads of sweat on his brow and body.

The girl snuggled into him, her arm across him. 'Have you ever had it as good as that?'

'No never,' he murmured. 'Never.'

'If I was your girlfriend you could have the same more often.' She slipped her hand down to the now flaccid member. 'Just imagine, Arthur, the fun we could have. I could even move in and look after you.' Leaning forward, she kissed him, softly running the tip of her tongue inside his lips.

He closed his eyes and enjoyed the sensuality of it all, yet thinking this is what real life should be like. This is what I've been missing all through that bloody brother of mine. Then, as the girl closed her mouth over his and kissed him, he knew he was going to grasp whatever was on offer. His hand closed over her breast.

'What's your name, love?'

Chapter Seventeen

On Monday morning, Arthur could hardly wait to share his good news with his friend Ben. Once he'd set up his stall, he hurried over to him.

'Morning, Arthur. You're looking very chipper.'

'I've got a girlfriend!' He stood beaming, waiting for a reaction.

'Good heavens! How did that happen?'

'I picked her up in a bar and took her home and she stayed the night. She wants us to be together.'

'What do you mean, together?'

'Well, after we had sex in bed, she suggested we continue our relationship.' With a lascivious grin he confided, 'I've never had sex like it, Ben. She was amazing! Anyway, this morning she said how nice it would be if she moved in with me, so she could look after me properly.'

Thinking that this could upset his plans of getting close to Arthur, Ben asked, 'What about Percy? He wouldn't like that one bit.'

'Well, he ain't here and won't be for some considerable time. I'm entitled to have a life!'

'I wouldn't rush into anything, my friend. If I were you, I'd enjoy going out together and having her stay over now and again, but living with someone does have its problems. Before you know where you are, she'll be bossing you around like your brother did. You might want to go to the pub for a drink with your mates and she won't like it.'

Arthur's eyes narrowed as he considered this. 'Mm. Maybe you're right. I'll wait a while and think that over. She can have my body any time she likes, but as yet, not my house.'

'No, Arthur, you've got it all wrong. She can have your body any time *you* like! You can't have people making decisions for you any longer. Be your own man!'

The trader laughed. And, slapping Ben on the shoulder, he said, 'You're a good mate. Looking after my interest like that. It's good advice, thanks! See you later,' and he walked back to his stall.

Phoebe, having watched this animated conversation, was curious and walked over to Ben. 'Your friend looks pleased with himself. What's going on?'

Placing an arm around her shoulders, he said quietly, 'He's got a girlfriend.'

Her eyes widened in surprise. 'No!'

He burst out laughing. 'He's not a bad-looking chap, some women might take a liking to him. In fact, one has done so, it seems.'

She thought about it for a moment. 'I suppose a good woman might make something of him.'

'Oh, I don't think she's a good woman at all.'

'Oh, I see. Percy wouldn't like that.'

'But Percy isn't here, and Arthur is enjoying his freedom. Frankly, I'm pleased for him. His miserable brother used to make his life hell, let him get a taste of freedom. It could be just what he needs.'

Now Phoebe laughed. 'You've got more faith in humanity than I have.'

'Well, you know what they say. No one is all bad and no one is all good.'

Her smile faded and she looked at Ben, cheeks flushed, eyes flashing in anger. 'Well, let me tell you, Percy Stanley is *all* bad. He hasn't a decent bone in his body!' She hurried away.

He was astonished at the sudden change in her, the venom in her voice. So unlike the Phoebe he knew. What was it with her and Percy Stanley that this man had such an effect on her? One day perhaps he'd get to the bottom of the problem.

Saturday was a miserable day. The heavy grey clouds gathered and before long it started to rain heavily. The wind became stronger and the traders were having trouble with the canopies covering their stalls.

Phoebe and young Tim tried valiantly to keep theirs from blowing away and soon both were soaked to the skin. Eventually they had no choice but to close the stall with Ben's help and go home – as did everyone else.

Tim was shivering beneath his wet clothes and Phoebe

made him go to his room to undress while she built up the fire, put on pans of water to boil to fill a bath to warm him and while she waited, she also changed out of her clothes, rubbing herself down with a towel, putting on a pair of pyjamas, an old jumper and a warm dressing gown. Then she put a pan of stew in the oven to warm.

Tim was immersed in a bath in front of the fire, pouring the hot water over his shoulders with a filled jug to warm himself. Phoebe rubbed him dry and put on his pyjamas and a dressing gown, then settled him on the sofa covered in a blanket, while she dished out bowls of stew for them.

'Eat up, Timmy. Can't have you catching a cold, can we?'

'No, Phoebe,' he said. Then he sneezed.

After they'd eaten, Phoebe took out the bottle of embrocation their mother always used and rubbed Tim's chest with it.

'There! Mum always swore by this. Let's hope it will stop you getting a cold.'

He screwed up his nose. 'The smell alone is enough to do that!'

She chuckled. 'Some cures are not always pleasant, Tim. But if they do the job, that's the main thing.' At that moment there was a knock on the door.

Wrapping her dressing gown even tighter round her, Phoebe opened the door.

'Bath time, is it?' Ben stood there grinning broadly.

Phoebe felt her cheeks flush with embarrassment. 'Best come in,' she said somewhat reluctantly.

Seeing Tim all tucked up on the sofa, Ben smiled at the

boy. 'Well you look cosy and no mistake.' He sniffed the air. 'What's that strange smell?'

'It's some rotten stuff Phoebe rubbed on me to stop me catching a cold!' the boy replied, with more than a note of disgust.

'Don't complain, lad, she's only looking after you.' He glanced over to Phoebe. 'You look very fetching, if I may say so.' He walked over to her and kissed her briefly.

She moved quickly away. 'You know that I don't. We were soaked to the skin. Nightclothes were the most sensible thing. Would you like something to eat?'

He declined. 'Thanks, I ate before I came, but a cup of tea wouldn't go amiss.'

After she'd made Ben his tea and fed her brother, she bundled Tim off to bed, tucking him in to make sure he'd be warm. 'A good sleep will soon put you right, young man.' She kissed him goodnight, turned out the light and left the room.

Ben was settled on the sofa and when she appeared, he patted the seat beside him. 'Come and sit with me.'

Phoebe did so and Ben immediately put his arm around her and pulled her close. 'I'll keep you warm,' he said as he nuzzled her hair.

It felt good to be within his arms. Safe and warm. Phoebe let her thoughts run away with her. How perfect this would be if it was permanent. But Ben had never talked of the future and suddenly she wanted to know what was on his mind.

'How long are you going to be working in the market, Ben?'

This took him by surprise. 'What do you mean?'

'Well, is it permanent or do you have other plans for the

future?' There . . . she'd said it!

He hesitated. What could he say? He knew what he wanted, but as yet wasn't at liberty to say, but he didn't want to lose this lovely girl.

He looked at her and asked, 'Do you trust me, Phoebe?'

'Yes, of course I do.'

'Then please be patient. Yes, I do have plans for the future, but at the moment I'm unable to talk about them.' He stared into her eyes and tipped up her chin. 'All I can say is that I intend to be around for a long time.' Then he gave her a long, lingering kiss.

When eventually he was ready to leave, he took Phoebe into his arms. 'You are not to worry about the future because I promise you have no need to.' He kissed her forehead, then left.

Phoebe settled back on the sofa. She was even more confused. Whatever did Ben actually mean? The only thing that was clear was that he wasn't leaving and that was a relief, but the rest? Why wasn't he able to tell her now? What was he hiding?

In Winchester Prison, Percy Stanley had no plans to stay around. His court case was coming up soon and he didn't relish spending the next few years behind bars. The time spent in hospital without all the usual restrictions and guards always doing their rounds was the only time he had any hope of escaping – and that's what he intended to do.

On Fridays, the dirty linen from the hospital was collected and taken outside the prison gates to be washed in a special private unit, to sterilise it. He had already managed to steal a white doctor's coat with a stethoscope in the pocket and hidden it. This he would wear to cover his prison clothes. He just needed a few moments to carry out his plan. If his timing went wrong, he wouldn't make it.

The door of the ward was unlocked while the collection was taking place and he'd noticed that the collectors left several huge linen baskets on wheels just outside the ward door. Normally the guard would take this opportunity during the collection to slip to the toilet. His one worry was the whereabouts of the nurse at this time. Today was Friday. Hiding the doctor's coat beneath his top, he glanced at the clock. Another hour to go.

Percy felt his heart thumping beneath his clothes as he waited. He'd removed the hospital slippers and put on his shoes, then he sat on his bed and waited.

Just after the laundry men arrived and started to collect the soiled linen, the nurse walked into the ward, carrying a tray of medication, bandages and a hypodermic. She placed it on the cabinet beside the bed. 'Right, Stanley, I'm here to change your dressing,' she said.

'But you usually do it after lunch,' he spluttered.

'Well, I'm doing it now. Then I'm off duty for an hour. But first I've got to give my other patient an injection and his pills.' She walked over to the bed of the only other patient.

Percy was desperate. Through the glass on the door he could see two linen baskets already full and the men had disappeared into a room to collect more laundry to fill the others. This was his only chance as the guard had slipped away to the Gents.

He quickly got to his feet, rushed over to the other bed,

grabbed the nurse and with one blow, knocked her senseless and placed her on the floor out of sight. He picked up the hypodermic and threatened the patient with it. 'One sound and you'll get this in your throat. Understand?'

The man quickly nodded.

Rushing to the door, Percy peered out, then quick as a flash he climbed into one of the almost filled baskets and piled the linen over him. Hearing footsteps he held his breath. More laundry was piled on top of him and the men continued their task until they'd completed it, then they collected the other baskets and started to wheel them from the building. Percy could hear gates being unlocked and relocked as they made their way to the van, where the linen was wheeled up a ramp into the interior. The engine started and eventually they went through the final exit, turned right and within a short time, slowed to a stop.

Percy felt the bile rise in his stomach he was so nervous. Would he be able to avoid detection? He had no idea what would happen now. The back door to the van was being opened.

'Hey, Charlie! Fancy a cuppa before we unload? There's one brewing here in the staffroom.'

Charlie was only too happy to accept. He pushed the door of the van almost shut and left it.

Percy quickly climbed out of the basket and hurriedly put back the linen that had covered him. Donning the doctor's coat, he opened the van door wider, carefully looking around.

This was a private laundry, not part of the prison itself, and the gates were open with no one standing guard. Percy placed the stethoscope around his neck and walked quickly away. He turned the first corner he saw and stopped. Leaning against a wall, he waited until his legs stopped shaking, then he felt nauseous. He fought the sensation, not wanting to draw attention to himself. In the distance he saw a small park and putting the stethoscope in his pocket, he wandered over.

Sitting on a bench, he lit a cigarette and tried to calm down. Well, he was free, but what now?

Chapter Eighteen

It wasn't long before the unconscious figure of the nurse was discovered and it was realised that Percy was missing. The hospital was searched and the laundry van that had taken the linen away. A couple of pillowcases were found on the floor of the van, which led everyone to surmise this had been the way the prisoner may have escaped. The guard was sent before the prison governor, being severely reprimanded for leaving his post during the collection.

Policemen searched the area, but to no avail. Stanley was not to be found. Southampton police were advised in case Percy tried to contact his brother. Everyone was on high alert and it was decided to keep the fact of the escape away from the press for a few days.

* * *

Later that afternoon, two policemen walked into the market and chatted to the stallholders as was their habit, not causing any undue concern from the traders. Eventually, they wandered over to Ben's stall. They quietly told him what had transpired as they chatted to him. He looked shocked.

'Keep an eye on Arthur,' he was told. 'We're keeping tabs on the house in case Percy tries to get back. As yet, the news of the escape isn't public knowledge, but we can't hide the fact for too long as the public could be at risk.' Then they sauntered off.

As the police left the market, Arthur wandered over to Ben. 'What did they want? They usually come and give me a bit of stick, but not today. Not that I'm bothered.'

'Oh, it was their usual walkabout; you know, keeping an eye on everything.'

'But when they spoke to you, you looked surprised, what was that about?'

Ben grinned and said, 'Apparently there's a stray dog causing a bit of havoc. He went into the butcher's down the road and ran off with some meat. They were just warning me to be careful if I saw him.'

This seemed to satisfy Arthur and he wandered back to his stall. But Ben was thinking about Phoebe and her reaction whenever Percy was mentioned and when he used to be around, her nervousness bordering sometimes on fear. He'd never got to the bottom of this mystery, but his gut told him that if she knew of Percy's escape, she'd be devastated. He wandered over to her stall.

'Wait for me tonight. I'll help you put your stall away and walk you home.'

'That's nice of you. What brought that on?'

'I just thought we could spend an hour together away from here. I've hardly had time for a chat today, we've been so busy.'

Marj sauntered over. ''As 'e proposed yet, love?'

'Oh, Marj, how you do go on!'

She put her hand on Phoebe's arm. 'The boy's in love with you, it's obvious. Surely 'e's given you some 'int about the future?'

Phoebe hesitated but Marj was such a good friend and she needed some advice, so she told her friend about Ben saying he couldn't say anything at the moment, but that he was going to be around for a long time.

Her friend looked puzzled. 'I wonder what 'e's keeping back?'

'I don't know, but he asked me to trust him.'

'Then you must! Whatever it is, 'e must have a very good reason. That young man has integrity. 'E wouldn't lead you up the garden path. I'd stake my life on it!'

Phoebe hugged her friend. 'Oh, Marj, I do hope you're right, because I am in love with him.'

Percy Stanley had been busy. He'd wandered into the men's department of a large store in Winchester and, mingling among the crowd of shoppers, had managed to steal a jacket and a cap. He'd then gone into a public toilet and changed out of his white coat, putting it into a bin in one of the cubicles. Putting on his cap, he pulled it down to cover his face as much as possible. He had a little money with him, which he'd taken out of the nurse's pocket, and went into a small cafe for something to eat, in case he didn't get another meal for a while. He'd seen several police walking around and surmised they were looking for him, but he avoided them. He was anxious to get back to Southampton to collect a stash of money he'd hidden in one of their secret lock-ups. This would enable him to get far away and avoid detection. Arthur had the key, that was the only problem. It was almost a certainty that his home would be watched, which made things difficult, but he had to try to get in touch with his brother somehow. That money was his way to freedom.

Arthur was having the time of his life. He was now enjoying the sexual favours of Ivy, his girlfriend who was only too happy to oblige as she was hoping to persuade Arthur to let her move in permanently. She even took some food with her and cooked him a meal one evening, just to show him she was as adept in the kitchen as in his bed.

Putting down his knife and fork, Arthur belched loudly. 'That was really tasty, Ivy love, I don't remember when I last ate dumplings.'

She smiled coyly. 'I'm not surprised. Men living alone can rarely look after themselves when it comes to food. A good meal is good for the soul. It makes for a happy man.' Getting up from her chair, she wandered around the table, slipped her arms around him, kissed his neck and playfully nibbled his ear, before sitting on his knee.

'Do I make you happy, Arthur?'

He fondled her breast. 'You do, Ivy, you do.' He slipped his hand up her skirt, but she stopped him.

'Not on a full stomach, love. You'll get indigestion!' She got up, gathered the dirty plates and, with a sly smile, took them into the kitchen.

* * *

Meanwhile, in Winchester, Percy Stanley went to the railway station and, after checking that there were no police hanging around, bought a platform ticket. He stood with his back against the wall, waiting for the next train, glancing around to see if anyone was looking at him. Then in the distance he could hear the sound of a train approaching. It pulled into the platform with a squeal from its breaks, then let out a cloud of steam, which gave Percy cover to climb on board. He stood in the corridor instead of taking his seat in a compartment, thus allowing him to look out of the windows at the following stops to see if the police were standing by. He eventually alighted at the small station at Otterbourne, handed the guard his platform ticket, pretending to talk to the lady in front of him as if he'd been there to meet her and then he headed for the exit and walked quickly away.

It was three days after Percy had escaped from the prison hospital. It was obvious to Ben that Arthur was unaware of this through his daily conversations, which consisted only of Ivy, her cooking and his sex life. But Ben knew that the report of the escape would soon be common knowledge, as the police would have to consider the safety of the public. If Percy, known for his brutality, was to come in contact with someone who might recognise him or get in his way, it could turn into a major incident.

Saturday was the usual busy day in the market and at lunchtime Tim went for his weekly order of fish and chips for him, his sister and for Ben, before sitting on the steps with his friend Laura to have their lunch break together.

Phoebe had invited the girl around for tea on the previous Sunday and watched her and Tim do their homework together, ready for school the next day. She was delighted with this new friendship, for her brother's only other friends were the boys who lived along the road, but they were often off with their father and mother. She knew that made him sad and only emphasised the fact that he was now an orphan. She did her best to fill the role of mother and sister, but she too had her own moments of great loss, although she hid these from Tim.

Toward the end of the day when the evening edition of the local paper came out, somebody had handed a copy to Marj, who put it down to read later. It was just before closing when, in a quiet moment, she looked at the headline. She let out a cry and hurried over to Phoebe.

She handed the paper to her. 'Will you look at that! The bugger 'as done a runner!'

With a frown, Phoebe wondered what on earth she was talking about . . . then she read the headline. MAN ESCAPES FROM WINCHESTER PRISON. Beside it, a picture of Percy Stanley.

Phoebe felt the blood drain from her body – then she fainted.

Marj yelled for Ben, who, seeing the prostrate figure on the ground, rushed over. He bent over Phoebe and held her in his arms, calling her name. He felt for a pulse as he did so. Tim, his face pale with worry, stood and watched.

Marj soaked a cloth in a bucket of water she had, and Ben put the cloth on Phoebe's forehead, talking to her all the time. 'What the hell happened?' he asked her friend.

She showed him the headline. As she did so, Phoebe

started to come round. She was confused but as she opened her eyes, she saw Ben's face.

'What are you doing?' she asked her voice trembling.

'You fainted,' he said.

With a frown she tried to remember. 'I did?'

Ben helped her to her feet and sat her on a chair that Marj brought over from her stall. One of the other stallholders handed him a glass of water and he gave it to her, holding it steady while she sipped it.

'You all right, Phoebe?' asked Tim, shaken by events.

She gave a wan smile. 'I'm fine, I don't know what happened.'

'You read the headline in the paper that Marj showed you,' Ben told her. 'It was about Percy Stanley.'

Her eyes widened and she stiffened. 'Oh my God! It said he'd escaped. Is it true?'

Ben kneeling beside her, took both her hands in his. 'Yes, I'm afraid it is. He's been on the run for three days.' Again he saw the look of fear he'd seen before. But Phoebe said nothing more.

Getting to his feet, Ben said, 'Right. I'll put my stall away and, after, Tim can help me with yours, then I'm taking you home!'

Phoebe began to argue but Ben just looked at her, daring her to argue further, then he walked to his stall and started packing up.

Marj stood beside Phoebe. 'What's wrong girl, because something certainly is? No one don't faint for nothing!'

'It was just such a shock. That's all.'

Her friend stood in front of her and with a hard stare spoke. 'You and me is best mates, you can tell me anything, you knows that. Right?'

165

Phoebe put her hand on her friend's arm. 'I do know that, honestly I do.'

Marj waited a further moment but when nothing else was forthcoming, she just grunted and walked back to her stall, but all the time watching Phoebe closely. She was no fool, there was something going on that just wasn't right but she'd no idea what – and it worried her.

Ben and Tim put the stall away, then collected Phoebe, returning the chair before leaving the market. Not a word was said as Phoebe, walking in the middle, her arms through those of her two men, headed for home.

In the meantime, Arthur had overheard the conversation about his brother escaping and rushed off to buy a paper. He was now a worried man. Percy had escaped custody. That could put an end to *his* freedom! He was livid. For the first time in his life, he was free, able to please himself. He had a woman who warmed his bed and cooked for him occasionally. He had a real friend in Ben, for the first time in his life. All of which his brother would have denied him. Well, he wasn't going to lose all that! Then, when he calmed down, he realised he'd be watched in case Percy tried to come back to the house or get in touch with him. The police would probably watch his house and him, scrutinising his every move. Already Percy was interfering with his life! He kicked the side of his stall in his anger, then packed up and went home.

Chapter Nineteen

When they arrived home, Ben insisted that Phoebe sit on the settee while he boiled the kettle and made her a cup of tea. He then cooked them bacon and eggs with mushrooms on toast.

Phoebe thanked him and sat quietly eating, saying nothing more. When they finished, Ben cleared away the dishes and, through the window, spotted the boys from along the road outside, playing football. He suggested that Tim might like to go and join them. The boy was delighted to do so and rushed out of the house.

Ben sat beside Phoebe on the settee and, putting an arm around her, said, 'We need to talk.'

Frowning, she gazed at him. 'Talk? What about?'

'Percy Stanley.' He felt her stiffen within his hold. 'It's time to tell me why this man frightens you enough to make you faint when you heard he'd escaped.'

'I don't know what you mean.'

'Yes, you do. When first I came to the market, you were just wary of him, as were others, but then something happened and you changed. I want to know what that was.'

'I can't tell you!' she exclaimed. 'Please don't ask.'

Her bottom lip started to tremble and he drew her closer. 'I'm not leaving here until you give me an explanation. Phoebe, darling, how can I protect you if I don't know what's going on?'

All her pent-up emotion spilt out. The murder, the fear of Percy finding out that she was a witness, her concern for Tim's and Mum's safety if he did, and now his escape. It was all too much and she burst into tears.

Ben held her and let her cry, wondering what on earth had caused such anguish, until eventually she stopped. He held her face and stared at her. 'It's time to share this, whatever it is. Now tell me, so I can help you.'

She hesitated for a moment, wondering if she dare share her secret, but knowing that now she couldn't cope alone any longer. 'I saw him kill a man!'

Ben was shocked, but his expression didn't change. His training in the force stood him in good stead. 'When was this, and where, Phoebe? Just take your time.'

She explained why she returned to the market to check if she'd locked her stall away safely. 'I heard raised voices coming from Percy's lock-up. I was about to leave when he and another man started fighting and tumbled outside. I hid behind a pile of cardboard boxes, but I could see what was happening through a space between them.'

'So what did happen?'

'Percy knocked the other man down and was holding

him by the throat. He couldn't breathe very well but he managed to get up and turned towards Percy.' She stopped and her voice broke as she said, 'Percy brought out a knife and stabbed him!' She started crying and between sobs carried on. 'He picked the man up and put him in the lock-up, then was about to walk away when I moved and one of the boxes fell.' Her eyes widened. 'I thought, I was going to die too but before he could come looking, a cat jumped down, crying, and Percy walked away. He thought it was the cat, I suppose. All I knew was that I was saved and needed to get away.'

'Oh, Phoebe. You must have been terrified.'

'I was. I was violently sick in one of the boxes, then I rushed home.'

'But why didn't you go to the police?'

'Percy didn't know I'd seen him, no one else was around. It would be his word against mine, because the next morning, the brothers went to their lock-up and opened the doors as wide as usual to collect their gear, so obviously the body was no longer there. They could deny it! Who would believe me? I had no proof of what I saw. Then I would be a danger to Percy. I had to think of Tim's safety. I couldn't tell anyone. I think it must have been the person whose body was found much later in the cemetery.'

Ben needed time to think of the implications of all this before he made a decision, but he was now aware of the burden that Phoebe had been carrying alone. He had to reassure her.

'You still don't need to tell anyone. Only the two of us know. We'll wait until he's captured before we decide what to do. The police will be watching the area closely. Percy won't dare come anywhere near here, so you've nothing to worry about.'

He saw the relief reflected in her eyes and he kissed her softly. 'I'm here to take care of you and Tim, so please will you stop worrying? I'll walk you home each night, if that would make you feel better?'

She clutched his arm. 'Oh, would you, Ben? I'm so afraid he'll turn up, because that one time he suddenly appeared and picked up some fallen stuff when I was packing up in my lock-up, I screamed. He grabbed me and asked me why I was so scared of him. What if he realises I was there and it wasn't the cat that made the noise?'

'Why would he, Phoebe? He didn't see you. The police didn't come looking for him the next day. He's probably forgotten the incident.'

'If only I could be sure.'

'You'll just have to trust me. Now, are you going to be all right if I go home?'

'Yes, I'm fine. As you said, he'd be foolish to come around this area and he is no fool.'

Ben gave her a hug, kissed her goodbye and left. He didn't go home, but walked to the police station and spoke to Detective Inspector Jack Bentley and told him what he'd just heard.

'I knew that bastard was guilty! But you did the right thing. We'll leave your young lady out of it for the moment until we catch Stanley. His brother obviously helped him to move the body. Arthur is a weak man. Knowing the facts, we'll soon break him, but we have to have his brother in custody first. Just watch over her until we do.'

* * *

Percy was feeling fraught. He'd slept rough the last few nights in Otterbourne, once in a derelict shed. Then he found a bicycle left outside someone's house and rode it to Southampton Common, where he dumped it among a load of bushes. He used the public toilet to freshen up, but even so he looked dishevelled, with several days' growth on his chin. But at last he was nearer to Arthur and his goal. He walked towards the town.

It was late afternoon and Arthur was tidying his stall when a small boy walked over and stood before it.

'Bugger off!' snapped Arthur.

'I've got a message for you,' the boy said and handed over a piece of folded paper. 'Some old bloke told me to give it to you and you'd give me a tanner for my trouble.'

Arthur opened the note and read it. He immediately looked round to see if anyone was watching, then handed the boy a sixpence and sent him on his way. Then he read the note again.

It gave the address of one of their secret lock-ups and a message. *Be there at midnight, bring change of clothes. Don't be followed!* He scrunched the paper up and put it in his pocket and continued to tidy his display, still gazing around casually. But no one was taking any notice of him. Inside he was fuming. Fucking Percy! Why couldn't he leave him alone? He had a good life now and again his brother was interfering with it. There was no way he could ignore it because Percy wouldn't leave him be if he did, this he was certain of. He had no bloody choice, he thought.

He locked his stall away at the end of the day and went to the nearest pub to down a few pints and wonder what

Percy had in mind. He'd better take a few pounds with him to give to his brother with the idea that Percy could use it to get away from Southampton and him. With a bit of luck, that would be the last he would see of him. He ordered another beer. Ben, being ever watchful, had seen the boy hand over a piece of paper, and the look on Arthur's face when he read it. It had to be from Percy, who else would do such a thing? Certainly not the girlfriend, surely? No, if it was from her, Arthur wouldn't behave so furtively.

He wandered over to Phoebe. 'Look, darling, I'm sorry, but I can't walk you home tonight. Will you be all right?'

She assured him that she would be, so Ben closed up early, allowing him to find a place to watch Arthur's movements unseen. He saw him go into the pub and hid away to wait for him. While he waited, he saw a policeman doing his rounds and stopped him, explained who he was and what he was doing, and asked him to inform the station that he thought something was going down and to let the police watching the house know. But to tell them if Arthur Stanley left his house, he wasn't to be stopped, just followed. Then he waited until Arthur left the pub and walked home.

The house lights were extinguished just before eleven o'clock. Ben surmised that if he'd been summoned by his brother, Arthur would try and sneak out by the back door, so as not to be seen, therefore he positioned himself where he could see the end to the alleyway at the back of the houses and waited.

Half an hour later, Arthur, clutching a bag, quietly opened his back door and closed it, then, at the back gate, he peered out and listened. There was no noise or movement. Closing the gate behind him, he crept along the back walls of the other houses until he came to the end of the alleyway. Here he stopped and poked his head round the corner to see if there was anyone there. Eventually he stepped out, and keeping close to the wall, walked swiftly away. His heart hammering, expecting any moment for a hand to grab his shoulder. When this didn't happen, he began to relax and congratulate himself on fooling the police, who would certainly be keeping a watch on the house.

Eventually he reached his destination and walking to the door of the lock-up, he stopped and looked around, calling softly, 'Percy! Are you there?'

A hand covered his mouth, making him jump.

'Shut your mouth, you stupid sod! Of course I'm here. Open the bloody door, will you!'

On hearing his brother's voice, Arthur fumbled in his pocket for the key and unlocked the door. Percy shoved him roughly inside and shut it behind him. 'I hope you were sure you weren't followed!' he snapped.

Arthur spun round and glared at his brother. 'Of course I wasn't, I'm not stupid!' Then, seeing the bedraggled state of Percy, he said, 'Christ, you look rough!'

'What do you expect, I've been on the run for days.' He walked over to a small chest of drawers, and turning it upside down, removed a bundle taped to the bottom.

'What's that?' asked Arthur.

'My way out!' Percy opened the bundle to uncover a wad of notes. He held them up for Arthur to see.

'You miserable bastard! You never told me about that. There's a small fortune there!'

Percy grinned. 'This was my emergency fund. In our game you never know when you need the readies to get you out of a mess. Now I need it.'

'What about me? What if I'd ever needed them?'

'You didn't, you had me watching your back instead.'

But Arthur was incensed. 'Watching my back? Lot of bloody good that was! Who murdered Frank Clarke? Not me! That was down to you!'

'You shut your face! I'm taking this. It'll buy me a passage out of here. You won't see me again. You can live your miserable life, I'll be glad to see the back of you.'

'That's bloody fine with me!' raged Arthur. 'I've never been so happy since you were arrested. I have a better life without you, so bugger off. I'm glad to see you go.'

He opened the door and they both stepped outside to be blinded by a mass of light from several torches.

'Arthur and Percy Stanley, you're nicked!'

Chapter Twenty

Percy tried to run but was soon stopped by several policemen and held to the ground. As he felt his hands being cuffed behind him, he yelled at his brother.

'You useless bastard! You were followed. I warned you about it, but you couldn't even get that right. I should have smothered you the day you were born!'

'Shut your mouth, Stanley!' snapped one of the policemen, as he hauled him to his feet. The brothers were placed inside a police van with two constables sitting with them and taken to the police station.

Arthur silently glared at his brother during the journey, his hatred for him growing by the second for getting him in this situation. Once they arrived, they were separated and taken into the cells to wait.

DI Jack Bentley was walking up and down in his office,

trying to think of the best way to question Arthur. It was obvious that he had no love for his brother and that since he'd been living alone he had enjoyed his freedom from Percy's domination. But if he was persuaded to confess to his part of the murder of Clarke, he too would serve a term of imprisonment. Would that be enough to make him cover for his brother?

The man in question was sitting contemplating his future. He was livid that Percy had now implicated him in helping an escaped prisoner. Prior to that, the police had nothing on him. Would that lead to a custodial sentence? His anger boiled up inside him. Percy had never had any consideration for him. It was always 'do this', 'do that', never 'would you like to', or 'shall we?' Not him! Then he sat up and began to smile. However, *he* now had the upper hand. For the very first time, he could decide his brother's future. Pay him back for the years of misery. But that would come at a price. Was he prepared to pay it? That would be what his brother was banking on – his fear of prison.

Arthur was hustled into an interview room. His handcuffs were removed, then he was told to sit down at the table. Opposite sat DI Bentley and another detective.

Bentley sat looking at the man before him, trying to ascertain his mental state. He saw a look of trepidation on the other's face. No wonder, he thought, Stanley knows he's in a really serious situation.

He took out a packet of cigarettes from his pocket and lit one, then seeing the look of longing from his prisoner across the table, he pushed the pack over to him with a lighter.

Arthur removed one with hands that trembled.

'I don't have to tell you, Arthur, that you are in a load of trouble, burglary being the smallest crime, I'm sure you know this, then aiding and abetting the escape of a prisoner for another – but covering up a murder, now we are talking about a serious crime.'

Arthur's eyes widened in surprise. 'I don't know nothing about a murder!' he exclaimed.

'Oh, come now! Lying at this time really is foolish. I thought you had more sense.'

'I haven't murdered anyone!' Arthur's voice got nervously higher.

'No, but your brother did.'

Arthur glared at Bentley defiantly. 'Prove it!'

'Oh, we can do that . . . we have a witness.'

Stanley paled at the comment. 'What do you mean?'

'We have a witness who saw your brother knife Clarke, lift his body and put it in the lock-up, then walk away. No doubt Percy came rushing home to you to help him remove the body to the cemetery. We know that you both cleaned up by the lock-up outside with sand and water, and then inside.' At the mention of the sand, Arthur looked stunned. 'You are seriously implicated, my friend. Your brother has placed you deeply in the brown stuff! Shame, really, because you're not like him. You don't have it in you to kill anyone. But there is blood on your hands, nevertheless.'

Arthur was shocked into silence.

'You're looking at serious time behind bars for something you didn't do. Now, I don't think that's fair. But of course, there is a way you could do yourself some good and perhaps the judge would be lenient in his judgement when the case comes before a court, which it certainly will.'

Arthur was now sweating profusely. Wiping his forehead with a handkerchief he asked, 'What do you mean?'

'Well, the way I see it: why should you carry the can for a crime you didn't commit? Your brother gave you no choice in the matter. Knowing the man, I'm sure he bullied you into helping him. What else could you do? However, if you make a statement, giving us the facts, the judge would most certainly take this help into consideration.'

Arthur glared at him. 'I'm still looking at a term inside!'

'You're going down anyway, but an accessory is a serious charge with a long custodial sentence, unless your statement was a help in solving the murder. Then it would be very different.' He let Arthur think about it for a while, then added, 'Just think, when eventually you do get out, Percy will no longer be around to interfere with your life. You are still a young man. You could do as you like, when you like and with anyone who takes your fancy. You could live, Arthur! Please yourself for the rest of your life!'

Bentley could see Arthur thinking about it all. It was a lot to ask and Arthur wasn't the brightest of men; however, he wasn't stupid enough not to understand the situation and the offer before him.

'Tell me about your brother,' Bentley asked.

Arthur looked puzzled. 'Like what?'

'As kids together, for instance. Was he a good older brother?'

With pursed lips Arthur answered. 'No! He was always a bully. If he couldn't get his own way, he'd beat me up. He scared away all my friends.'

'He ruined your childhood, then?'

'If Mum gave us money for sweets, he'd take mine too!' Arthur was growing more resentful with every memory, playing into the hands of the detective.

'What about girlfriends? Did he have any?'

'Women were scared of him. He was a wicked bugger. He expected everyone to do as they were told. No woman likes that. If they upset him, he'd give them a slap, so they stayed away. In the end he used brasses for sex. Otherwise he wasn't interested.'

'Not like you and your girlfriend, Ivy?'

Arthur smiled. 'She likes me. Wants to move in and take care of me. No one ever said that to my brother!'

'I can understand that. After all, you're a fine figure of a man. 'Arthur looked pleased at the compliment. 'I'm sure you'd be kind to a woman. Think, one day you could have a family of your own if you so wished, but of course this couldn't happen if you were shut away for years – and believe me, Percy won't appreciate your keeping quiet. By keeping quiet you're not doing *him* any favours. He's going to be arrested for murder, anyway. All you're doing by keeping silent is just adding more years that *you* have to serve in prison, which seems to me pretty pointless.'

Bentley and his companion rose from their seats. The detective pushed a writing pad and a pen over to Arthur. 'I'll give you some time to think about it. Keep the cigarettes.'

Outside the room he turned to his associate. 'With a bit of luck, he'll come clean. We'll leave him be to stew on it. Come on, I desperately need a cup of tea.'

After their break, the two detectives entered another interview room and waited for Percy to be brought in. This

179

time the handcuffs stayed in place. Percy glared at the two men, waiting for them to speak.

Bentley smiled softly. 'I cannot tell you how happy I am today. I knew you'd killed your mate Clarke and now I can put you away.'

Percy wasn't fazed. 'Don't give me that old bull. You don't have any proof. You're all mouth!'

Bentley leant back in his chair. 'You couldn't be more wrong. We have a witness!'

Percy laughed. 'Of course you do.'

'Let me tell you what happened. You quarrelled with Clarke, it came to blows and you ended up outside the lock-up. You actually had him on the ground, by the throat at one point.' At this piece of detailed information, Percy looked stunned. 'But he managed to get to his feet,' Bentley continued. 'He turned towards you and then you took out a knife and stabbed him.' Bentley paused to let his words sink in. 'After, when you realised he was dead, you picked him up, put him in the lock-up and walked away. That was when you got your brother to help you take the body to the cemetery and clean up the blood.'

'It's a pretty story,' Stanley bluffed. 'So who is this mysterious witness you're supposed to have?'

'I'm not at liberty to say. You will find out when we go to court.' The detective leant forward. 'I can already hear the trapdoor opening!'

Percy tried to get to his feet. 'You bastard!' But a constable standing behind him pushed him back onto the chair.

'Oh, and by the way, don't think your brother is going to help you. As we speak, he's writing out a statement, which, with a bit of luck, will have the judge place his black cap on his head as he passes sentence on you.' He rose to his feet. 'Charge him,' he told the other detective and left the room.

After he'd been charged, Percy was sent back to his cell before being transported to a prison to await his trial. He'd been shaken to be told there had been a witness at Clarke's murder. The very fact the detective knew he'd had Clarke down on the ground and held by the throat could have only come from someone who was there. But who? In his mind he went over the scene. There was no one around when Clarke had arrived and as far as he knew they were alone when they had their fight. Then he remembered the cat jumping down after a box tumbled onto the ground. That was it! There had to be somebody hiding and who'd disturbed the pile. He'd taken it for granted the cat had been the cause. It was the only answer to the mystery. But who the hell could it have been? Who would have had reason to be there? The market was long closed. The stalls put away, the place empty. It had to be a passer-by or . . . someone who had a reason to be there and that could only be a stallholder. That girl, Phoebe someone, was the only one to store her stuff just along from his lock-up.

He sat up straight. Of course! That would explain why she'd been terrified when he'd appeared to pick up some of her fruit and handed it to her in the lock-up that time. She'd screamed with fright! That would explain her behaviour ever since the event. It had to be her. His eyes narrowed. Why hadn't she gone to the police the next day? He cursed the fact that he hadn't realised before.

* * *

In the meantime, Arthur had been thinking. He wasn't about to commit himself to any written word without some detail of how long a judge might consider he'd have to serve if he gave the police the information they wanted. After all, he now held the upper hand. A real bargaining point. No, he'd wait. He wasn't very intelligent, but he was a good salesman.

Detective Inspector Bentley entered the room with his associate and was disappointed to see an empty pad before his prisoner. He sat down, looked at the pad and then at Arthur.

'What's all this, then?'

Arthur looked at him. 'It seems to me that I could have a serious piece of information that you require to close your case. I'm not saying I do, only that it's a possibility. However, you haven't really offered me anything concrete in return. All you've said is a judge would take a statement from me into consideration. That's not enough!'

Bentley stared at him, thinking, *You are a cunning little sod*. 'So what do you want in return?'

'What are you offering?'

Bentley thought for a moment. 'No charge brought against you for burglary.'

'You've only proof that my brother sold the goods. None that I had anything to do with it. You have to do better than that.'

'We'll drop the charge of aiding and abetting the escape of a prisoner.'

Arthur wasn't impressed and it showed. He waited.

'You had nothing to do with the murder, only in covering it up and helping to hide the body.'

With a sly smile Arthur said, 'That doesn't sound to me like a crime that would be enough to put me inside for very long and . . . *if* I were to help, then it would be even less, wouldn't you say?'

The detective had to agree.

'In your estimation, how long?'

'A couple of years with time off for good behaviour, probably eighteen months would be my estimate.'

Arthur lit a cigarette and sat back. He puffed slowly on it, enjoying his moment as the others waited for his answer. 'Eighteen months, you say?'

Bentley nodded.

Although he hated the thought of prison, Arthur thought eighteen months wasn't nearly as bad as he'd expected. After that, his brother would be out of his life and he would be a free man.

'Very well, Mr Bentley, you have a deal,' and he picked up his pen.

The two men left the room, leaving Arthur to write out his statement. Once outside, Bentley spoke. 'Cunning bugger, but in all honesty, I don't blame him. He's no threat to the public, unlike his brother. It will be my great pleasure to see him go down and now we've got him!'

Chapter Twenty-One

Later that day, Ben was called into Bentley's office and told the good news. 'Arthur Stanley has made a statement, giving us the facts and naming his brother as the murderer of Frank Clarke and describing how they disposed of the body in the cemetery.'

'What about Miss Collins? Will she have to appear at the trial as a witness?'

'I'm afraid so. After all, she was the only one who actually saw Stanley kill Clarke. Her evidence is vital. You'd better prepare her.'

'I'll go and see her now.'

As Ben left the station, he realised that at last he could tell Phoebe the truth about who he was and why he'd been in the market. Finally, he could be himself without any further subterfuge and that was a great relief. He only hoped she'd understand. However, he couldn't tell her at her stall, they needed privacy for such a conversation.

While Ben had been at the meeting, in Kingsland Market, Marj had been talking to Phoebe.

'Where's your boyfriend been these past couple of days, then? Ever since the two brothers have been arrested, 'e too has disappeared. What's going on?'

Phoebe looked perplexed. 'I've no idea. I've not heard from Ben at all. I hope he isn't poorly. I don't know where he lives or I'd call and see if he was all right.'

Glancing over Phoebe's shoulder, Marj said, 'No need, 'ere 'e comes now.'

Turning, Phoebe saw Ben approaching and wondered why he looked so serious.

'Ben! I was worried about you. Are you all right?'

He placed an arm around her and kissed her cheek. 'I'm fine. I'm sorry I've not been in touch, but can we meet this evening? I can explain.'

'Yes, of course. Come round after seven, by then I'll have got Tim settled and we'll be on our own.'

'Excellent! I'll see you then. You all right, Marj?' he called.

'All the better for seeing you, young Ben! We missed you.'

'I missed you too.' He turned to Phoebe. 'See you tonight.'

Marj wandered over to her. 'That boy's got something on 'is mind. I wonder what it is?'

'He's coming round tonight to tell me why he hasn't been in touch.'

'Mm. Be prepared to be surprised,' Marj warned.

'What do you mean?'

'I don't really know but I've a feeling in my water that

186

'e 'as a tale to tell, which you're not going to expect.'
She walked away, leaving Phoebe feeling puzzled. Marj
wasn't usually wrong about things. It was as if she had a
sixth sense. She said it was coming from Gypsy stock that
had given her such an insight.

Tim, dressed in his pyjamas, opened the door to Ben that
evening. He was delighted to see him and gave him a hug.

'All ready for bed I see,' said Ben as he stepped inside.
'I've brought these for you, but you had better wait until
tomorrow to eat them or Phoebe will be angry with me.' He
handed over a small bag of sweets. The boy was delighted.

'I'll take them to school with me.'

'Come along, Tim,' said Phoebe. 'Time for bed. You can
read for a bit. I'll come up and put your light out in a little
while. Cup of tea?' she asked Ben.

'Not just now, maybe later. Come and sit beside me on
the sofa,' he said. 'I have some explaining to do.' He took
her hand in his. 'I've not been able to be strictly truthful
with you from the day we met.'

'Whatever do you mean?'

'I'm not a market trader, as you well know – I am a
policeman, a detective, and I was in the market to keep an
eye on the Stanley brothers.'

This information floored Phoebe and she was speechless.

'I was undercover, so unable to tell anyone. I am sorry,
but I had no choice. Then, when you told me you had seen
Percy murder that man – I'm sorry, darling, but I had to
report it to my superiors.'

Her eyes widened. 'You what?'

'I had to, Phoebe. As an officer of the law I couldn't

possibly keep it quiet. You had vital information that would convict a killer, a man who was a menace to society. The very fact we now had you as a witness allowed us to arrest Percy for the crime and coerce Arthur into writing a statement, naming his brother as the murderer and hiding the body in the cemetery. Without you, we couldn't have done that. Do you see how important it was?'

She looked horrified. 'Now I'll have to go to court and tell everything in public. Oh Ben, how could you betray my confidence like that? I trusted you!'

'I am sorry, Phoebe. But you were witness to the actual stabbing.'

'You knew how frightened I was, how worried by it all, yet you still told your superior.'

'I'm a policeman, I had no choice, *can't* you see that? I couldn't possibly withhold this information, it was too important. And what's more: it was knowing there was a witness that made Arthur confess and name his brother, so Percy will never be free again to do any further harm. No longer will he be around to scare you by his presence. You'll be able to carry on without out any worries about him.'

'That's easy for you to say! Sometimes I have nightmares, when I see it all happening again. I'll *never* be free of him!' She pushed his hand away and, getting to her feet, walked over to the stove, picked up the kettle and made a pot of tea.

Ben was wracking his brains trying to find a way to make her realise his position in all this. 'I know it's hard for you to understand and I'm sorry you're still haunted by what you saw that night, but you don't have to handle all of this alone. I told you, I intend to be around for a long time. I'll help you through it.'

She cast a hostile glance at him. 'Really? I'm not sure that's a good idea. How can I ever trust you now?'

He looked shattered by her words. 'You can't mean that, Phoebe. I had such plans for the future – for you and Tim, for us to be together. I love you, you must know that by now?'

She looked at him with tears brimming. 'Yet you threw me to the wolves!'

Ben rose from the sofa and went to walk towards her, but Phoebe held up her hand to stop him. 'I think it's best we leave things as they are for the moment, Ben. I think you should go.'

'Phoebe!'

'Please, Ben, don't say any more. Just leave . . . please.'

As he shut the door behind him, she collapsed onto the sofa in tears.

As he walked down the street, Ben was desolate. He couldn't believe that Phoebe hadn't been able to understand why he'd had to inform his superiors that she'd witnessed the murder. He'd been so happy that now he could tell her the truth about his job, that he was now free to plan their future together – all three of them. He'd had to wait, to pretend, and he'd hated that. She needed time to take it all in, he told himself. Well, he'd give her a couple of days and then he'd talk to her again.

During a lull in the market the following morning, Marj wandered over to Phoebe.

'Well, by the look on your face, I was right about young Ben! But I didn't expect you to look so bloody miserable about it. What's up, love? It's best you get it off your chest.'

Phoebe told her the whole story. As she got to the part about the murder, Marj let out a cry of horror. 'You saw it? Oh girl, come 'ere.' She took her into her arms. 'No one should 'ave to see such a terrible thing.'

When Phoebe had recovered enough, she told her the rest of the tale.

'But that's great! It was because you told Ben what you saw that eventually that bastard was brought to justice.' Then she saw the anguish on the face of her friend. 'So what's the problem? Is that the end of your beautiful friendship? Does 'e now want to walk away. Is that it?'

'No, quite the opposite, but somehow I feel he betrayed me. I told him about the murder in confidence; he said it would remain between us. But he reported it!'

Marj looked at her in amazement. 'Phoebe Collins! I've known you from a young child, 'elping your dad on the stall; I've seen you take over as the breadwinner and bury your dear mother, God rest 'er soul – but I've never ever thought you were stupid . . . until now!'

Phoebe was taken aback by the anger in her friend's voice.

'You 'ad just given Ben the means of solving a murder, to put away a man who is a danger to the public – and you are affronted by this? I can hardly believe it! Just think. If 'e hadn't reported it and it came out eventually, 'e probably would 'ave lost his job for withholding vital evidence and Percy Stanley would still be strutting about the place. You would see him every day, knowing what 'e'd done. You'd end up a basket case and leave that bugger free to top someone else who upset him! Why can't you see this? I don't understand.'

She could see that Phoebe wasn't convinced by her argument. 'And . . . what if Percy eventually realised that you'd seen 'im? You were always on pins when 'e was about. In time 'e might 'ave caught on. What then? 'E might have topped you too, then where would poor Tim 'ave been, answer me that!'

Phoebe burst into tears. 'I can't think any more!'

Putting an arm round the girl, Marj tried to comfort her. 'I'm not surprised, love, after what you've been through, but at least you won't 'ave to see the brothers no more. In time, you'll feel better, especially with Ben by your side. That man loves your bones and those of Tim too. The boy needs a father and you need someone to look after you for a change. Don't throw it all away or you'll regret it for the rest of your life.' She walked away, leaving Phoebe to think about her advice.

The headlines in the early edition of the local paper had everyone talking.

MAN CHARGED WITH MURDER.

Beside it, a picture of Percy Stanley. It went on to tell of his criminal record, about his previous term in prison, the fact that he was already charged with burglary.

The traders in the market couldn't stop talking about it. It was only then that Phoebe realised she would be implicated in all this mayhem. She bought a paper and took it home to read. It didn't mention anything about a witness, only that Arthur Stanley was also being held in custody. So far, only the police knew she was involved.

Two days had passed, and Phoebe hadn't heard from Ben. It seemed strange in the market without the brothers' stall, but it was the empty spot where Ben had been that saddened her. She missed his cheery smile first thing in the morning. His very presence pleased her when she would look over to him. Now there was an empty space and she hated it. She'd had time to consider his position and realised that, as he'd said, as a policeman there was no way he could have kept the information she'd given him to himself. She only hoped he'd call to see her so she could apologise.

Marj could tell she was missing Ben and had now come to terms with everything.

'Don't you worry none, love. Ben will come back. 'E's just giving some breathing space, that's all. Mark my words.'

Phoebe just hoped she was right.

Tim too was missing Ben. On the next Saturday he said as much as he helped his sister. 'Where's Ben, Phoebe? He isn't here and he hasn't been to see us. Has he gone away?'

She didn't think she had the right to explain Ben's real position, so she made up some excuse.

It was to his chum Laura the boy gave vent to his real feelings when she asked him why he was looking so glum.

'It's because of Ben. He isn't here and he hasn't called at the house. I wonder if he and Phoebe have fallen out.'

'Would that matter if they had?'

He nodded. 'I really like Ben and I thought he liked Phoebe. I hoped he'd ask her to marry him, then I'd have a dad like all my friends. Ben took me to watch the cricket not long ago. It was great, just me and him. He's kind and he'd take care of Phoebe too.'

'You can share my dad, if you like, Tim.'

He smiled at her. 'Thanks, Laura, but I want one of my own, if you know what I mean.'

She smiled sympathetically. 'Here, have one of my chips.'

It was Sunday morning and Phoebe was cleaning the house when there was a knock on the door. She opened it to see Ben standing there.

'Hello, Phoebe. May I come in?'

She stepped back. 'Of course you can.'

Tim had just finished his breakfast and he ran to Ben and flung his arms round him. 'Ben! Where have you been? You weren't in the market yesterday and you haven't been round here, either.'

Ben looked at Phoebe, who just raised her eyebrows at him as if to say, 'It's up to you.'

Sitting down at the table, Ben pulled up another chair for the boy. 'Well, you see, Tim, I was there doing another job, really, apart from selling stuff from the stall.' He then proceeded to tell Tim his story.

Tim was thrilled at the tale. He thought it sounded exciting. 'A detective! The brothers are in jail and that Percy killed a man! Did you know that?'

'Not at first, but he was a suspect.'

Tim looked at his sister. 'Did you know all this, Phoebe?'

'No, as a matter of fact, I didn't.'

Ben was pleased to hear that the remark wasn't said with any malice.

'I couldn't tell anyone, Tim. But now the case is closed, and I can go back on duty. No more standing in the cold.'

Tim looked disappointed. 'I won't be able to buy your fish and chips for you. I'll miss you, Ben.'

'Well, I'm keeping my fingers crossed that your sister is going to allow me to call on her again.' The two of them looked expectantly at her.

With a slow smile she said, 'I don't see why not.'

'Have you any plans for today?' Ben asked.

Shaking her head, Phoebe said, 'I've not yet given today a thought. Why?'

'How about we all go to the pier, get some fresh air, play on the slot machines, look at the stalls, have some lunch and later we can go to the cinema?'

Tim jumped up and down with joy. 'Oh, Phoebe, let's do that, please?'

'How could I possibly refuse,' she said.

Chapter Twenty-Two

It was a lovely morning, with the June sun shining on the water as they arrived at the pier. The warm weather had brought others out to enjoy themselves. Ben brought a supply of pennies and he and Tim played the slot machines and put money in one with a grab mechanism, hoping it would pick up one of the treasures inside the glass case, without any luck. They put a penny in another and the clown looking back at them laughed loudly. His body bounced up and down with glee, making them laugh. They bought ice cream and sat in deckchairs, eventually wandering along the pier to a cafe to have some lunch.

While Tim was tucking into his meal, Ben looked at Phoebe. 'Am I forgiven, then?'

She looked embarrassed. 'Yes, of course. I now realise you didn't have a choice and that I was being less than understanding.' She pulled a face. 'Marj gave me a good talking to!'

'You told her everything?' He looked surprised.

'Yes, I know she'll not say a word to anyone. I've known her for years and she's like a second mother to me.' Laughing she added, 'I felt like a naughty child when she'd finished telling me how stupid I'd been.'

'I knew I loved that woman for a reason! But let's put all this behind us now and move on with our lives. We'll plan for the future soon, I promise.'

They finished their day out at the pictures and when Ben eventually left, he took Phoebe into his arms and kissed her. 'I love you, Phoebe – and Tim. Just remember that.'

A little later, as Tim got ready for bed, he looked at his sister. 'We had a lovely day today, didn't we?'

'We did indeed.'

'Are you friends again with Ben?'

She saw the worried expression on his face. 'Yes, why do you ask?'

'I want him to be my dad, that's why.' He turned and went upstairs to his bedroom.

Phoebe sat with a cup of tea and thought about the longing in the voice of her young brother. Of course he needed a father. He could hardly remember his own and she knew he felt the loss of a father figure when he saw his friends with theirs. Ben loved Tim, hadn't he told her so? You only had to see them together to know how they had already bonded. That had been apparent at the loss of her mother and at the funeral. She loved Ben, he was the man with whom she wanted to spend the rest of her life, but what would she do about the stall? Would they move from the house? Could Ben afford to marry her and look after Tim as well?

Her head was spinning. So much had happened over the past weeks that she was unable to think. So many thoughts raced through her mind. Phoebe rose to her feet. She needed to sleep. Today had been so good, she'd go to bed and think of that and try to put her worries aside.

While Phoebe was trying to understand how her life might change, Arthur Stanley was in Winchester Prison living his. He was awaiting his trial and was learning what life in a small cell without any freedom was like.

On admission, he'd been stripped and searched, deloused and bathed. He was given a set of prison clothes, one change of underwear, a pillow and a blanket and then led to his cell. Gates were unlocked and ahead was a huge space with cells either side of a broad, empty alleyway. On the way he'd passed other prisoners who looked at him through the grille in their doors. Some yelled disparaging remarks; others just stared at the new arrival. The warder led him up an iron staircase to the upper floor. Their footsteps echoing, the warder's keys rattling. But what was the most frightening was the air of menace. This was not a happy place.

The cell door was opened by the warder. 'Right, this is your new home, Stanley. Now don't give me any trouble or you'll be sorry.' The door clanged behind him and the sound echoed as the key turned.

Arthur saw a middle-aged man sitting on the bottom of two bunk beds, reading. He glared at Arthur and motioned to the upper bunk. 'That's yours.' He pointed to a large bucket in the corner. 'You piss in that – not in your bed! We slop out every morning.'

'Slop out? What's that?'

The man sighed. 'Jesus! I've got a prison virgin to cope with.' He looked at his new cellmate. 'We have to empty the bucket every morning . . . that's slopping out! Now make up your bed and leave me alone.'

With some difficulty, Arthur climbed up onto the bunk and eventually lay on his side looking around. There was a tiny barred window on the back wall. A small table, two chairs – and the bucket. Nothing more, apart from a couple of shelves with two framed pictures on one of them. He lay there wondering how he was going to survive in this? He was hungry. He'd been given some breakfast before leaving Southampton, but he'd been too nervous to eat much of it, which he now regretted.

Leaning over his bed, he looked down at the top of the head of his cellmate. 'What happens at mealtimes?'

With a deep sigh the man answered. 'The cell doors are unlocked and we go to the dining room and line up. You take a tray, a plate and some cutlery and stand in line. You take what you're given, find a seat and eat. Then, when you're told, you line up, return the tray and cutlery and line up again to be let out in the quadrangle for an hour's break. Then you return to your cell until dinner. Got it?'

'Got it!' said Arthur.

It seemed for ever before the cell doors were opened for the prisoners to eat at lunchtime. Arthur very nervously followed his cellmate, not knowing the procedure. The prisoners filed into the dining room. There were long tables set up in lines with bench seats, and at the end of the room cooks stood in a line behind a counter, serving from hot dishes. Arthur put his plate down. The server didn't even look up as he slopped a large spoonful of what looked like brown mush onto the plate. Arthur frowned but moved on. Mashed potatoes came next and at the end some vile-smelling cabbage. Following behind his cellmate, he sat down and looked at the contents of his food.

'What the hell is this supposed to be?' he asked.

'Beef stew,' he was told.

After a couple of mouthfuls, he said, 'I reckon a cow just walked through this, because I can't see no meat here.'

'You're not in a bloody hotel, you know. You'll get used to it.'

Another convict, sitting on the other side of Arthur, spoke up. 'Listen, son. Take my advice, if you don't want to cause trouble. Just eat your grub and be grateful. The pudding's usually better.'

Arthur looked at him. He was elderly, with round shoulders, his face lined, hair thinning, but he smiled kindly at Arthur. 'You'll get used to it all in time.'

'How long have you been here?'

'Fifteen years.'

Arthur was stunned into silence, wondering whatever crime the man had committed to have been incarcerated for so long? The sponge pudding and custard were at least edible, even if the custard was thin.

After filing back with the empty dishes, the prisoners were led out of the dining room into the quadrangle, a square open space with high fences. The men dispersed.

Some stood together chatting, others wandered off and sat down on the concrete to have a cigarette or just look around. The old man from the dining room led Arthur to a bench and they both lit up a cigarette.

'What's your name son?'

'Arthur. Arthur Stanley.'

'Your first time in the pokey, ain't it?'

Arthur nodded.

'Well, take my advice. Keep yourself to yourself, don't upset no one and you'll probably be all right.'

With a frown Arthur asked, 'What do you mean, probably?'

The old boy shrugged. 'Inside you can never tell. A wrong look at the wrong person at the wrong time can be deadly.' He got up and walked away.

Arthur stayed where he was, almost too scared to look at anyone. He'd quickly glance around then look away, trying not to meet any gaze from another prisoner. By the time the bell went for them to return to their cells, he was a nervous wreck.

He sat at the small table and wiped the sweat from his brow. Looking up, he saw the other man grinning.

'Did old Henry put the fear of God in you in the yard?'

Arthur told him what he'd been told.

'He's right, of course, but just keep your mouth shut and find a spot on your own.'

'Who is the old boy and why is he here?'

'His name is Henry Evans. He killed his wife and mother-in-law. Said he couldn't stand their nagging any longer! He's in for life!'

Arthur was speechless. 'That nice old boy did that?'

The other man burst out laughing. 'That nice old boy throttled his wife in their bed, then went and did the same to the mother-in-law in hers. After, he went to sleep. Said it was the best night's rest he'd had since the day he got married.'

'Blimey!' was all Arthur could say, but then he looked at his cellmate, wondering why he was inside and for what reason? But he didn't ask, thinking he'd rather not know. As he lay on his bunk, he wondered how his brother was coping. Knowing Percy, he wondered how he'd react to being given orders. With a sly smile he knew he wouldn't like it at all.

Percy had been taken to Wormwood Scrubs prison and put in solitary confinement, which suited him, not having to share space with a stranger. Here, alone, he could fume about his brother giving him up to the authorities and probably gaining remission for the evidence. If he could only get his hands on the little bleeder, he'd do for him!

At lunchtime, a warder opened his cell door and shoved a plate of food at him.

Percy looked at what was on the plate. 'What's this? Pig swill?'

The warder looked disparagingly at him. 'Eat it or leave it! I couldn't give a toss.'

Getting to his feet, Percy glared at him. 'Who do you think you're talking to?'

'Don't try and come the big I am to me, sunshine. In here you're a nobody. Just a number! The sooner you get used to that the better it'll be for you.' He went out slamming the door shut.

Percy picked up the plate, sniffed the food and then, picking up a fork, tasted some of it. He immediately spat it out and threw the plate and the contents against the wall. It splattered everywhere, the walls, the floor and some of it onto his bedding.

Later the warder returned. He opened the cell door, looked around and saw the mess. He picked up the plate and the fork, glared at Percy and left without a word.

As the hours passed, Percy regretted his outburst as he slipped on some food on the floor. The smell from the rest of it permeated the room, making him feel sick. He wiped some off his blanket on the bed and lay down. The rest of the day passed without anyone bothering him and finally the lights went out and he was in darkness, apart from a shaft of moonlight through the small barred window in the cell. He slept badly.

The following morning, Percy could hear a sound of activity outside on the landing and wondered what was going on. There was a sound of cell doors opening and closing, voices, steps of people walking, getting nearer each time. He sat on his bed and waited.

Eventually his door was unlocked. Two warders stepped inside followed by a man dressed in a smart suit. The warder looked at Percy.

'Stand up, this is the governor.'

Percy rose to his feet.

The dapper gentleman looked at him, then at the mess in the cell. He looked at the warden.

'The prisoner doesn't like our cooking, sir!'

The governor glared at Percy. 'I will not tolerate such

behaviour in my prison. You will wash down this whole cell until it gleams.' Seeing the defiance on Percy's face he continued. 'Until my warders are satisfied that your cell is habitable again, you will not be given anything more to eat. You will not be allowed out to exercise, you will stay confined here until you satisfy my staff!' He turned and left.

Half an hour later, Percy was taken out of his cell to a room, given a bucket, some soft soap, a long mop and a couple of floor cloths and a scrubbing brush. Then he was taken into another room where he had to fill the bucket with hot water before being led back to his cell.

'I'll be back in two hours,' he was told by the warden.

Although he was furious at being given such a task, Percy set about cleaning up the mess because he couldn't stand the smell of it any more. He washed down the walls, scrubbed the floor, but by now the water was too dirty to be any good so when the warder returned, he was taken to refill the bucket to finish the job. It took him nearly all afternoon before the warden was satisfied. He lay on his bed, completely shattered.

A while later, the door was unlocked, and the warder walked in with a tray. 'You missed supper time.' He placed the tray on the table. Walking over to the table, Percy, now very hungry, looked at the plate. There was a sandwich, a cup of watery tea and a biscuit. He sat down and devoured the lot. Was that it? He was still hungry. He banged on the door of the cell until the face of the warder appeared in the grille in the doorway.

'What's all the noise about?'

'I'm still hungry. Is that all the food we get?'

'You should have eaten your lunch. Now don't go

banging on this door any more, because I've got better things to do than listen to you.'

Percy sat on his bed. He'd not had any breakfast due to the mess he'd made of his cell and he was ravenous. Now he realised he'd have to eat whatever was given to him to keep up his strength. He had no choice.

Chapter Twenty-Three

Phoebe was sorting out her stall and cleaning it as was her habit on Monday mornings. She wasn't feeling well. Her head was pounding and she'd started sneezing.

'What's up, love?' asked her friend, Marj.

Phoebe drew up a stool she had at the back of the stall and sat down. 'I don't know. I've got a thumping headache and I feel chilled. I was fine yesterday, but when I woke this morning I felt dreadful.'

'Go 'ome, darlin'. Mondays are quiet, you won't miss much business. Make a 'ot drink and go to bed. Go on, staying 'ere won't help.'

Reluctantly, Phoebe took her advice. When she got home, she made a pot of tea, took a couple of Aspirin tablets, then went to bed, leaving a note on the kitchen table for Tim. She soon fell into a deep sleep.

* * *

Tim let himself into the house, saw the note on the table, read it and walked quietly upstairs. Phoebe had left her bedroom door ajar, so he crept in and looked at the sleeping figure of his sister. For a moment he had a feeling of panic, remembering his mother having to take to her bed before she was taken to hospital – where she died. Peering at the face of his sister he thought she looked all right and decided not to disturb her yet.

Downstairs, he looked in the larder and saw a bowl of soup, which he placed in the oven to warm. He'd eat, do his homework, then wake Phoebe if she still slept; just to be sure she wasn't seriously ill.

Later he was just about to go upstairs when there was a knock on the door. To his great relief, he saw Marj standing there.

'Phoebe's in bed asleep,' he blurted out. 'Do you think she's sick like Mum was?'

Marj stepped inside and put her arm around the boy. 'No, love, she's just caught a chill. It's probably just a cold. I'll go and look at 'er in a minute but I've brought a couple of pies around. 'Ave you eaten?'

'I found some soup, that's all.' He looked longingly at the pies as she unwrapped them.

'Right! Get a plate and a knife and fork and eat one of these while I looks in on your sister.'

'I made a pot of tea,' the boy told her. 'There's some left in the pot.'

Marj poured one into a cup with a little milk and sugar and went upstairs. Putting the tea down, she gently shook Phoebe. 'Wake up, girl!'

Phoebe gradually opened her eyes and frowned before she realised where she was. 'Marj! What are you doing here?'

'I brought a couple of pies round from the pie shop in case you didn't 'ave any food in the house for you and Tim. 'E's digging into 'is now. 'Ow you feeling, love?'

Phoebe sat up and took the cup of tea that was offered. 'My headache's gone, thankfully, but I still feel chilled.'

'You need a couple of days in bed, girl.'

'But the stall—' Phoebe began.

'Bugger the stall! You go back tomorrow, before you know it, you'll be in bed for a much longer time. Young Tim's already wondering if you're going to pop your clogs like his poor mum.'

'Oh no! Oh poor Tim. He must be worried sick! But I've got to feed him. I can't do that if I'm in bed.'

'Now, don't you fret none. The boy's had some soup and now a pie. 'Ave you got bread in the house for him to 'ave for breakfast?'

Phoebe nodded. 'Right. Give him some money to buy fish and chips for you both at lunchtime and I'll cook something for your supper. I've brought a piece of cheese to 'ave with the bread. Can you manage on that in the morning?'

'Oh Marj! What would I do without you?'

'You'd do the same for me. We're mates, ain't we? Now I'll stoke up the fire ready for the night. Does Tim know 'ow to work the damper so it don't burn away?'

Phoebe nodded. 'Tim is used to having to take care of himself and things in the house.'

'Good. Now wrap up warm if you 'ave to go outside to the lavvy. I'll be back tomorrow after I close. I'll send young Tim up with a pie for you to eat.'

At noon the next day, Ben went to the market but when he saw the empty place where Phoebe usually had her stall, he hurried over to Marj. 'Where's Phoebe?'

'At 'ome in bed. She caught a chill on Sunday and I made her go 'ome yesterday. I'm taking food to 'er tonight and Tim is buying fish and chips during 'is school break at lunchtime.'

He looked at his watch. 'I've got time to pop round, but she'll have to get out of bed to let me in.'

'Don't be daft, lad. People don't lock their doors round 'ere. Let yourself in, but call upstairs to let her know it's you.'

He hurried away.

Opening Phoebe's front door, Ben stepped inside and called out. 'It's only me, Phoebe! Can I come upstairs?'

It was Tim who answered. 'Come up, Ben, we're having our lunch.'

Ben walked into the room to find Phoebe sitting up in bed eating fish and chips with Tim doing the same seated beside her on a chair. Ben was relieved to see that she was looking just a little pale but as she smiled he could tell she wasn't too unwell. Leaning forward, he kissed her cheek. 'I was worried when you weren't in the market,' he said.

'Marj sent me home. I must say she was right to do so as I'm feeling a lot better now.'

Tim looked at her bedside clock and got up. 'I have to get back to school,' he said.

'You run along,' Ben told him. 'I'll take care of your sister. I'll see you tonight.' He sat on the chair.

'The sooner we sort out our future the better,' he said, frowning. 'If we were married, you wouldn't be in this situation. You both need taking care of and the sooner we get that sorted, the better!'

With a broad grin Phoebe asked, 'Is that a proposal?'

Ben started laughing. 'I suppose it is, but it certainly isn't how I planned it.' Taking her hand he asked, 'Will you marry me, Phoebe?'

'Yes, of course I will.'

He rose to his feet and kissed her. 'But we'll wait until you're fit and well before we start planning. Now, I have to leave as I'm on duty, but I'll be back tonight. All right?'

She nodded. 'I'm not going anywhere.'

When at last she was alone, she leant back against her pillows. 'I've just got engaged,' she said quietly. 'In bed with a chill – I've just got engaged!' She started to laugh.

Ben and Marj arrived at the house at the same time that evening. With Tim's help, Marj set about sorting the dinner she'd prepared as Ben raced up the stairs to his new fiancée.

'How are you, darling?'

'Feeling much better. In fact, I'd like to come downstairs to have my supper. I'm fed up being here.'

He helped her out of bed and into a warm dressing gown, then he gathered her into his arms. 'Shall we break the happy news to Tim and Marj?'

'Oh, Ben, let's do it. Tim will be so happy, and Marj too.' They went down the stairs and into the kitchen. Phoebe was settled in a chair with a blanket and they waited for her friend to serve the meal.

Just before they started eating Ben spoke. 'Phoebe and I have something to tell you both.' Tim and Marj stopped what they were doing.

'We are engaged! I asked Phoebe to marry me earlier today and she said yes!'

Tim let out a cry of joy. 'That means you'll be my dad!' He scrambled out of the chair and flung his arms round Ben.

Marj had tears in her eyes. She got up, hugged and kissed Phoebe, then did the same to Ben. 'Congratulations! I'm so very 'appy for you all.' Sitting down she added, 'Now let's eat before this chicken goes cold.'

Tim was ecstatic. 'Will you play football with me and take me to another cricket match?'

'Of course, but not at the same time!'

Tim grinned at him. 'I didn't mean that, silly!'

Ben ruffled his hair. 'I know, Tim, I was only teasing. When Phoebe's better, we'll go out to dinner and celebrate. But it will only be a sandwich and a glass of lemonade because I have to buy Phoebe a ring first.'

The look of disappointment on Tim's face made them all laugh.

'He's teasing you again,' Phoebe said, then she looked at Ben. 'Well, I hope you are?'

'Well, maybe two sandwiches each!'

Watching everyone tucking into the food she'd made, Marj was thrilled to see how happy they all were. Her dream for Phoebe and Ben had come to fruition and Tim would have the father figure he craved. Ben was a good role model for the boy, and he'd make sure Tim was well looked after . . . and Phoebe. My God, it was about time! These past years had been hard on the girl, but she'd kept the family going after her father went to war and didn't return and even after the loss of her dear mother. Now someone would look after her.

At the end of the meal, Marj took Tim into the kitchen to help her wash the dishes, leaving Ben and Phoebe alone. They cuddled up together on the sofa.

'When Tim has his school holidays in August, I'd like to take you both to visit my parents,' he told Phoebe.

She looked concerned. 'Will they be pleased about us marrying?'

'Why wouldn't they be?'

'Well, having a bride is one thing, Ben, but taking on another man's child is another.'

'I don't see it like that, darling. As far as I'm concerned, you come as a package – if I can use that expression. I couldn't consider one without the other, it has never occurred to me to do so.'

'Tim thinks the world of you, you know that, don't you?'

'I do and I'm thrilled that he does. He's a fine boy and will grow into a fine man, we'll see to that, together.'

They sat over a final cup of tea, then Tim and Phoebe went to their beds and Ben insisted on walking Marj home.

As they left the house, she tucked her arm through Ben's. 'I can't tell you 'ow thrilled I am that you and Phoebe are getting married.'

'Thanks, Marj. I'm a lucky fellow. Phoebe's a lovely girl.'

'And you're not 'alf bad either, love!'

He burst out laughing. 'Marj, you're incorrigible!'

'I'm not at all sure what that means, Ben, but if it isn't rude, I'll take it! But what I want to know is why did you take so long to propose? It were obvious to me you was in love with the girl ages ago.'

'I couldn't while I was undercover. I had to wait until my job was done and I could be truthful as to who I really was. When the Stanleys went to prison, I could tell her.'

'Those two! And that bastard Percy. My God, to think that poor girl saw 'im top that bloke and not be able to tell anyone. No wonder she was so jumpy in the market.'

'True, but at least the public have no knowledge of that, or Phoebe would be hounded by the press and she wouldn't have a life to call her own.'

'My lips is sealed, love, don't you worry about that! Ah 'ere we are, I'm 'ome. Thanks for the escort. Blimey! I've 'ad a police escort 'ome, I've just realised! Best not tell the neighbours, they'd get the wrong idea! Night, Ben!'

'Goodnight, Marj, sleep well.'

While everything was settling down in the lives of those in Southampton, trouble was already brewing in Winchester Prison. Arthur had no idea what was in store for him.

Chapter Twenty-Four

Arthur had more or less settled to prison life in the few days he'd been there. He kept close to his cellmate on the way to the dining room each mealtime. He chatted to Henry Evans, but not to anyone else. He was a little in awe of him after discovering his background. It quietly amused the old lag, who was aware of this, but he didn't say anything about it. To his mind, Arthur was an innocent when it came to crime and was completely out of place in a prison yard with full-time criminals. In a way, he felt sorry for the young man.

When he was in the quadrangle, Arthur was usually on his own as his cellmate had his own small circle. He would wander off and find a quiet place to sit and have a cigarette, making sure he didn't get involved with anyone, not staring too long at anybody who might take offence. After a few days, he began to relax and feel less nervous.

'Got a light, mate?' The sudden voice made him jump. Standing in front of him was an older man, holding out an unlit cigarette. 'I've left me matches in me cell,' the prisoner said with a smile.

Arthur handed over his matches.

The man took them, lit his cigarette, returned the matches and, to Arthur's surprise, sat beside him. 'Thanks. I really enjoy a smoke outside, rather than in me cell. Seems more normal somehow. I try and forget this is a prison yard. What's your name?'

Looking at him somewhat uncertainly, he answered. 'Arthur.'

The man held out his hand. 'I'm Bill.'

Arthur had no choice but to shake his hand. Had he not done so he might have upset him, and he didn't want any trouble.

They sat quietly together, just watching the passing scene in front of them as men walked around, some in gatherings chatting, and some even laughing together.

Arthur stole a quick glance at his companion, but Bill didn't look back at him, just continued to look around. When he'd finished his cigarette, he got to his feet.

'Thanks, Arthur. Might see you tomorrow?'

Arthur nodded and Bill walked away. As he watched him, he thought, well he seems harmless enough. He was quiet, not belligerent in any way. It would be nice to have a friend to chat to.

In the queue at lunchtime, Arthur heard a familiar voice behind him and turned. Bill was there, talking to another prisoner. 'Hello, Arthur, I thought it was you. You all right?'

'Yes, fine, thanks.' He collected his food and found a place at a table that was beginning to fill up. Bill came and sat beside him. They chatted, complained about the food and as they rose to return their trays and dishes, Bill asked, 'Going outside for a smoke?'

'Yes, I look forward to getting some fresh air, don't you?'

'Best part of the day for me. It don't matter to me if it rains, even. I finds a sheltered spot and hunker down.' They joined the cue for the quadrangle together.

Once settled, Arthur was looking at a building in the far distance, wondering what it was. It didn't look like any of the other cell blocks. He asked his new friend.

'What's that building over there? I've been wondering for days. It looks different from the others.'

'That's the execution block. That's where they hangs you if you're sentenced to death.'

Arthur went cold and shivered. Would his brother end up at the end of a rope? If he did, it was his evidence that put him there! The enormity of the fact overcame him. He rushed to the corner of the building and was violently sick.

After, he stood, his hands to his head, still feeling nauseous and slightly feverish. Taking a deep breath, he walked back to Bill and sat on the ground.

'You all right? Blimey, I've seen reactions from many people when they know what that place is, but never one like yours. Sorry if I upset you, but you did ask.'

'It's all right, really. It just came as such a surprise.'

Bill put a comforting arm round his shoulder. 'Don't take on so. It's obvious to me this is your first time in prison. It takes some getting used to. Here, have a fag.'

Knowing how difficult it was to come by such things, Arthur looked at him in surprise. 'Are you sure you can spare it?'

Bill grinned broadly. 'Don't you worry none. When you know your way around a prison, it ain't that bad, really. If you've got money you can buy most things. You need anything, you come to me. After all, we're mates, aren't we?'

Arthur nodded. 'Yes, of course we are.'

The bell rang and the prisoners lined up, tightly packed together.

'Blimey! Not much room is there?' Arthur grumbled.

'No, but it won't be long, we're moving now.' Once inside they departed for their separate accommodation.

Two days later the prisoners were let out in groups and taken to the bath house. A building with cubicles for each bath, but without doors so the warders could see the men at all times.

Arthur had climbed out of his bath and was getting dressed when Bill popped his head round the door. 'Hello, mate! Bet you feel better now?'

Doing up his trousers, Arthur agreed. 'It's nice to feel refreshed and clean.'

The next day in the quadrangle, Bill came and sat beside Arthur as was his habit now. Arthur was grateful for the company as he didn't have to worry about upsetting anyone. The other prisoners ignored them. It helped to bring a feeling of normality, being in the fresh air out of the prison block or locked away in a cell.

In a strange way, Arthur was now less nervous of his surroundings. He knew just to eat the food in front of him, not to try and make conversation with anyone other than his cellmate, Henry, and now his new friend. It made for easier living. Not that he didn't long for his old life. The market, his own home. Ivy. But he felt quite proud that he was able to take each day as it came. So far it was liveable. If his sentence was a short one, as he'd been led to believe, he now felt able to cope.

But a prison was never peaceful for long. There was always an undercurrent and it didn't take long for a scene to turn into a riot. The following day outside during the exercise break, two men started fighting. Others gathered round, taking sides, urging the men on.

Arthur was horrified as he watched and quickly found a quiet corner to hide in. Very soon warders came rushing out to try and stop the fight, which had now grown as others took the opportunity to pay back a slight that had once upset them and which they'd not had an opportunity to settle.

Eventually there was a sound of gunfire as warders fired into the air, thus stopping the affray. Prisoners were lined up and sent back to their cells, watched by the warders, some of whom were now armed.

Arthur was shaking and was greatly relieved when at last he walked back inside his cell, the door slamming and being locked when his cellmate had joined him. But the noise coming from those now incarcerated was almost as frightening to Arthur, who had never experienced such behaviour.

'It's part of prison life,' his cellmate remarked. 'You'll get used to it!'

But Arthur knew he wouldn't. Just as he was settling and now this. It didn't bode well for the time he eventually would have to serve.

Things quietened down for a while and Arthur, although nervous when he was in the yard, began to relax again. He was sitting alone looking around at the usual normal scene in front of him, remembering the day when it all changed – and how quickly things had developed. One or two prisoners had been injured with the use of home-made weapons. Cells had been searched and privileges taken away. But now all was peaceful again.

It was at slopping out time some days later that things changed. Len, Arthur's cellmate, wasn't well and had stayed in bed, so Arthur was on his own at the back of the queue. Emptying the contents of the bucket, he felt the need to pee, so he undid his trousers to use the urinal. As he stood enjoying using a proper toilet, he heard a movement behind him and before he realised a prisoner was up close to him, trying to grope him.

'Oh, Arthur, I just knew you were a big lad.'

Arthur let out a scream and a warder appeared. 'What the bloody hell's going on?' Then he saw. 'You dirty bastard, back to your cell now!'

'You,' said the warder to Arthur, 'get back to your cell and be careful in future when you want the toilet!'

Hurrying back to his cell, Arthur was shaking when he realised how close he'd come to being assaulted sexually.

He then remembered the warnings of the detective when first he'd been interviewed about him being in prison and being approached.

He'd never been more horrified. A fist fight was bad enough, but being accosted sexually was terrifying and beyond his comprehension. He knew about homosexuals. Living in a seaport town they were not unknown, but he'd never mixed with any. He and Percy didn't socialise much. It was only when Percy was inside and he was alone he was free to do so and, for him, his delight was women.

As he was released for exercise the next day, Arthur was feeling tense and nervous, wondering if anyone would bother him, but nobody came near him. With a sigh of relief, Arthur sat down. Henry Evans joined him.

'If you're worried about that bloke from yesterday, he's not coming out to play!'

Arthur looked at Henry and saw a look of amusement on his face. 'What's so funny?'

'Watching you being led to the slaughter, like a lamb.'

'You knew and you stood back and watched?' Arthur was livid.

Henry just shrugged. 'You take any amusement you can get in here, my son. I knew you weren't in any real danger. Too many warders about. Now if it had been him,' he pointed to a big man crossing the yard, 'that would have been a different matter.'

Looking at the man, Arthur shuddered. If it had been him, he'd have been terrified. He'd be certain never to be near him, ever.

'So what's happened to that bloke, then?' he asked Henry.

'He'll lose his privileges for a few days, that's all. After all, he didn't do you much harm. Put it down to experience.'

'It's all very well for you!' Arthur retorted. 'No one bothers you, they're too bloody scared.' He realised what he'd said and became fearful.

Henry just smiled. 'It's all right, son. You've no need to worry. I'm all for a quiet life without any trouble. I sorted that in the first few months when I was sent here.'

'I'm not cut out for prison! I'm not sure I can do my time when I'm sentenced.' Arthur was on the verge of tears. 'I'm not tough like you and my brother. Now, he wouldn't put up with anything.'

'Does he visit you?'

Arthur gave a derisory laugh. 'He'd have a job, he's in Wormwood Scrubs waiting for his trial. He's up for murder.'

'So what are you in for?'

'I'm a witness at his trial.'

Henry frowned and was silent for a moment. 'I don't understand.'

'He came to me after he'd topped the bloke and I helped him move the body. I told the police what had happened.'

'You shopped your own brother?'

'Don't look at me like that. He killed this man all because he told my brother he was a nobody. He involved me when I'd nothing to do with the murder. He wasn't even sorry he'd done it. I wasn't going to spend my life behind bars for him!'

'You'd better hope that no one here finds out what you did. Shopping someone is treated with contempt among prisoners. My advice is don't tell anyone else.'

'I've told you!'

'Yes, and be thankful I'll keep that information to myself. You're no criminal and I hate to see anyone inside for something they didn't do, but you keep your mouth shut if you don't want any trouble.' He walked away.

But now Arthur was really worried. It was still a while before the trial and then after he'd be inside again. How was he going to survive? After the trial it would be in the papers. The information could eventually seep into the prison. What then? It didn't bear thinking about. He sat brooding and cursing his brother.

Chapter Twenty-Five

It was August and the school holidays. Ben had arranged to take Phoebe and Tim up to Gloucester to meet his parents. Tim was thrilled and excited, but Phoebe was filled with trepidation. It was asking a lot of anyone to take on a young boy who wasn't his. Ben wasn't at all bothered, she knew that, but she tried to put herself in Ben's mother's shoes and knew if it were her, she'd be concerned.

Marj tried to calm her. 'You ain't marrying 'is family love, you're marrying Ben and you've both got it sorted. Just go up there, be yourself, enjoy the change. Putting the stall away will be a real treat. It'll do you good. Once Ben's parents see 'ow 'e and Tim are together, they'll understand. If they don't, it don't matter. Ben loves you both, it won't make a difference to 'im, mark my words.'

Tim could hardly wait for Saturday to share his news

with Laura, his friend. 'We're going on a train tomorrow to Gloucester to meet Ben's parents. I've never been on a train and Ben says it's a long journey.' He beamed at her. 'They'll be my grandparents! How exciting is that?'

Laura pulled a face. 'My grandfather is a misery. Whenever we go to see him and Gran, which isn't often, he grumbles the whole time about something or other.'

'What about your gran?'

'Oh no, she's lovely. She makes the most wonderful cakes and always gives us some to bring home. Now, that really upsets my grandfather, but Gran just smiles and ignores him.'

Tim's world suddenly wasn't so bright. What if Ben's parents didn't like him? Or worse, what if they didn't like his sister?

As they were packing up the stall, Ben came over to check final arrangements for the next day and noticed that Tim's enthusiasm for the trip had waned.

'What's wrong, young man? You've suddenly gone very quiet.'

'Perhaps your parents won't like you getting married to Phoebe and perhaps they won't like me.'

Putting his arm round the boy's shoulder, Ben tried to cheer him. 'I'm sure that won't be the case, Tim, but even if it was, it wouldn't make any difference. I love you both and we're going to be a family.'

The boy clung to him, but was so overcome with relief, he couldn't speak.

The train journey was long. They changed trains at Waterloo for the final leg of the journey. Waterloo was bustling and Tim's eyes grew wider, watching all the people rushing around. He'd never ever been in such a crowd or heard such noise and clung tightly to Ben's hands in case he lost him. Eventually they settled in a carriage. Tim sat next to the window, avidly watching the countryside as they passed by. He was amazed at all the cattle and sheep wandering around in the fields, but it was when he saw a field with several horses he became really excited.

'Do they belong to just one person?' he asked.

'Probably,' he was told.

'I'd love to ride a horse one day,' he said wistfully.

The train eventually pulled into the station and they alighted with the other passengers. Picking up their cases they headed to the exit and climbed into a taxi. Ben gave the driver the address and they sat back as the vehicle moved off.

Phoebe was feeling very nervous and glanced at Ben. He saw the uncertainty in her expression and took her hand and squeezed it.

'Everything's going to be fine,' he assured her.

Tim was silent as he watched out of the window. They drove out of the busy town. Here the houses were different, many built in a soft-coloured stone, with lovely gardens. The vehicle came to a halt outside one such house. He then looked at Phoebe for reassurance. She smiled at him.

'Come on, Tim, let's go and meet the family.' She took him firmly by the hand and followed Ben up the path.

The door was opened before they got there. A middle-aged woman with brown hair, flecked with silver, wearing a skirt and blouse greeted them with a warm smile.

She kissed Ben and hugged him. He quickly introduced Phoebe and Tim to her. Turning to Phoebe, she said, 'Do come in. You must be longing for a cup of tea after your journey.' Then she looked at Tim. 'I expect you'd rather have lemonade, young man, wouldn't you?'

Tim beamed at her. 'Oh yes, I would, thank you.'

'Come with me,' she invited and led them into a large kitchen with a cosy settee in an alcove and a big table in the middle with chairs. The aroma of cooking filled the air.

'Make yourselves comfortable,' she said as she put on the kettle to boil. 'I just need to turn my roast potatoes'. She placed a glass on the table and a jug and to Tim she said, 'There you are, help yourself. There's plenty more, I made it this morning.'

'You made this yourself?'

It was Ben who answered. 'Mother has always made her own lemonade, Tim. It's so much nicer than shop-bought. Try it!'

The boy carefully poured a glass full and took a sip. His eyes brightened. 'Golly! This is lovely.'

Ben's mother beamed at him. 'Oh, thank you. You can come here anytime. Anyone who likes my lemonade is always welcome!' She took the potatoes out of the oven, turned them, put them back and made a pot of tea.

'I do hope you like lamb?' she asked, looking at her visitors.

'Oh, how lovely,' said Phoebe. 'It's ages since we've had any.'

At that moment the kitchen door opened, and a tall man entered. He took off his boots and put on a pair of slippers, then walked to the table, where he greeted his son warmly with a hug.

Ben took him over to where Phoebe was sitting. 'Dad, this lovely lady is my fiancée, Phoebe, who I've told you so much about. Phoebe, this is my father.'

'I'm happy to meet you, Mr Masters.'

He shook her hand. 'Please call me Hugh and I'm delighted to meet you too.' He looked across at Tim. 'Hello, young man, you must be Tim. Ben's told me all about you.'

'Hello,' said Tim shyly.

'I do hope you're hungry, Tim, because my wife likes her guests to eat well.'

Tim beamed at him. 'Oh, thank you, it all smells so good I'm sure I'll eat *everything*!'

Hugh burst out laughing. 'A man after my own heart. I must just wash my hands, I've been gardening.'

'Can I do anything to help you, Mrs Masters?' Phoebe asked.

'No, thank you, my dear, I'm all organised, and do please call me Ellie.'

'That's a pretty name,' Tim said. 'I haven't heard it before.'

'It's short for Eleanor, but I prefer Ellie. Now, let's have that tea. It's such a lovely day, I think we should have it in the garden. Ben, will you put everything on a tray and bring it outside? I'll carry the pot.'

Just outside the kitchen door was a small patio with a round table and chairs. They all settled there. Phoebe looked round the garden, which was full of colour. There were shrub roses, some hybrid tea roses, and small lavender bushes, which scented the air. A mass of white tall Shasta daisies and other flowers. It was like an artist's canvas.

Phoebe walked over to get a better look. 'This is so very beautiful. So much colour.'

Hugh came and stood beside her. 'And so much work! But I love working in the garden. It soothes my soul.'

'I can imagine that it would,' she agreed. 'I've never had a garden.'

He heard the longing in her voice. 'Maybe one day you will, my dear.' He turned to Tim. 'Come and look at my fish pond.' They walked off down the garden together and Phoebe sat at the table with Ben and his mother.

'Hugh is so proud of his pond,' said Ellie, smiling. 'He will be delighted to have someone new take a look. You know what men are like!'

Phoebe looked around. 'It's so beautiful here, so unlike Southampton.'

'The Cotswolds are known for being picturesque and of course, you live in a seaport, which I'm sure has its own character.'

'Yes, that's true, but here, it has an air of peace about it.'

Ellie excused herself to look at her cooking, leaving Phoebe and Ben alone.

He reached for her hand. 'There, didn't I tell you there was nothing to worry about?'

'Your parents are lovely, Ben. They've made us feel so welcome.'

'That's because they know I'm happy and that makes them happy. Now relax and enjoy.'

An hour later, they sat at the table in the kitchen ready to eat. Tim watched in awe as Hugh carved the leg of lamb, which he placed on the plates. Various dishes held a selection of vegetables from which the diners could help themselves.

'Hugh grows most of the vegetables himself,' Ellie informed them.

Tim was helping himself to some peas. 'Did you grow these?'

'Indeed, I did. I had a good crop this year.' He also grew the carrots, parsnips and cauliflower that were served, which impressed his visitors.

To Tim's delight, the dessert was apple pie and ice cream.

He looked at Ellie. 'You are a really good cook, even better than Phoebe, and she cooks very well.'

Everybody started to laugh. 'Thank you, Tim,' Ellie said. 'That's the nicest thing anyone has ever said to me.'

'Really?'

'Really.'

During the evening, Ellie produced a family album. Ben was horrified but Ellie said, 'Your fiancée should know of your background if she's to take you on!'

Apart from the pictures of Ben as a boy, there were pictures of him in his police uniform, taken before he was a detective. Another showing him receiving a medal for bravery, which he quickly dismissed and to his relief, the rest was of family holidays.

Phoebe and Tim were fascinated by it all.

'We don't have many pictures,' she said, with some sadness. 'My father went away to the war and didn't come home. After that we didn't take any.'

'War is a terrible thing,' Hugh stated. 'It destroys family life, leaving children like Tim fatherless, and for those who return, they're never quite the same. But hopefully there won't be any more.'

* * *

At bedtime, Tim and Phoebe shared a room next to Ben's. She was told to sleep as long as she liked, that Ben would see to them in the morning as Ellie had an appointment.

Both of them slept soundly, but Tim woke first. His movement woke his sister and after using the bathroom they dressed and went downstairs. The smell of bacon frying filled the air and they found Ben cooking in the kitchen.

He kissed Phoebe. 'I hope you slept well?'

'Like a log! It's so quiet and peaceful here,' she told him.

'Dad's feeding his fish, Tim. Will you go and find him and tell him breakfast is in five minutes?'

The youngster rushed out of the kitchen to do as he was asked.

'Tim is loving it here,' Phoebe remarked. 'It's a whole different life for him.'

'When we're married it will be different again – and for you. You won't have to work in the market, for a start.'

'I won't miss that. No more standing out in the cold. Marvellous!'

She'd been the one to keep the family going for so long and now all of a sudden the realisation that she was no longer required to do so was overwhelming and tears filled her eyes.

Seeing her emotion, Ben walked over to her and held her close. 'Those days will be over, Phoebe. It's time someone looked after you for a change and I'm the lucky man to be able to do it. Now, please cheer up or my father will think I've been unkind to you and I'll be in deep trouble!'

This made her laugh and at that moment Hugh and Tim arrived.

* * *

230

All too soon, the visit was over and the three of them were back on the train heading homewards. Tim was full of the things he'd seen and done, but feeding the goldfish was his greatest treat and he talked about it most of the way home.

'Next week, you'll be getting ready for school,' Phoebe reminded him, 'but you can come with me to the market in the morning and give me a hand.'

He beamed at her. 'I can tell Laura about our trip, if she's there, she will be surprised!'

Ben looked at Phoebe and smiled, pleased that the boy had enjoyed himself so much.

In Winchester Prison, Arthur Stanley was not having such a good time. The news that he'd ratted on his brother had seeped through the prison grapevine and he was discovering just how it was received by his fellow inmates.

Chapter Twenty-Six

Arthur lined up at exercise time and walked outside into the quadrangle. It was a warm day with blue, cloudless skies. He found a quiet spot and sat down, enjoying the warmth of the sun on his body. It wasn't long before he noticed several of the inmates looking at him and talking quietly. That in itself was strange, but what unsettled him was the expression of hostility on their faces when they did so.

Henry Evans strolled over to him. 'A warder from Wormwood Scrubs prison has just been transferred here. He was on the same wing as your brother, now everyone knows why you're here.'

Arthur's face paled. 'That's why people are looking at me and talking,' he stammered.

'Just watch your back, that's all,' Evans warned, as he walked away.

To make matters worse, Arthur saw that the convict who'd groped him in the bathroom was now back and he was in the midst of one of the groups. He glanced at Arthur and sneered as he chatted to a couple of men, who then looked over at him.

Almost paralysed with fear, Arthur looked away, knowing he was now in deep trouble and wondering what would happen to him – and when?

The hour passed and no one approached him, but he was terrified of the line up to return to the cells. Anyone standing near him was in a position to do him some harm and when the bell rang, his legs were shaking so much, he could hardly stand. He didn't know if he should stand in line now, or join it at the end.

'Come on, lad, you walk with me.' He jumped at the voice and saw it was Henry Evans. Evans motioned with a nod of his head. 'Stand in front of me, you'll be all right. No one will touch you if I'm there.'

Arthur walked to the line of men and took his place, but he was shaking. He felt Henry standing close behind him. No one said a word as they filed into the prison and once safely inside, Arthur hurried off to his cell, half expecting a knife in his back at any moment. Once in the cell, he climbed onto his bed with a sigh of relief, fighting off the feeling of nausea rising from his stomach. He managed to keep it under control and lay quietly.

Len, his cellmate walked in. He glared at Arthur. 'Not only do I have a first-timer but it seems I have a snout as well! You are a rotten bastard, dobbing your brother in like that. I've got no time for a squealer, they're the worst kind, so don't talk to me, 'cause I don't want anything to do with you!'

The warder came along and shut and locked the door. Only then did Arthur relax, but then he had to face tomorrow and the other convicts once again.

Breakfast was an ordeal. As Arthur handed over his bowl, the prisoner on kitchen duty slapped a couple of ladles of porridge in it, then looking at Arthur, he spat in it, then glared at him, daring him to say anything. His mug of tea was only half-filled and when he sat down, no one sat near him. It was as if he had some dreadful disease and was in quarantine.

It was much the same at lunchtime. His food was slapped on his plate so hard it splattered his clothes and again he sat alone, dreading the fact that very soon, he'd be outside, surrounded by men who now despised him. His hands trembled as he ate . . . and then the bell rang.

As he lined up to be let out with the others, no one spoke but he was jostled as he waited. Each time someone knocked against him, he waited for the pain from some hidden weapon that one of the convicts had either stolen or made, but as he walked out into the fresh air, he was still unharmed. By now he was sweating profusely and couldn't stop trembling. He walked to his usual spot, sat down and hurriedly tried to light a cigarette. His hand was shaking so much, it took several matches before he was steady enough to light it.

A group of cons stood nearby. 'Perhaps we should set up a noose like the one in the execution block, so our little canary here will understand what it feels like to get the death penalty.'

They all laughed loudly and moved on.

Arthur looked round and saw a prison warder on duty. He rushed over to him. 'Get me out of here, my life's in danger. I want to be put in solitary confinement until my trial!' He grabbed the man's jacket 'Please!'

The warder pushed his hands away. 'Go and sit down.'

Arthur pleaded with him. 'They're all out to get me. I've been threatened! Can't you ask the governor? A murder wouldn't be a good thing to happen, especially if the press got to hear. Please!'

The warder looked at him. 'All right, I'll have a word when everyone is back in their cells, now go and sit down.'

As he walked back there were sounds of a chicken clucking being made by all that he passed.

When the bell rang for the inmates to return to their cells, Arthur looked round for Henry Evans, but he was nowhere to be seen. Now Arthur really panicked, knowing that Henry had been his saviour the day before. He waited until he was the last in line. At least then, there was nobody at his back. To his surprise, there were no taunting or threatening comments from those ahead of him and he walked to his cell with a sigh of relief. But as he walked inside, the door was slammed shut and two men stood facing him!

Later that day, Ben was sitting at his desk working when DI Bentley sent for him. Ben knocked on the man's door.

'Come in and take a seat,' he was told.

'Something wrong, sir?'

'You could say that. Arthur Stanley has been murdered. They found him bleeding profusely in his cell. He'd been stabbed several times, but by the time they got him to the hospital, it was too late.'

'Oh my God!'

'Well, you know what this means, don't you? Miss Collins is now our only witness. We do have Arthur's testimony, but we've taken advice and because he isn't here to collaborate it and be cross-questioned, it's inadmissible. I'd like you to visit her and inform her before the news gets out. I'm sorry.'

Ben rose from his chair. 'I'll go now.'

As he walked towards the market, Ben was dreading having to tell Phoebe of Arthur's death. His statement, had he been able to appear, would have strengthened her evidence. He was worried about her standing in the witness box with Percy in the courtroom too, in the dock, listening to her. Knowing how the man scared her, he wondered if she would be able to cope, giving her evidence and with the cross-questioning that would follow? How quickly things could change, he thought. Only a few days ago, Phoebe and he were celebrating their engagement with friends, happily planning a future, and now this!

Ben entered the market and walked over to Phoebe's stall. She was serving a customer, so he waited. Marj looked over and frowned. The last time she'd seen Ben was when several of them went out to dinner and Ben placed an engagement ring on Phoebe's hand to make it all official. Now he looked as if he carried the worries of the world on his shoulders. She waited and watched.

Phoebe, having served her customer, came from behind the stall and kissed Ben on the cheek. 'Hello, darling! What are you doing here in the middle of the day?'

He took her hands in his. 'I've some bad news, I'm

afraid. Arthur Stanley was murdered today. They found him in his cell. He'd been stabbed.'

Phoebe put her hand to her mouth. 'Oh, that's awful! I've no time for the man but I wouldn't see that happen to my worst enemy. I am sorry.'

Taking a deep breath, Ben continued. 'You don't understand, Phoebe. This means you are now the only witness.'

She let out a cry and just stared at him, speechless, as she realised what he'd said.

'I'm so sorry you'll have to go through this, darling, but now only you can put him away. Without your evidence, we don't have a strong enough case. Before the trial, a solicitor will help prepare you to take the stand and I'll help you too. We have to put him away and I know you can do it.'

She gave a wry smile. 'Oh, Ben, and things were going so well!'

'Never mind. When it's over we can get on with our lives. The case shouldn't be far off now. I'll try and find out when it's on the list. Look, darling, I have to go, but I'll be round later tonight.'

As he walked away, Marj sidled over to Phoebe. 'Everything all right, love?'

Shaking her head, Phoebe said, 'No. Arthur Stanley was murdered in his cell today. Now I'm the only witness.'

'Bloody 'ell! What 'appened?'

'He was stabbed, apparently. That's all I know.' She let out a deep sigh. 'Oh, Marj!'

Marj put an arm round her. 'You'll be all right, love. All you can do is tell the truth, then that rotten bugger will get what 'e deserves.'

'I know. There's poor old Arthur paying for his brother's dirty deed. It doesn't seem right somehow.'

'It don't seem fair, but there you go. Now don't you go worrying yourself sick about going to court. You'll be doing everyone a favour.'

In Wormwood Scrubs, Percy had been summoned to see the governor, to his surprise. As he was taken there by a warder, he couldn't possibly imagine why the governor would want to talk to him. Was he perhaps being moved to another prison? But if so, why?

The warder knocked on the office door and opened it, leading Percy in by the arm.

Looking up from the work on his desk, the governor stared at him, studying him for a moment before speaking.

'I'm not sure if what I have to tell you is upsetting or not, but I'm sorry to tell you that Arthur, your brother, passed away earlier today.'

Percy just stared back at him, his expression unchanged. 'What did he die of?'

'He was stabbed several times, and the doctor was unable to save him. I'm sorry for your loss.'

'Is that all?' Percy asked.

'Yes. Take him back to his cell,' the warder was told.

When he was alone, the governor shook his head. 'Cold-hearted bastard,' he muttered.

As he was escorted back to his cell, Percy could hardly keep the smile from his face. Now that Arthur was dead, his testimony was not such strong evidence without him sitting in the witness box, telling his sad tale! Sad news? Bloody wonderful news!

The warder let him into his cell. 'I can see you're broken-hearted about your brother,' he said, then he locked the door.

Percy sat on his bed, thinking, plotting. He would emphatically deny the murder. He'd say it was self-defence. A clever brief could sow the seeds of doubt in a jury's mind. Enough to give reasonable doubt, and they'd have to let him off, then the only charge would be the burglary and him selling the stolen goods. A prison sentence for such a misdemeanour wouldn't be that long. After, he'd be free. But then he remembered: the police said they had a witness. If it was that girl in the market, then he was in real trouble.

Well, the only way he'd find out would be when he was in court.

Chapter Twenty-Seven

Percy Stanley's case was on the court list for late September at Winchester assizes. Once there was a definite date, Phoebe was unable to put the idea of appearing in court to the back of her mind. What stressed her more than actually giving evidence was knowing that Percy would be in the court room listening to her. It kept her awake at nights and when eventually she did sleep, it gave her nightmares.

One morning in the market, Marj seeing the circles under her friend's eyes, walked over to her.

'You look like the wreck of the *'Esperus*, love. You're fretting about going to court, ain't you?'

With a grimace Phoebe nodded. 'It's keeping me awake at nights. He'll be there, Marj, listening to every word. What if he escapes again? He'll come after me!'

'No, come on, love. Don't you think the police, knowing 'e did a runner before, will take the necessary steps to be sure 'e doesn't get the chance. Nah! They'll be sure 'e can't escape again. There'll be a policeman standing in the dock, keeping a close eye on 'im.'

'I have the same nightmare every night, Marj. Percy's chasing me down the street and I'm screaming for help . . . and there's nobody there!'

Her friend put her arms around Phoebe and patted her on the back as you would a small child. 'Now then, now then! It's just nerves, darlin'. You'll be fine. For God's sake, Phoebe, think what you've been through. You lose your dad, you take over the stall, you carry on looking after Tim when your poor mum died. You became 'is parents as well as 'is sister. You are a strong woman! Percy Stanley is just dirt under your shoe! You are in a position to put him away and probably save some other poor bugger from a similar end.'

Phoebe hugged her friend. 'Oh Marj! What would I do without you?'

'Damned if I know!' She walked back to her stall, chuckling softly.

Preparing the supper, Phoebe tried to be cheerful for Tim's sake. He was not aware that she'd seen the murder take place and she wanted to keep that fact away from him as long as possible. If he knew, he'd question her about it and it was the last thing she wanted to talk about and secondly, she didn't want him worried.

Ben soon arrived and joined them for a meal. They kept the conversation light until Tim had done his homework and was safely in his bed. It was only then they discussed what was ahead.

'The trial shouldn't take that long,' Ben explained. 'After all there is only your evidence. The coroner's report, then mine about being undercover and seeing the outside of the lock-up cleaned around the time we imagine the murder took place, which ties in with what you saw. But it's your testimony that will put him away.'

'But you said I'd be cross-questioned.'

'Yes, you will. Stanley will be given a solicitor to fight his case. He'll try and prove his client's innocence. It's what he's paid to do.'

'But to do that he'd have to make me out to be a liar!'

'He'll certainly try and trip you up, but if you just answer his questions and stick to the truth, you'll be fine. You just need to keep your head and not get flustered.'

'And Percy will be there listening to it all!'

'Yes, Phoebe, he'll be sitting in the dock with a policeman guarding him. Don't ever look at him. Keep your eyes fixed firmly on whoever is asking the questions. If you look at Percy, he'll do his best to distract and intimidate you, hoping you'll make a mistake.'

Letting out a deep sigh she looked crestfallen. 'All that's bad enough but after it'll be worse. It will be in all the papers, everybody will know. Poor Tim will be teased at school again. It was bad enough when Mum died, but this will be worse because it'll be a sensation.'

'I've thought about that. When the case is over, I'm taking some leave and we'll go off to Gloucester and stay with my parents for a week. You'll need a break and I'll have a word with Tim's headmaster, who's a very understanding man, and we will leave it all behind. We can make plans for the wedding. The sooner we get married the better, then we can all three of us start a new life together.'

Phoebe gazed at him. 'Oh, Ben, I do love you! Especially when you say the *three* of us.'

He looked at her with surprise. 'But it is the three of us!'

'I know, but it's wonderful that you think that way, a lot of men wouldn't.'

'Then they'd be wrong. We are already a family and in time we'll have children of our own – and Tim will be an uncle. He'll love that! We'll move to a bigger flat and eventually our own home. You won't have to work in the market any more; you'll be too busy looking after the men in your life.'

She looked concerned. 'Can you afford to keep us without my money coming in?'

Ben started to laugh. 'I can see you'll be a good housekeeper, Phoebe. Yes, darling, I can afford to keep you and Tim, otherwise I wouldn't have proposed to you.' He looked at his watch. 'I have to go, I'm on an early shift. It's one thing you'll have to get used to, I'm afraid. I don't work business hours and, if we have a case, I could be away for a few days sometimes.'

'That's all right, I'll have Tim to keep me company.'

'There you are! Whoever was stupid enough to say that three's a crowd?' Getting to his feet, he pulled her into his arms. 'Try not to worry, darling. It won't be long when all this unpleasantness will be a seven-day wonder and we can get on with our lives.'

'I can't wait,' she said as she walked him to the door.

* * *

The day of the trial drew nearer. Phoebe had an appointment with Edward Phillips, the solicitor, who informed her he'd be helping a barrister called James Harding, who was prosecuting the case, then they went through her evidence together.

'When he questions you, Miss Collins, I want you to give him a precise answer. Don't add anything else. The same thing goes when the defence questions you. Just answer the question. If you don't know, say so, don't try and make excuses as to why you don't know. Counsel will lead you when he questions you, so you know exactly what he's asking. You just give him an answer and no more, unless he asks. Do you understand?'

'Yes, it sounds so easy sitting here talking to you, but I dread going into the court and taking the stand.'

He smiled at her. 'I do it all the time. It's *my* Kingsland Market, I suppose! But for you and others it can be a bit intimidating. Just think of it as a rather grand room where business is being conducted. Yes, there is a sort of theatrical feel with the barristers wearing wigs and the judge in his rather splendid wig and robes, but we are all there to see justice served, that's the most important thing. This man has killed someone in cold blood. He already has a record for violence and has served time for that. He's a danger to the public and must be put away. Thankfully, you were witness to the unspeakable deed. Sadly, Arthur Stanley met an unsavoury end all through his brother, so that's another murder he was the cause of, but because of this Arthur can't be there to tell his story himself. Unfortunate for you, but fortunate for the law – you can. Do you realise how important your evidence is?'

'Yes, I do, I really do. I just don't want to mess it up.'

'Having spent some time with you, Miss Collins, I'm sure you'll do just fine. Once you're led to the stand and take the oath, take a deep breath, it will help to calm you. Please don't worry, we're there to take care of you. You must trust us.'

Phoebe smiled at him. 'I do, I promise.'

He rose to his feet and shook her hand. 'Good! I'll see you in court.'

Chapter Twenty-Eight

The day of the trial arrived. Phoebe arranged for her neighbour to look after Tim when he came home from school. She told him she had an appointment, but didn't tell him for what reason, and then she met Ben at the train station so they could travel together to Winchester assizes.

It was a brisk September day and Phoebe felt cold, but she knew it was more through nerves than the chill of autumn. They didn't chat a lot as they travelled, until they arrived at the court house. There the solicitor was waiting. He introduced her to James Harding.

Phoebe had forgotten they'd be dressed in wigs and gowns and for a moment was taken aback by the change. It only made her realise even more the importance of the occasion. They sat outside the courtroom where they would be called to give their evidence. Ben held her hand as James Harding sat beside them.

'I know this is an ordeal for you, Miss Collins, but you'll be fine and today we will see justice served. You were brave to keep this all to yourself for so long, seeing Stanley in the market every day, knowing what he'd done, that took great courage. I need you to be as strong today. Remember what you've been told about just answering the questions put to you and no more?'

She nodded. 'Yes, I do.'

'Good. Now as you know, Stanley will be in the dock watching. Just forget he's there. Don't even glance in his direction. Just look at the person in front of you asking the questions. All right?'

'All right.'

'Remember, after taking the oath, take a deep breath and we'll begin.' He grinned at her. 'After this is all over, I'll take you both out for a couple of stiff drinks!'

This was so unexpected, Phoebe laughed. 'We'll probably all need a drink by then.'

James got to his feet. 'I'll see you later.'

Ben put his arm round Phoebe. 'The worst will soon be over, darling. Then we can get on with our lives.'

'I know, but I can't help being nervous.'

'That's understandable. Appearing in court for any reason is a bit daunting. But I don't see it lasting more than a few days.'

'A few days?' She was shocked. 'I thought it would be all over by this afternoon!'

'I'm afraid the law takes a little longer than that on a murder case. Yes, if you were being fined for some piffling misdemeanour, but not murder.'

'No, I suppose that was rather stupid of me. I could only think about getting it over.'

'You'll only be called once, but before that others will have to give evidence. Indeed, you may have to wait until tomorrow, it all depends.'

She let out a deep sigh. 'I could do with one of those drinks now!'

There was a frisson of excitement inside the courtroom. A murder trial was serious. The press were there in force and the public gallery was full. Everyone stared with interest as Percy was led up some stairs and into the dock. Their expectation heightened as the jury was led in to take their places. Percy glared at them as they settled. Then the door at the side opened.

The voice of the clerk of the court echoed as the judge walked in. 'All stand!'

The judge took his seat, sorted his papers and waited as Percy was asked if he pleaded guilty or not guilty.

'Not guilty!' he proclaimed.

Looking at both barristers, the judge nodded. 'Shall we begin, gentlemen?' It was an order rather than a question.

James Hardy rose from his seat and approached the jury.

'Gentlemen, we are here today to see justice done. The prisoner, Percy Stanley, is charged with the murder of one Frank Clarke. During an altercation, Stanley produced a knife and stabbed him in cold blood. After, to cover his crime, he and his brother hid the body in a local cemetery and carried on with their daily lives. He's not shown a shred of remorse for this heinous crime and I believe he should pay the price for taking this man's life.' He walked back to his seat and sat down.

The counsel for the defence approached the jury.

'Gentlemen, what my learned friend has told you is partly the truth. Percy Stanley did indeed stab Frank Clarke, but it was purely in self-defence. He was in fear for his life and as a last resort he used the only thing that would save him. This was not done in anger, but only for survival. After, he panicked and hid the body in the belief that no one would believe it was an accident. This man is no murderer; he's only in the dock for trying to defend himself.'

He turned and walked back to his seat.

James Hardy stood. 'I'd like to call my first witness, Mr Charles Gates.'

A voice could be heard at the door of the court. 'Charles Gates!'

Into the court walked a middle-aged gentleman in a smart grey suit with spectacles perched on the end of his nose. He walked to the witness box and took the oath.

Hardy approached him. 'You are Charles Gates, the coroner?'

'Yes, I am.'

'You examined the body of Frank Clarke on March 24th of this year?'

'Yes, I did.'

'Will you please tell the court your findings?'

The coroner went on to explain that the body had decomposed after being left in the cemetery for several weeks and gave more detail about the state of the body but then said that he'd found the cause of death to be a stab wound to the heart that had been fatal.

'Thank you,' said Hardy. 'No further questions.'

The counsel for the defence rose to his feet.

'Mr Gates, I realise that the state of the body made your job more difficult, but could you say if this man could have been strong enough to put up a good fight, had he needed to?'

Gates peered over his glasses. 'He was well built and in his forties. But that's as far as I could possibly deduce.'

'Thank you, sir. No further questions.'

Mr Gates left the witness box.

Then Ben was called. He stood in the witness box, took the oath and waited.

Hardy walked up to him. 'You are Detective Benjamin Masters.'

'Yes, I am.'

'Will you tell the court what you were doing working as a stallholder in Kingsland Market.'

'I was there to observe the two Stanley brothers, who were under suspicion for burglary. I was watching their every move, looking for anything suspicious.'

'Working undercover, is that right?'

'Yes, sir.'

'Did you notice anything suspicious after the day of the murder?'

'Yes, I did. The two brothers were on edge. They argued, which wasn't unusual, but this time it was different. Young Arthur looked decidedly nervous and jumpy and this angered Percy. But this time, they were arguing quietly and there was a sense of urgency about their exchange. But what made it even stranger was that Miss Phoebe Collins, who was another stallholder, was also behaving differently. She too was on edge and somehow I felt that it had something to do with the brothers.'

'Did you have any evidence of this?'

'No, sir. Just a gut feeling. But after the market closed and everybody had gone home, I went back to check on the Stanleys' lock-up. I discovered remains of damp sand on the ground in front of it, which was strange. Then I realised that, only outside the lock-up, the ground had been carefully cleaned. I couldn't imagine why, until it was discovered that a murder had taken place and it all made sense. If the murder had been committed in front of their lock-up, there would have been a loss of blood from the victim, which would have had to be cleaned up. Sand would absorb it, then it could be washed away.'

'Anything else happen to raise your suspicions at that time?'

'Yes, it was Miss Collins' behaviour. She was on edge the whole time and then Stanley came through the market carrying goods and called out "Mind your backs", just as he was behind Miss Collins. She was so startled, she dropped a bag of goods, but it was because I saw her hands trembling as she picked the stuff up, that made me realise she was really scared of him and I wondered why.'

'Thank you. No further questions.'

The counsel for the defence stood up. 'These findings of yours, they are all supposition, aren't they? You don't have any proof that this is the truth, do you?'

'No, sir. But it made sense.'

'But that was just your opinion, you had no evidence. No further questions.'

Ben left the witness box and sat in the court. He glanced across at Percy, who just stared back at him.

James Hardy stood. 'I would like to call Miss Phoebe Collins to the stand.'

On hearing her name called, Phoebe entered the door of the courtroom and was let inside by a policeman, standing by the door. He showed her where to go. As she walked down the aisle between the seats, her heart was pounding. She kept her eyes on the witness box ahead, not looking anywhere else, until she arrived and stood in the box. After taking the oath, she stared at the table where Hardy and his team were sitting. He smiled at her and rose from his seat, then walking over to her, he spoke.

'You are Miss Phoebe Collins of 28 Union Street in Southampton?'

'Yes, sir,' she replied, looking straight at him.

'You have a fruit and vegetable stall in Kingsland Market?'

'Yes, sir.'

'Let me take you back to February 2nd. You had finished work for the day and you had gone home. What happened then?'

'It had been a busy day and I was late leaving. I was in a rush to get home to look after my young brother. It wasn't until later when I was checking a list of goods for my stall, that I realised I might have forgotten to lock up. I put on my coat and walked back to the market.'

'About what time of night would that have been?'

'After eleven, as all the pubs were closed and the streets were empty.'

'What happened then?'

'When I arrived, I was heading for my lock-up when I heard angry voices. When I looked towards the sound,

I saw that the door of the Stanley brothers' lock-up was open. I stopped to listen. There was a furious argument going on. I recognised Percy Stanley's voice, but not the other. Then there was a crashing and a banging. I was about to run away when they both came hurtling through the door, fighting one another.'

'Did they see you, Miss Collins?'

'Fortunately, no, but I was scared, and I saw behind me a pile of cardboard boxes piled high, waiting to be cleared in the morning, so I hid behind them. But I could see what was going on through a space in the boxes.'

'What happened next?'

'There was a lot of cursing and shouting as they exchanged blows, then Percy hit the other man, sending him to the ground. He climbed over him, sitting astride him, and held him by the throat. The man couldn't breathe and was fighting for his breath. I thought he was going to die, then with a mighty heave, he managed to push Percy off him and stagger to his feet. Once he'd regained his balance, he turned to face Percy, but to my horror, before he could move, Percy drew a knife and plunged it in him!' With trembling fingers, she took a sip of water from a glass on a shelf in front of her.

'The other man didn't attack Mr Stanley once he'd got to his feet?'

'No, sir, he didn't have time.'

'What happened next?'

'The man collapsed and lay on the ground. Percy leant over him but he didn't move. Percy cursed loudly, then he hauled the body up and dragged him into the lock-up.'

'What did you do?'

Her eyes widened at the recollection. 'Nothing! I was too scared to move.'

'And then?'

'After a while, Percy walked out of the lock-up, put the padlock on and turned the key, but as he was walking away, I moved my cramped leg and to my horror, a box tumbled down. He stopped and looked over. I was terrified and thought I'd be next, but at that moment, a cat jumped down with a squawk from the wall behind the boxes. Percy stopped, looked at the cat and left the market. When I felt it was safe, I crept out, but then I was violently sick in one of the boxes. After, I ran home and locked the door.'

'Why didn't you inform the police? After all, you'd just seen a man die.'

'I was too frightened. Percy didn't know I was there. I thought I'd wait until the morning when the market opened and he had to open his lock-up – but to my surprise, everything was normal. There was no body! Who would have believed me? I had no proof it happened, there wasn't a body to show people. It would have been his word against mine and what's more he would then know I'd seen him. My life would have been in danger. I had a mother and young brother to care for, I couldn't take the chance.'

'But how did you manage to work that day, knowing that across the way was a man who was a murderer?'

'I was on edge all day long, worried that he'd discover somehow that I knew what he'd done. I was a bundle of nerves.'

Edward Phillips was watching the jury closely. They

looked across at Stanley sitting in the box. His face was like granite, but his eyes narrowed as he stared at Phoebe.

Edward whispered to his clerk. 'The jury don't like him!'

'It was several weeks before the body was discovered. However did you manage to carry this dreadful secret with you?'

'It was because of my family. I had to be sure that I was around to take care of them.'

'But eventually you did tell someone?'

'Yes. Ben Masters and I had become friends. I didn't know he was a policeman, I thought he was a stallholder, like us. He was worried about me, my health was suffering. I couldn't sleep at nights and Ben sat me down and made me tell him what was wrong. By then I knew I could trust him and to share this burden was such a relief. But of course, being a detective, he had to report it and then it all took off from there.'

'But, Miss Collins, because of it, we are at last able to bring a murderer to justice. Thank you. No further questions.'

The judge spoke up. 'Ladies and gentlemen, now is a good time to break for lunch. Court will be adjourned until two-thirty.'

'All rise,' called the clerk of the court and everyone waited until the judge had left the chambers. Then the jury filed out. Ben waited for Phoebe. He kissed her and said, 'Come on, I'll buy you a lemonade and a sandwich. You will be cross-examined, so I can't get you anything alcoholic.'

They walked to a nearby pub and sat down. After Ben had collected their order, she sipped her drink. Her mouth felt dry and she was thankful for the cool liquid, but she was worried about having to face the cross-questioning that would follow on their return to court and said as much to Ben.

'All you can do is answer his questions and don't elaborate. He can't get away from the fact that his client killed a man, but is claiming it was in self-defence. It's the only argument they have. Then it'll be up to the jury to decide the verdict.'

They eventually returned to the courthouse and Phoebe once again took her place in the witness box. The counsel for the defence stood before her.

'Please remember, Miss Collins, that you are still under oath.'

She nodded and waited.

'Let me take you back to February 2nd when you were hidden behind those boxes. Would you say the fight between the two men was violent?'

'Yes, I would.'

'Both exchanging blows with great force?'

'Yes.'

'Were you surprised, when Percy Stanley had the man on the ground, that he was able to recover and get to his feet?'

'Yes, sir.'

'Why was that?'

'Mr Stanley had him by the throat and he was having difficulty breathing. I thought he was a goner.'

'Mr Stanley must have been surprised, too, wouldn't you think?'

'I really couldn't say.'

'So, when he did get to his feet, what happened then?'

'The man got his balance and turned to face Percy, but as he did, Mr Stanley drew his knife and stabbed him.'

'Would you say that it was probably the only way he could have stopped him?'

'I have no way of knowing that.'

The counsel stood and looked at Phoebe, who looked back at him.

'I have no further questions at this time,' he said and sat down.

Phoebe was told she could leave the stand. She walked over and sat with Ben.

'Well done, darling. You did very well.'

James Harding got to his feet. 'I've no further witnesses, My Lord,' he said addressing the judge.

The judge looked at his watch. 'Very well, court is adjoined until ten o'clock tomorrow morning.' He turned to the jury and warned them that they were not free to discuss the case with anybody.

Everyone stood as the judge left the room, followed by the members of the jury. As Phoebe turned to walk away, she inadvertently looked up and saw Percy Stanley about to be taken from the dock, back to the cells. He paused and glared at her, before being hurried down the steps. She felt a shiver down her back.

Once outside, she turned to Ben. 'Why did the judge close the proceedings?'

'He knows that Percy Stanley is to be called and that could take some time. It's best to keep it to the same day. It makes life easier for everyone. At the end, the jury has to go away and decide the verdict. With a bit of luck, it could be over sooner than we think.'

'What am I going to tell Tim about being away again tomorrow?'

'I think we have to tell him the truth. He'll have to know sooner or later.'

Chapter Twenty-Nine

By the time they'd returned from Winchester, Tim was already at home. They found him eating a sandwich as he did his homework.

Phoebe gave him a hug. 'You are a good boy. We stopped at the pie shop on the way home. I'll just cook some potatoes and vegetables, then we can eat.'

'Where have you been?' asked her brother. 'I thought you'd be home when I came back.'

Phoebe glanced at Ben, who sat beside the boy. 'You remember the body that was found?'

'Oh, you mean the man that was murdered, that Percy Stanley killed?'

'Yes, that's right. Well, Phoebe was in court today as a witness.'

The boy frowned. 'A witness to what?'

Phoebe walked over to him. 'I actually saw Percy commit the murder.'

Tim looked stunned. 'You saw him do it?'

'Yes, I'd gone to lock up because I'd forgotten to do so, and I saw it all.'

'Now, Tim,' said Ben, 'you're old enough to understand how dreadful that was for your sister and now she's had to stand up in court and tell the jury what she saw. Not an easy thing to have to do.'

'You didn't tell anyone after it happened?'

'No, Tim, because the next morning there was no body to be seen. Who would have believed me? And Percy would have known I was a witness.'

The boy looked horrified. 'He would have killed you too!'

Ben hurriedly intervened. 'But we don't know that and it's best you don't even think about it. Phoebe told me in the end, and that was when we were able to arrest him.'

Turning to Ben, Tim's voice trembled as he asked, 'Will Percy be locked up?'

'Yes, he will, so there's no need to worry. He will be locked up for a very long time, so he won't be free to do any more harm.'

The boy got up from the table and flung his arms around his sister. 'So will you be safe?'

Holding him tightly she assured him. 'Yes, Tim, I'll be safe, there's no need to worry.'

'We have to go back to court tomorrow, Tim, but when this is all over, Phoebe and I will get married and we'll all start a new life. Then I can take care of both of you. Now,

I don't know about you, but I'm starving. Let's lay the table while your sister cooks the potatoes so we can eat.'

When it was time for Tim to go to bed, Ben followed him to the bottom of the stairs. He took hold of the boy by the arm. 'I want you to know that I will *never* let anyone harm either you or Phoebe, as long as I live – and that's a promise.'

The boy held him tightly. 'I do love you, Ben.'

'And I love you too, Tim. Now off you go. I'll see you soon.'

'Is he going to be all right, do you think?' asked Phoebe.

'I think so. It was a lot for the boy to take in, but the fact that he knows you are safe will be enough to settle him, I hope.' He gathered her to him. 'It'll soon be over and we can put it all behind us. Tomorrow will be difficult, because Stanley will be in the witness box and he'll try to lie his way out of being a murderer.'

'Will the jury know he has already been in prison for hurting someone?'

'Grievous bodily harm or GBH, as it's known. No, they aren't told about it.'

'Do you think he'll get away with a plea of self-defence?'

'I've no idea, but we'll find out the verdict before long. I'm off to have a bath and get ready for the morning. I'll see you at the court. Try and get some sleep.'

When she was alone, Phoebe made a cup of tea and settled in the armchair near the fire. It had been a long day and she was weary, but her mind wouldn't settle. Knowing that Percy was a devious character, she wondered what he'd say when questioned. He'd lie if he had to. Being on oath wouldn't mean anything to him!

* * *

At ten o'clock the next morning, the court was in session, judge and jury in their place. There was a charged atmosphere in the courtroom as the counsel for the defence rose to his feet.

'I call Percy Stanley to the witness stand.'

The jurors sat forward, looking at him as he left the dock and walked across the room. He was dressed in a somewhat shabby suit and a white shirt and a tie that was slightly askew. He took the oath, and stared at his counsel.

'You are Percy Leonard Stanley of 31 Orchard Lane, Southampton?'

'Yes!'

'You and your late brother made your living as market traders in Kingsland Square market?'

'Yes.'

'I'd like you to tell the jury what happened in the market, late on February 2nd.'

'Frank Clarke came to see me to do some business.'

'What kind of business?'

'I had some jewellery I wanted to sell.'

'Can you please tell the jury why you two argued?'

'Clarke wanted to buy the stuff at a knock-down price. He was cheating me out of a fair sale, and I objected.'

'Surely that wasn't enough to warrant a fight?'

'No, not on its own, but he disrespected me, and no one does that,' he stated arrogantly.

'How did he show his lack of respect?'

'When I argued about the price he was offering, he laughed at me. He said I should be thankful that he'd made an offer at all, what I was selling was a pittance, hardly worth bothering with, that I was small-time . . . a nobody!' Percy couldn't hide the anger in his voice.

There was a rustling among the jury as they reacted to this.

'So what happened next?'

'He insulted me again, so I hit him!' He glared at the jury as he heard one or two gasp at his remark.

'Then what happened?'

'He hit me back, of course! Then we started to fight. He kept hurling insults at me, calling me names and eventually we ended up still fighting, outside the lock-up. I had him on the ground at one point, but he got up and came at me. He looked bloody livid, so I took my knife out of my pocket to defend myself. I thought when he saw it, he'd stop but he didn't, so I had no choice but to use it to save myself.'

'You say he came at you – the last witness says he just turned to face you and that you used your knife then.'

'Well, she's wrong; he came at me in a bloody rage.'

'Were you in fear for your life, Mr Stanley?'

'Yes, I was!'

'Let's be clear on this point. If Mr Clarke had stopped, would you have used your knife?'

'No. Of course not! I only used it to scare him. I certainly didn't intend to kill him.'

'But why use the knife at all? Couldn't you have fought him off again with your fists; you'd managed to do so before.'

'To be honest, I didn't have the strength. He was in good nick and I don't mind admitting, he hurt me. I didn't think I could better him again with my fists. The only thing I had left to defend myself was my knife. I didn't have a choice or he'd have done for me, of that I'm certain.'

'No further questions My Lord.' The counsel returned to his bench and sat down.

James Hardy rose to his feet and stood for a moment staring at Percy before walking slowly over to him.

James smiled at him. 'You and your brother ran this stall for several years, isn't that right?'

'Yes.'

'Can you make a good living doing this?'

Percy looked puzzled. 'We get by.'

'But you don't make a great profit. Am I right?'

Scowling at James, Percy replied. 'I'm not a rich man like you. No!'

James chuckled and the jury tittered at this.

'You say that Mr Clarke came to buy jewellery from you? That was the jewellery that was stolen, I believe?'

'Objection!' The defence counsel was on his feet.

James looked at the judge. 'The prisoner is already being held for the robbery of the jewellery, My Lord. I just want to clarify that these are the same pieces.'

'Overruled.'

James stared at Percy. 'Well, was it the same jewellery?'

Percy looked furious. 'Yes, it was.'

'And Frank Clarke is what is commonly known as a fence. A man who buys stolen goods.'

Percy just glared at James.

'Answer the question, Mr Stanley,' the judge ordered.

'Yes, he is.'

'A man, no doubt, who deals with many a stolen article, maybe much more expensive goods than you were offering. Perhaps that's why he called you small-time, a nobody. You tell us he continued insulting you and that is why your fight was furious and why it ended up eventually outside the lock-up, where it continued for some time until you had him on the ground, trying to choke the life out of him. We've been told he could hardly breathe. You hoped to finish him off for disrespecting you, as you called it, didn't you? After all, as you said yourself – nobody does that! You are a man of great self-importance; it's obvious that you were *enraged* at being spoken to like this.'

James strolled over to the jury, then turned back to Stanley. 'I put it to you that Clarke surprised you by getting to his feet, you thought you had him – that you could finish him off – make him pay for his insults! Show him who he was dealing with. When he got up and struggled to regain his balance, he didn't come at you as you say he did. He didn't have time, you had only one chance to kill him and you took it! You plunged the knife into him before he had time to fight back. Your arrogance and your temper have led you here today and one human is dead because of it.'

'That's not true. He came at me. It was an accident!' Percy yelled at him, banging his fist on the front of the box, his face puce with anger.

Hardy, now having riled his man, carried on.

'This was no accident. The previous witness clearly stated that Clarke had only just regained his balance and turned towards you. That's when you saw the advantage and you took it! You plunged the knife into him!' Hardy showed the court by pretending to hold a knife and use it with great gusto. There was an intake of breath from some. He turned back to Stanley. 'Then, when finally your victim had taken his last breath and lay still, you realised you had a body to deal with. You then panicked, locked the body away and went to fetch your brother to help you move it, which you then callously hid in the nearby cemetery. What

I don't understand, Mr Stanley, is if this was an accident, as you say and you stabbed Frank Clarke in self-defence – why didn't you call the police?'

Percy, still angry, just glared at James. 'Don't be ridiculous! They'd never have believed me with my record.'

Hardy was delirious at hearing this. Percy's past record couldn't be used unless someone introduced it – and Percy had just done so.

'Your record, Mr Stanley? Do you already have a police record?'

Percy suddenly realised his great mistake. He looked over at his counsel, who just shook his head in despair.

'Mr Stanley, I asked you a question. Do you have a police record?'

'Yes.'

'Perhaps you'd be good enough to enlighten the gentlemen of the jury?'

'I've served time for GBH.'

'That means grievous bodily harm, gentlemen,' James told the jury. Then, turning back to Percy, he said, 'I believe the man you attacked was so badly injured, he had to stay in hospital for some considerable time.' Percy didn't answer but just glared at him. James carried on. 'It has been proven you are a violent man. You've already served one term in prison because of this. I think you are an arrogant and angry man who does not like being crossed, and when Frank Clarke told you were a *nobody*, you lost your temper and killed him in cold blood. You've not shown one ounce of remorse during all the time you've spent in the witness box, because you don't have any. I think you are a menace to society and should be put away for a *long* time.' He went back to his bench and sat down.

The defence counsel stood. 'I have no further witnesses, My Lord.'

The judge glanced over to James Hardy, who got up and walked over to the jury. 'Gentlemen, you've heard the evidence. You've seen the man accused of the murder of one Frank Clarke, a man who came to Southampton to purchase stolen goods. A trade agreement, although an illegal one. Nothing that one would expect to have such dire consequences. But as you've observed, Percy Stanley has an uncontrollable temper. He's already severely injured one person and put him in hospital – and served time for doing so. Perhaps we are fortunate that we were not gathered here at an earlier date on a charge of murder, but we are here today. Frank Clarke is dead because Percy Stanley lost his temper yet again and attacked him with a knife. Not in self-defence, as he claims, but in pure rage because, as he said, he was disrespected.

'We've already heard from a previous witness that Stanley once had the victim on the ground fighting to breathe. Had he not struggled free, I feel sure that he would have died from strangulation instead of stabbing, because Stanley was so enraged, he would have killed him then. The defendant claims that Frank Clarke got up and came at him, but Miss Collins stated under oath that Clarke didn't have the time to do so before he was stabbed. This was no accident. Had it been so, Stanley would have been full of remorse. Did you see any of this in his demeanour? No, neither did I.

'This man took the life of another in a fit of rage, because he felt he'd been insulted. No other reason. This man is a danger to society, and I believe he should pay the price for

the life that he took so deliberately – and without pity.'
James walked back to his bench and sat down.

The defence counsel took a moment to face the jury. He
knew there was little chance of winning the case, but the
public could be unexpected, and a jury and its deliberations
was always an unknown factor.

He stood in front of the twelve men. 'Gentlemen, my
learned friend has made a strong case against my client and
much of what he says is true. Mr Stanley has served a prison
sentence for grievous bodily harm. We don't dispute that he
has a temper and is quick to anger. Yes, he felt insulted and
it ended up in fisticuffs, but – and this is important – Mr
Stanley at no time intended to kill Frank Clarke. He was
only defending himself when Clarke managed to get to his
feet. You can imagine how angry *he* was as he turned to my
client. After all, he'd taken a beating and that goes against the
grain in any male. He ignored the knife in Mr Stanley's hand,
and came at the defendant. What choice did he have but to
use it to save himself? It was used purely in self-defence and
nothing more. He does *not* deserve to be tried for murder!'
He walked away and sat down.

The judge addressed the jury. 'Gentlemen, it is time for
you to come to a decision. But before you do, I need to
explain the law to you.'

This he did briefly, using layman's terms for the jurors
to understand. He explained the burden and standard of
proof and the legal ingredients of the offence charged.

'What the prosecution claims was a severe assault
resulting in death. The accused is charged with murder.
What the defendant described was lawful self-defence and
not murder.

270

'You have heard the witnesses give their sworn statements and you have heard the defendant give his. One witness stated that Mr Clarke didn't attack Mr Stanley when he got to his feet after being punched to the ground, the defendant disputes this. Taking all this into account, if you think the prosecution evidence is true – without reasonable doubt – then the verdict is guilty. If you think that the defendant's evidence *might* be true, then he's not guilty. Please take your time. Go through the evidence carefully before making your decision.'

The judge, followed by the jury, left the courtroom. Percy was taken below to the cells to await the verdict. Ben and Phoebe went to a nearby cafe with the solicitor and the counsel for a welcome cup of tea.

'What happens now?' Phoebe asked.

'We have to wait for the verdict, and no one knows how long that will take.'

Ben leant forward. 'Have you any inkling as to what that will be?'

James Hardy smiled softly. 'I've learnt not to jump to conclusions. One can never tell what goes on in a jury room. But I will say that Stanley came across as an angry man. He wasn't sorry for what he'd done, and it showed, but we'll wait and see.'

Three hours later, the jury returned and everyone took their places to hear the verdict.

Chapter Thirty

There was a feeling of tension in the courtroom. The press were ready; pens poised waiting for the news that would be printed the next day. Those in the public gallery were almost afraid to breathe, wondering what the verdict would be. Percy Stanley stood in the dock, now pale and drawn, knowing that he could face the gallows if there was a guilty verdict.

The judge's voice echoed in the silent room. 'Gentlemen of the jury, have you reached a verdict?'

The foreman stood. 'We have.'

'What is your verdict?'

'Guilty!'

Percy Stanley looked shocked and he grabbed hold of the front of the dock as his legs almost gave way. He could scarcely breathe as he waited. Would the judge put the black cloth on his head? Was he to be hanged?

The judge spoke. 'Percy Stanley, you have been found guilty of murder. You took the life of another in cold blood and have not shown any remorse for this heinous crime. It is my duty to keep the public safe and I feel you are a menace to society.' He paused. Not a sound could be heard. 'I therefore sentence you to life in prison.'

The policeman standing with Percy had to hold him up as his knees gave way with relief.

Phoebe suddenly felt dizzy and gripped hold of Ben's hand.

'Are you all right, darling?'

'No, my head is spinning.'

'Let's get you out of here,' he said, but as Phoebe tried to stand, she staggered. Ben immediately lifted her into his arms and carried her outside. Someone rushed for a glass of water as Ben made her sit and bend her head down to her knees until she felt better.

She sipped the water and looked at her fiancé.

'Is it really all over? Is he going away for the rest of his life?'

'Yes, darling. It's over.'

'It's not that simple, Ben. I still have nightmares about the murder. It's not something I can forget that easily.'

'I know it will take time, but at least you'll never see Percy ever again. Eventually you'll be able to put it to the back of your mind.' He hugged her. 'You'll be too busy looking after Tim and me.'

At that moment, James Hardy and Edward Phillips joined them.

'Are you all right, Miss Collins?' James asked.

'Yes, thank you. When I heard the verdict I suddenly felt faint, but it's passed now.'

'Good! Now I think we all need that drink I promised. I know I need one and a brandy will soon put you back on your feet, Miss Collins. Trust me.'

While they walked to the nearest pub, Percy Stanley was about to be taken back to Wormwood Scrubs. As he stepped outside the back entrance to the courtroom, Detective Inspector Bentley stood waiting. He looked at Percy with distain.

'I told you, you'd go down one day, and I was right. If I'd been the judge, you'd be swinging from a rope! But your worst punishment is yet to come. In prison you'll be a nobody – just another piece of trash with a number. Nobody special, and you'll hate that, but let's say in another thirty years or so, maybe you'll have got used to it. After all, you'll be an old man by then.'

Percy began to curse and swear at Bentley, but he just laughed and walked away as he watched Percy struggle as he was pushed into a police van.

The policeman sitting opposite him didn't speak and Percy was relieved. He was still in a state of shock. He hadn't expected a guilty verdict; he'd convinced himself that the jury would say it was self-defence. He'd escaped the gallows, but now he'd live the rest of his years cooped up inside prison walls. He was in his early thirties, a fit man. A long and lonely future stretched ahead, shut away with a load of criminals. He didn't for one minute consider himself to be one. Still smarting from the detective's words, he muttered to himself. 'A piece of trash, am I? A nobody? You couldn't be more wrong!'

James Hardy held up his glass. 'A toast. To a successful verdict!' They all repeated it and drank. He turned to Phoebe.

'You did so well as a witness, Miss Collins, but I must warn you that for a little while you will be subjected to a certain amount of notoriety. The press will be wanting interviews, the public will be curious about you. There will be a certain amount of gossip from those who can be scathing.'

She looked concerned. 'What should I do? How can I handle it?'

'I would choose one reporter from a decent paper and give an exclusive interview and at the end of the interview say it has been a terrible ordeal and you want to be left alone to forget about it. Then refuse to speak to anyone else from the press. In a short space of time something else will become news and you will fade out of the picture. There will always be someone somewhere who will remember but in time it'll be forgotten. Besides, you have Ben to look after your interests. He's not going to let anyone harass you.'

'I can't quite get used to someone taking care of me for a change. It's a comforting feeling, I must say.'

'He's a good man; I hope you'll be very happy together.'

'Thank you, I'm sure we will.'

Phoebe felt a great relief as she walked into her house at the end of such a stressful day. Ben put the kettle on as young Tim came rushing into the house. He looked scared as he asked, 'What happened?'

Phoebe went over to him and put her hands on his shoulders. 'Percy Stanley was sentenced to life in prison.'

The boy burst into tears.

Phoebe held him close. 'Oh, Tim, please don't cry. It's all over now, we can forget about it and the brothers.'

'Now you'll be safe,' he cried. 'I was so worried he would murder you too!'

This brought Phoebe to tears also as she held on to her brother, unable to speak.

'Now, come on you two,' Ben chipped in. 'There's no need to cry, we have a holiday to look forward to. I can't arrive at my parent's house if you are all red-eyed from weeping! What would my father think? He might think I've been unkind to you and I can't have that. I expect he'll ask you to help with his fish pond, Tim.'

The boy wiped his tears. 'I'd like that,' he said. 'Will your mother have some of her lemonade, do you think?'

'Oh, my goodness, yes. She always has a jug ready in summer.'

Two days later, suitcases packed, the three of them made the journey to Gloucester and were warmly greeted by Ben's parents. Everyone relaxed in the cosy kitchen, eating freshly baked scones and sponge cake – and for Tim, a glass of lemonade.

The days spent in the Cotswolds felt like a healing. Phoebe relaxed at last and Tim was in heaven, helping Hugh with his fish pond and digging in the vegetable garden.

Ben had quietly taken his parents aside and told them what had happened.

Hugh shook his head as he listened. 'What a terrible ordeal for that poor girl. It'll take some time for her to get over all this.'

'I know, Dad, but I want us to get married soon so we can all start a new life together. I hope you both will be happy for us?'

Ellie hugged him. 'Of course we are. Phoebe is a lovely girl and young Tim is a delight. He adores you, son. We only have to see you together to know that there's already a great bond between you.'

The week seemed to fly by before they were on their way back to Southampton. Ben was due back on duty the next day, Tim started school again and Phoebe was off to the market to sort out her stall. Some of her goods would now not be fit for sale after the days spent in court and the week away, but some should still be fine. She needed to get back to normal.

She and Ben had decided to get married in November. In the meantime, he'd look for a larger flat until the following year when, as a wedding present, Hugh had offered to give them the money for a down payment on a house. Until then, Phoebe would work in the market as she'd said she needed to keep busy.

Phoebe was greeted warmly by Marj on the Monday morning as she wheeled her stall onto its pitch. Marj flung her arms around her friend and kissed her cheek.

'Oh, my love, I 'ave missed you!'

'I've missed you too, you old devil! Let me look at you. You look fine. What's been going on while I've been away?'

'Well, love, it was all that news of the trial. It was in all the papers. It was the talk of the town, never mind the market! Such an ordeal for you. Are you all right?'

'Still a bit shaky, Marj, to be honest, but the week away with Ben's parents was lovely and it did help.'

'So when's the wedding?'

Phoebe beamed at her. 'Sometime in November. We have to go and see the vicar and sort out a date. You best buy a new hat!'

'I've got one already! I knew I'd need it one day, I just 'oped I wouldn't have to wait too long to wear it.' Her smile faded. 'I suppose that means you won't be working no longer in the market?'

'I'm afraid so. I am pleased, of course, not to have to face another winter out in the cold, but in another way I'll miss it, it's been my life for so many years.' She caught hold of her friend's hand. 'But most of all, I'll miss you, Marj. You've been more than a friend, more a guardian angel, looking out for me when I had to take over from Dad.'

'Oh, bless you, love! You were so young and so brave, 'aving to earn to keep your family. It was a great responsibility, and you worked so 'ard to do so, and you were successful. I'm just so thrilled you 'ave that lovely man to take care of you both. I couldn't be 'appier for you.'

'What about you and Tony? Do you still go out with him?'

With a mischievous look she said, 'Oh yes, we're getting along very well, thank you.'

'How well? Or shouldn't I ask?'

'You can ask, love, but I'm saying nothing! Now you best sort out your veg or you won't do no business today.' She walked away chuckling softly.

While she was sorting her stall, several of the other stallholders came over to talk to her. All were very sympathetic for the ordeal she'd suffered, but remembering James Hardy's advice, she answered them briefly, thanking them for their concern, saying she wanted to put it behind her and just get on with her life. She carried on sorting the vegetables to be thrown away, and some that she could give to the children who came searching for handouts, but there was enough to stock her stall for a couple of days until she refilled it.

During play time at school, Tim was surrounded by boys who knew about the trial and Tim's sister being a witness, but this time he wasn't upset because the boys, being children, were thrilled with it all. After all, a murder was exciting and his sister was a bit of a heroine in their eyes.

On the way home, Phoebe had to shop for food as her larder was empty. As she did so, she was aware of several women staring at her and whispering. She overheard one.

'I'm sure it's her. I saw her picture in the paper.'

She left the shop as quickly as she could, realising that this was going to happen for a while, as James had predicted. In the market during the following days it was even worse. Folk would gather in groups a few feet away, looking at her and whispering. She ignored them.

One day Marj had reached the end of her tether with such folk. She walked round the front of her stall and glared at the gathering. 'You lot shopping or are you just gawping? If you don't want to buy – move on and make way for those who do!'

Marj in a temper was not to be messed with and they all hurried away. Hearing the sound of laughter behind her, Marj turned round, to see Phoebe doubled up trying to stop laughing and failing miserably.

'Oh, you are a caution! You scared the living daylights out of those women.'

'Well, they make me sick! They are like a lot of vultures looking at a dead carcass!'

'Oh, thanks, Marj! Is that how you see me? Not very flattering, I must say.'

The two of them started giggling. 'I hope Ben doesn't see me like that!'

'If 'e did, it would have been my stall 'e'd 'ave come to, not yours! I'd have given 'im 'is money's worth and no mistake!'

Wiping her tears of laughter away, Phoebe said, 'You really are a naughty woman!'

'Not me, love, I'm as pure as the driven snow!'

'Oh my, I'm going to miss you. You'll have to come and visit me often when I'm a married lady.'

'You have my word on that, young lady. Now I best get back to work.'

Phoebe stood leaning against her stall viewing the market, remembering when she first came here as a child when her father worked the stall, and the years that followed when he went to war and she took over. This place had been her life for so long, she knew that leaving it behind wouldn't be easy. There was a great camaraderie between the people who worked here. It was like an extended family, apart from the brothers. She couldn't help feeling sorry for Arthur. He wasn't a bad man like his brother, just a weak one who, through his brother's greed and temper, had paid with his life. How sad that was just as he'd begun to enjoy himself, left on his own. He'd even had a girlfriend. Phoebe gave a wry smile. At least he'd had a few months of freedom and she was pleased for him.

She picked up an apple and bit into it. It reminded her of the time when she'd dropped a box of fruit in her lock-up and

Percy had picked some up and walked into return them and taken her by surprise. She clearly recalled the terror she felt as he looked at her. She closed her eyes as she tried to shut out the image. Well, he'd spend the rest of his life with time to think of what he'd lost. She hoped he would go through hell.

Chapter Thirty-One

Percy Stanley waited in his cell for the door to be unlocked for the day. He'd been placed in a block used to house the most dangerous prisoners. Those who'd committed murder or manslaughter. Others were serving time for grievous bodily harm and some were awaiting trial for some heinous crime.

It became clear to him almost immediately that there was a decided pecking order among the inmates. The leader, Harry Matthews, an older man who'd been inside for many years, serving a life sentence for killing a family after breaking into their house. He was thickset and balding with hooded eyes and bushy eyebrows. There was a certain aura about him as he walked about, and it was obvious to newcomers that he was held in respect and with a certain amount of fear from his fellow prisoners. This did not sit well with Percy.

On the third day, at breakfast, he nudged the prisoner sitting next to him. 'What's so special about him?' he asked, nodding over to where Harry was sitting surrounded by his closest followers.

The man looked at him in surprise. 'You must be new here. That's Harry Matthews. You mess with him and you are in trouble.'

'What right has he to be the big I am?'

'How long are you in for, mate?'

Percy glared at him. 'Too long!'

'Then let me give you a bit of advice. Keep clear of him. Don't upset him, and remember: what he says, goes. If he tells you to step aside, do it! If he tells you to get his food, do it!'

'I'm not waiting on anybody. I'm not a bloody servant!'

'Then, my friend, you are in for a very hard time in here. These are hard men, mostly in for a long time, some for life. They haven't anything to lose. You'd best remember that.'

Percy watched the other table as he ate his porridge. Matthews sat at the end of the long table with its bench seating. Percy watched as he drained the tea in his cup and just handed the empty to the person sitting beside him, who without hesitation, picked it up and went to get a refill. He returned and placed it on the table, without a word being spoken.

As Matthews picked it up to drink, he glanced around the room and saw that Percy was watching him. He didn't look away, but seemed to study this newcomer. Percy just stared back at him. The old lag's eyes narrowed as he recognised the hostility there. The corners of his mouth twitched in a half-smile, but it was far from friendly.

At that moment the bell went and the men stood in lines ready to return their empty dishes, apart from Matthews, who got up and walked out, leaving one of the others to take his.

Percy couldn't help feeling a certain admiration for the power that he had, but he realised that sooner or later, the two of them would clash.

As Percy walked back towards his cell, he was called to by a warder and told to go and get a mop and bucket of hot water as he'd been assigned to scrub and mop one of the corridors.

'I'm not a bloody housewife,' he snapped.

'Don't come it, Stanley! You've been inside before, you know the drill. You all have a job to do to help keep the prison running smoothly and that's yours!'

Percy duly filled the bucket, took a scrubbing brush, mop and soap and, following the warder, walked to his work area – a large square with cells either side. It was in the centre of the block, therefore busy with prisoners and warders walking through. The prisoners returning to their cells after completing their daily tasks and the warders on watch, walking to and fro. Not ideal for the person trying to wash the floor.

'Get off there, you stupid idiot! Can't you see it's wet?' Percy yelled at one of the prisoners who just walked over a newly washed area. The man ignored him.

Muttering angrily, Percy carried on. Just as he'd finished and stood back looking at his work and feeling pleased, someone walked behind him and in passing, kicked the bucket of dirty water over. The water swirled around Percy's feet and all over his newly cleaned floor. He spun round and looked straight into the eyes of Harry Matthews, who just glared at him and walked on, followed by three other men who were laughing.

Percy's hands gripped the handle of the mop so tightly his knuckles were white. How he longed to use it on bloody Harry Matthews. 'Bastard!' he muttered quietly, but he knew there was nothing he could do and that really made him angry. He mopped up the water, swearing quietly to himself until he'd finished and returned to his cell. He kicked his chair over and sat on his bed, still fuming. He could wait, he thought. What was it that detective said? In time, everybody makes a mistake.

It was now early November and there was much excitement in the market and the Collins household as the wedding of Phoebe and Ben was to take place in three weeks' time. Marj and Phoebe had gone to London for the day, hunting for a wedding dress. They'd been to several big stores and small shops but without success. Nothing had quite fitted the bill until Marj whisked her friend off to a back street, then up a rickety staircase and into a room that was stacked with rails of clothing. Materials of different types, from satin, velvet, different coloured nets, spilt out of boxes. It took Phoebe's breath away.

'Oh, Marj! This is like Aladdin's cave. It's wonderful!'

'Marj!' A woman emerged from behind a railing full of dresses. 'Well, you old tart! How the devil are you after so long?'

The two women embraced. 'Dolly, I want you to meet my dearest friend, Phoebe. She's looking for a wedding dress. Phoebe, this is Dolly, an old mate of mine.'

'Hello, love! Now, when's the wedding?'

'In three weeks' time. It's a quiet affair, just friends and family. I'd like something that I can wear again and I'm aware it will be on a cold day, although we don't have far to walk to the hotel.'

'For God's sake, Phoebe, this is your wedding day, not a birthday party. Don't you want to be frivolous?' Marj looked at her in despair.

Dolly held up her hand and, turning to Marj, she said, 'Now just leave the girl alone. Of course she feels frivolous, but she's being sensible too. I wore my wedding dress only once and now it's in a box. What bloody good is that?' And to Phoebe, 'Come here, love, take off your coat and let me measure you. Marj, you sit down and shut up!'

Phoebe was in her element as Dolly produced one dress after another while asking Phoebe about her fiancé. 'Oh, a detective! You'll be going to a police ball every year, so we'll choose a dress that is fitting for that too. Now let me see . . .'

She took down a pale, coffee-coloured gown made of lace, with a round neck, long sleeves, dropped waist and a handkerchief skirt just below the knees. To this she added a rich brown velvet coat. The ensemble looked classy and expensive. Dolly looked at the girl in front of her, then disappeared, only to return with a cloche hat the same colour as the coat.

'Here. Put this on.'

Phoebe did so and stood back looking at her refection in the mirror. 'Oh, my goodness! Is that really me?'

'Oh, Phoebe, love, you look just like a model. Ben will fall in love with you all over again when 'e sees you in that outfit!'

'She's right, love,' Dolly agreed. 'You couldn't do no better than that.'

'I love it, Dolly, but how much is it?'

'You never mind about that,' said Marj. 'This is my wedding present to you.' Tears filled her eyes. 'I've waited so long to see you settled with a good man, one who will be kind to young Tim as well. Now I can relax and stop worrying about you.'

Phoebe hugged her friend, close to tears herself. 'Oh, Marj, thank you so much.'

Dolly packed the outfit into a box with a handle for easy carrying. 'Good luck, girl! Have a great wedding and a good life.'

On the train home, Phoebe was trying to sort out her plans for before the wedding. 'Next week, we move into the new flat that Ben has rented. I've been packing everything away in boxes. Tim and Ben have helped too, otherwise I wouldn't have been ready in time. Ben is staying at a friend's house until the wedding. It'll give me time to sort out the place for him to come home to.' She sat back against the seat. 'I can't remember living anywhere else. It'll be strange to leave. The house is full of memories of my parents. Tim being born, Dad going off to war, Mum filling the kitchen with her washing. It's sad to go in one way, leaving all that behind.'

Marj reached for her hand. 'But just think, love. You'll be building new memories, your life with Ben, not your parents, God rest their souls. It's the start of a new life, it's exciting.' She looked a little sad. 'I wouldn't mind starting another one meself.'

Phoebe looked at her. 'You could, you know. Tony idolises you. You're good together. You bounce off one another. You'd make a great team.'

'I'm just not sure about living with a man again after so long, having to consider another person. I've become used to pleasing meself.'

Phoebe looked at her. 'Do you want to be alone for the rest of your life, Marj? That can be very lonely. Coming home after a long day, no one to talk to. I know you're used to that but as you get older, you need someone to come home to, to sit by the fire with, talk to. You should think seriously about it.'

Marj didn't answer but she sat back, deep in thought.

Chapter Thirty-Two

It was the day of the wedding. It was a crisp November day, the sun was shining, albeit without much warmth to it. Marj was with Phoebe, helping her to dress and seeing that young Tim was all suited and booted as was fitting for his sister's wedding. He had a new navy suit, a white shirt and navy patterned tie. He stood in front of the mirror, looking at his reflection, feeling very grown up. He was to give his sister away and was filled with pride at the privilege, especially as at the rehearsal, the vicar had praised him for doing a good job. Ben's parents were coming from Gloucester and were staying at The Star hotel, where the wedding reception was to take place after the ceremony at St Michael's Church. Ben had a fellow policeman as his best man.

The ceremony was at noon and Marj had arrived early and insisted that Phoebe and Tim sat down to tea and toast to sustain them until the wedding breakfast. She was resplendent in a dress, coat and an amazing hat with a broad brim and a feather that draped across the brim. She looked stunning and was delighted when both Tim and Phoebe poured praise upon her as she gave them a twirl on her arrival.

Eventually the car arrived to take them to the church. Tim and Phoebe sat in the back and Marj in front with the chauffeur. The car was bedecked in white ribbons, as was fitting.

When they arrived, Marj waited for the bride to get out and gave her a hug. 'I'm off to my seat now, darling. Next time I speak to you, you'll be Mrs Masters!' Her words caught in her throat. 'I'm away now or I'll make a fool of meself. Enjoy this moment, Phoebe. It's so special.' She kissed her on the cheek and hurried into the church.

The curate was waiting by the door. 'Are you ready, Miss Collins?'

Phoebe just nodded.

He gave a nod to the organist and the air was filled with the opening chords of 'The Wedding March'. Phoebe took Tim's arm. 'Ready?'

He beamed at her. 'Ready!' They started to walk slowly down the aisle of this splendid church. As they did so, Phoebe glanced at members of the congregation, some of whom were the stallholders, a few friends of her mother, and Ben's guests, whom she'd yet to meet. At the far end stood Ben and his best man. He turned and smiled at her as she neared him and when she arrived at his side, he took her hand.

'You look lovely,' he whispered and gave her hand a squeeze.

Phoebe smiled back, feeling her body relax as the vicar began the ceremony.

'Dearly beloved, we are gathered here today . . .'

Eventually, after signing the register, the bride and groom walked back down the aisle and stood on the steps of the church as the congregation spilt out of the building and the photographer began to take his photographs. Ben's parents quickly gave Phoebe a hug and kiss, then stood in line as the photographer did his job, and at last the couple walked down the path to be showered with confetti before they escaped across the road to the hotel. As they reached the entrance, Ben drew Phoebe into his arms and kissed her.

'Hello, Mrs Masters!'

She chuckled softly. 'I do like the sound of that; in fact, I think I could get used to it very quickly.'

The doorman interrupted them. 'They're ready for you, sir, in the dining room.'

The two of them followed and then waited inside to greet their guests.

The meal was served. The mushroom soup was welcome, as it had been a chilly walk to the hotel, and the chicken that followed was succulent, served with mixed vegetables, followed by lemon tart and fresh cream. Bottles of white wine were placed on the tables and champagne served as the best man stood to give his speech. He regaled the guests of stories of Ben when he first joined the force. Many that were hilarious and then a couple that told of Ben's bravery in given situations of which Phoebe had no knowledge but only proved to her what a brave man she'd married. Then he asked the guests to stand and toast the bride and groom,

Phoebe and Ben. Which they did. Then Ben rose to his feet.

He began by thanking his guests for being there and sharing what was the happiest day of his life. 'Sadly my wife's father is no longer with us as he died fighting for his country, but if he was he would have been bursting with pride. His daughter Phoebe took over his place by looking after her family, her brother Tim and her mother, who sadly passed away not that long ago. She became the head of the house at a very early age and I'm the lucky person with whom she decided to share the rest of her life. But not only have I gained a wife today, but a son also, so I am doubly blessed. I hope to be as good a man to him as was his father. I am now in the position of being the man of the house instead of Phoebe and at last the responsibility for this family is mine. I could not be more proud and happy to do this. I ask you to drink to my new family, Phoebe and Tim!'

The guests stood to give the toast, a few of the women quickly dabbing their eyes with a handkerchief at his heartfelt speech.

Phoebe looked at Ben. 'That was so lovely of you,' she said, tears brimming her eyes.

Ben took her hand and kissed it. 'It's now your turn to sit back and have me shoulder any responsibilities and I couldn't be happier. I love you, Phoebe, and I love Tim too. You see, we'll all be so happy together.'

The wedding party moved into another room where there was a three-piece band playing softly and a bar had opened at one end of the room. The guests mingled and chatted until it was time for the bride and groom to have the first dance. Ben took his bride in his arms and held her close as they danced slowly to a waltz, to be joined eventually by many of the guests.

Tony, who'd gone along with Marj, took her onto the dance floor. 'What a splendid day this has been, love. It's great to see two people so happy – well three, really, because young Tim is in seventh heaven too.'

'I can't tell you 'ow delighted I am to see the girl settled,' Marj answered. 'She's been through so much and now she 'as a man to take care of her and Tim.'

Tony looked down at the woman in his arms. 'Don't you think, love, that it's time for us to make our relationship more permanent?' He saw the look of surprise on her face and continued. 'Listen, Marj, neither of us is getting any younger. I don't want to die a lonely old man. I love you, you daft woman, and I think it's time we got married!'

She started to argue. 'You've just got carried away with the day, you daft bugger. Besides, I've been on my own too long. I've got selfish doing what I want when I want.'

'But we could do that together. You know I'm an easy-going chap, I won't make demands on you. We'll sort out a way to live together and be happy. Oh, Marj, be brave, girl! I'm good husband material, trust me.' He beamed at her. 'You won't get a better offer, so don't let me slip through your fingers or you'll live to regret it.'

She stopped dancing and looked at him, then she lifted her hand and stroked his cheek. 'You're a good man, Tony, and maybe you're right. I do get lonely and Phoebe was only telling me off about it quite recently.' She leant forward and kissed him softly. 'All right – if you're sure?'

'I was sure the day I moved into the market!' He picked her up and swung her round. 'Come on, let's get a drink to celebrate, but we'll keep this to ourselves today. We don't want to take any limelight from the newly-weds.' They walked off together to the bar.

Ben's family stayed overnight in the hotel so they could take Tim home with them and allow Ben and Phoebe to spend a few days in London. As it was winter and near to Christmas, they decided to do this and then they could go away in the summer with Tim for a good holiday. They all said their goodbyes after breakfast the following morning.

While Ben and Phoebe had been celebrating, in Wormwood Scrubs the atmosphere was very different. There was always a feeling of menace about the place. It was like sitting on the edge of a volcano, waiting for it to erupt . . . and finally it did!

Harry Matthews was aware that Percy was resentful about his power over the other inmates and he intended to teach him a lesson, as he always did with any newcomer who was trying to show his supremacy. He waited until Percy was scrubbing the floor outside of his cell and he walked over to him and said, 'My cell floor wants scrubbing down. See to it!'

Percy looked at him, his face puce with rage. 'You can fuck off, Matthews! I'm not one of your lackeys. I scrub down the corridors and nothing else!'

Quick as a flash, Matthews bent down, picked up the bar of soap and rammed it into Percy's mouth, nearly choking him as he did so.

Percy could scarcely breathe and Matthews pushed it down his throat a bit further.

'Now, you do as I say or you'll be taking your last breath. Do I make myself clear?'

Percy just nodded and gasped as Matthews removed the bar from his mouth and tossed it in the bucket of water, which splashed all over Percy's prison clothes. Matthews hauled him to his feet. 'In here, you do as I say when I say if you want to stay healthy. Understand?'

Unable to speak, Percy just nodded.

'Then what are you standing about for, get in there and scrub!' He shoved the bucket nearer with his foot. 'And do a good job or you'll have to do it again!' He walked away.

Percy tried to swallow. His throat hurt and he heaved as he tasted the part of the soap that had stuck to his gullet. But beneath the fear that he'd felt, he was seething. Nobody treated him like that and got away with it. His turn would come and when it did, he'd take it with both hands!

Chapter Thirty-Three

It was Christmas Eve and the newly-weds were well settled in the home they now shared. Phoebe and Tim had decorated the tree and Ben had helped with the room decorations. Now, Phoebe and Tim were preparing the vegetables and stuffing the turkey, waiting for Ben to come home. Beneath the tree were presents wrapped in Christmas paper and on the wireless Christmas carols were being played.

Ben arrived soon after, his coat collar turned up against the cold outside. 'Oh my, that smells good,' he said, sniffing the air.

'I've made a shepherd's pie for dinner,' Phoebe told him as he leant over and kissed her.

'You all right, Tim, are you being a good lad and, helping your sister?'

'I've peeled the potatoes, the carrots and the parsnips.'

'He's been a great help,' Phoebe said. 'I'll make a chef out of him before I've finished.'

Tim pulled a face. 'I didn't want to stuff the turkey, though.'

Ben burst out laughing. 'No, son. I wouldn't fancy that either.' Turning to his wife he asked, 'What time are Marj and Tony arriving tomorrow?'

'About noon. I thought we could all have a drink, then open our presents before lunch.'

Tim's face was a picture of dismay. 'Do I have to wait until then?'

'We wouldn't be that unkind, Tim,' said Ben. 'You can open yours before breakfast and we'll open our main present, saving the other small thing for later.'

They sat together to eat their dinner. The shepherd's pie and vegetables were followed by bread and butter pudding. As Ben finished his, he looked at Phoebe. 'That was really lovely, darling. I knew you were a good cook long before we married because Tim told me so. He also told me what a good housekeeper you were. Naturally, I couldn't let another man discover such a gem, so I decided to propose.'

Phoebe looked at her brother. 'What on earth made you do that?'

He beamed at her. 'I did it so Ben would marry you. I wanted a dad and I wanted him as my father . . . and it worked!'

'You devious little monkey!'

The boy looked at Ben. 'What does devious mean?'

'It means that you were extremely clever, and I owe you a debt of gratitude, young man, because you were right.'

'Oh, you two!' she exclaimed. 'I'm outnumbered when you get together.'

'We men have to stick together, isn't that right, Tim?'

The boy giggled softly. 'Yes, that's right – sorry, Phoebe.'

She just shook her head, but smiled as she did so, then the plates were cleared. 'As you two have decided to stick together, you can share the washing-up, I've finished for the night,' and she sat down.

Ben looked at Tim with a look of mock horror. 'We've been rumbled, old son, so I think it's best that we do as she asks or we won't get any turkey tomorrow. Come along. I'll wash and you wipe!'

Phoebe sat and listened to the banter coming from the kitchen and was content. Considering Ben had never had children he was so natural with Tim. No one would know he wasn't his real father and she knew how lucky she and Tim were. She said a silent prayer of thanks and thought that her father wouldn't object that another had taken his place, not with Ben. They would have liked one another had he been alive to meet him, of that she was certain.

Christmas morning arrived and, like most children at this time, Tim was up early. When he came downstairs in his pyjamas, he found that Ben was already up and had lit the fire and was preparing the breakfast.

'Merry Christmas, Tim! Phoebe will be down in a minute. Would you like a cup of tea while we wait?'

'I'll have one!' Phoebe had arrived. 'We can open the presents and then have breakfast, what do you say, Tim?'

He was already on his knees in front of the tree, shaking any gift with his name on it, trying to guess what was inside.

301

Phoebe went over to the tree and picked out a couple of presents. 'Come on, Ben, hurry up!'

They sat on the floor in front of the fire. Phoebe handed a big square parcel to her brother. 'You start!'

The boy was so excited he tore the paper off as fast as he could, so anxious was he to see what mystery was inside. When at last he opened the box, he gasped with glee as he looked at the Hornby train set with its engine, rails and carriages and with a small station building to complete the set. 'Oh! Oh! I've always wanted one of these!' He got to his feet and hugged and kissed his sister and then Ben. 'Thank you so much!'

Phoebe then handed a parcel to Ben. 'I hope you like it.'

Inside was a warm navy dressing gown, tied with a cord belt. 'That's for when you get up early in the morning,' she said, 'your other one was old.'

Ben put it on over his pyjamas and paraded around pretending to model it, to their great amusement. He then bent down and retrieved a parcel for his wife and handed it to her.

Inside was a beautiful nightgown in pale ivory, trimmed with lace. Phoebe took it out of the tissue paper and held it up against her. 'Oh, Ben, it's beautiful. Thank you.' She went and kissed him. 'But I won't be modelling it now, if you don't mind! I'll wait for later.' She gave a knowing look to her husband.

While Ben cooked breakfast, Phoebe put the turkey in the oven and started to lay the table in the dining room in readiness. Then, after eating breakfast and clearing away, they all got dressed, ready for the day ahead.

* * *

Marj and Tony arrived at noon and were greeted warmly by all. 'I've not seen you since the wedding,' Phoebe cried as she hugged her dear friend.

'Well, you've been away and then getting settled, it takes time. Everything all right, love?'

'Oh, Marj, I couldn't be happier. Ben's such a lovely man and he and Tim get along so well, you'd think Ben was his real father.'

'Just as I thought it would be. But now we've brought this with us.' She looked at Tony and grinned as she produced a bottle of champagne. 'It's to celebrate.'

'What are we celebrating?' Ben asked. 'Anything in particular?'

Tony walked over to Marj and put an arm around her. 'We're celebrating another wedding. Marj and I tied the knot last week!'

For just a moment there was a shocked silence, then everybody started talking at once. Marj held up her hand. 'Tony proposed to me while we were dancing at your wedding. He persuaded me that we could be happy together and, to my surprise, he actually said he loved me!'

Phoebe hugged the pair of them. Ben kissed Marj and shook hands with Tony. Tim was prancing around with joy.

'We went and got a special licence and grabbed a couple to be witnesses, then we went off to the Polygon for a champagne lunch. Tony has sold his house and we're living in mine,' Marj told them. 'I haven't chucked him out, as yet, so the future looks promising!'

Ben quickly produced some glasses and they all drank a toast to the happy couple – even Tim was allowed a little sip from a glass.

It was a day filled with happiness. They exchanged gifts after lunch and sat chatting and drinking by the fire as Tim set out his railway. He'd been given one or two pieces in his extra gifts to add to the station scene and his train chugged around the track all the afternoon.

It was quite late when eventually Marj and Tony left to go home. Everyone was tired but relaxed, pleased that there would be another day to rest before returning to normal. Phoebe was happy not to have to face the market in the cold ever again. Tony and Marj had said they'd continue for a while before retiring. Phoebe was delighted for her friend. She liked Tony and was sure he was the right person to take on her lovely but fiery friend. She climbed into bed and snuggled up to Ben. 'Thank you for such a lovely Christmas.'

He held her close. 'I enjoyed it too. To have my own family made it really special, and then to learn about Tony and Marj made it even better. Now go to sleep, darling, you've worked hard today.' He nuzzled her neck. 'I will be waking you in the morning, so get some rest!'

It was a new year and Phoebe settled down to married life. At first she missed her friends in the market, but not having to stand in the cold. Marj sometimes popped round on her way home to keep in touch and Ben was busy with a new case.

There had been some pilfering in the docks. In a warehouse, cases of wine were being stolen before shipping, and Ben with some of the force had been keeping watch on the warehouse. After some time and several shipments safely delivered, without results, the team was stood down.

Ben hated unsolved cases and one evening before he went home, he entered the docks, chatted to the policeman on the gate and walked to the warehouse to take a look. There was an eerie feel about the place. Usually during the day, the docks were buzzing with workers, cranes moved goods, trucks arrived and left. Ships docked and unloaded their cargo. Ships funnels blew their mournful cry . . . but now, nothing. Only strange shapes against the skyline, the odd cat fighting for scraps or chasing rats and mice. For once the noisy gulls were silent.

Just as he was about to leave, he heard the sound of a vehicle approaching and hid away in the dark.

A van pulled up in front of the warehouse. Ben realised it would have had to show a pass to get through the man on the gate, so he waited. The van slowed and backed up to the door of the warehouse. Two men got out. With a pair of wire cutters they broke the chain across the door and then smashed the lock before entering.

Ben realised he didn't have time to call for backup and looked around for something he could use as a weapon. He found a heavy piece of wood. Gripping it tightly, he entered the warehouse. The men were just in front of him, looking at the stacked cases of wine.

'Police! What do you think you are doing?'

They turned, at first startled at the voice, but after seeing Ben was alone, they pounced on him. He tried to fend them off but between them they knocked him to the ground, hitting and kicking him. Eventually, he cried out in pain and lay still. The men took one look at his bloodied countenance and ran out of the building, leaving Ben slipping in and out of consciousness.

At last the policeman from the gate found him. He'd become suspicious when the driver of the van had seemed in a great hurry to leave the dock and he came to investigate. He immediately called for an ambulance and reported his finding to headquarters.

He waited with Ben, trying to comfort him when he came to, but he was concerned; not knowing how seriously injured Ben was, he didn't try to move him. He just covered him with his tunic to try and keep him warm until the ambulance arrived.

Chapter Thirty-Four

Phoebe woke suddenly and sat up in bed. She realised that someone was banging on her front door. Grabbing her dressing gown, she hurried downstairs as Tim came out of his room and followed her. Opening the door, she saw a policeman standing there.

'Mrs Masters? Can I come in?'

Her heart sank and she opened the door wider to allow him to enter. He asked her to sit down.

'What's wrong? It's Ben, isn't it?'

'I'm afraid so. He's been injured and is now in the hospital. If you get dressed, I'll take you there.'

'Is he dead?' she asked, her heart beating like a hammer.

'No, Mrs Masters, he's been injured during a raid and is now in hospital. He was attacked by a couple of criminals. That's all I know, I'm afraid.'

She and Tim rushed upstairs and hurriedly dressed. Neither of them spoke in the rush to get ready.

Once in the hospital, they were led to a waiting room, given a cup of tea and told to wait until someone could see them. The two clung together for comfort for what seemed an eternity, until a nurse came to them and sat beside Phoebe.

'What's happened to my husband?'

The nurse held her hand. 'It's too early to say anything about his condition,' she said. 'Your husband was attacked and sustained some injuries, nothing life-threatening, but we had to wait for the X-ray. He's now in surgery. I'll send for a cup of tea for you both, but you'll have to wait until he comes out of surgery. Try not to worry, he's in safe hands, I promise.'

Tim started to cry. Phoebe held him close, unable to speak, because she knew if she tried, she'd be in tears too, which wouldn't help her brother.

Getting to her feet, the nurse said, 'This might take some time, so make yourselves comfortable. I'll bring you a couple of blankets to keep warm.'

Wrapping themselves in the blankets, the two of them tried to make themselves comfortable. Phoebe made Tim lie on a settee and covered him.

'Try and get some sleep, Tim. We may be here for a while.'

'If I fall asleep, you will wake me when somebody comes, won't you?' he asked anxiously.

'Of course I will. I promise!'

* * *

Dawn was breaking and the staff in the hospital were arriving for the change of shift. With people walking to and fro it gave the place a feeling of normality, which helped to ease the trauma that Phoebe was suffering. Tim was sound asleep, but Phoebe, although weary, was awake still.

At last a surgeon appeared, walked over to her and sat down. She quickly woke Tim.

'I'm sorry you've had to wait so long, Mrs Masters. The operation went well. Your husband is somewhat battered and bruised. He has a couple of broken ribs and a broken shoulder. We've operated on and bound his ribs and now he's in recovery. I'll let you look in the room to see your husband, just to reassure you, then I suggest you and the boy go home, get some sleep and come back this afternoon.'

He took them along the corridor to a room and put his hand on the handle. 'Just five minutes, that's all until later this afternoon.'

She and Tim approached the bed, where they looked down at the pale features of the man they both loved. Tim slipped his hand into his sister's.

'He's going to be all right, isn't he?'

She put her arm round his shoulders and tried to sound positive. 'Yes, Tim, but he needs time to heal. Now, come along, let's go home, have some breakfast and get some sleep, after all we want to look our best for Ben when we return.'

Ben wasn't the only one suffering from injuries. Percy Stanley was in a sorry state. He'd been beaten up by Harry Matthews's boys when he'd refused to run an errand for the gang boss. He'd been told to go and fetch something for Matthews from his cell by one of his men.

Percy looked at the man. 'You do it! I'm not one of his lackeys,' he'd replied.

The convict looked at him. 'You can't be that stupid to actually refuse to do this?'

'I ain't stupid. But I don't run after anyone, so bugger off!'

That evening before lockdown, two men came to his cell to teach him a lesson. They gave him two black eyes and covered him in bruises. They left him on the floor of his cell, moaning with pain. Consequently, he had to have stitches put in a deep cut over his right eyebrow.

Despite this, Percy was filled with rage and not repentant in any way. If anything, it only strengthened his resolve to get even. No one was going to take his manhood away, making him into some kind of servant! He deserved respect too. Harry Matthews would have to accept that.

Phoebe, now rested after having eaten and slept, returned to the hospital with Tim later that afternoon and they were shown into a side room and told not to stay for too long today.

Ben was propped up on pillows. He smiled when he saw them. 'I'm sorry, darling, to be such a nuisance.'

'Oh, Ben, we've been so worried. How do you feel?'

'As if I've been run over by something heavy, but I'll be all right, eventually. It'll just take time.' He looked at Tim. 'Don't look so worried, Tim. We'll still be able to play football and cricket, but not for a while.'

While Ben was trying to placate Tim, Phoebe started

unpacking the toiletries she'd brought with her and two pairs of pyjamas. She placed them carefully in the locker for when he was able to use them.

A nurse stepped inside the door. 'Five more minutes, Mrs Masters.' She shut the door as she left.

Ben looked weary and Phoebe turned to Tim. 'We best go, we can come back tomorrow after I pick you up from school.'

They both said their goodbyes, then left, but outside the hospital, Phoebe stopped. She couldn't face going home at this moment. All she wanted was the comfort of her friend.

'Let's go and see Marj,' she said to Tim.

His little face, drawn and pale, brightened and he nodded.

The market was reasonably busy as they walked towards Marj's stall. She'd just finished serving a customer and when she saw them approaching, she smiled and waved, then she saw their faces and stopped smiling.

Phoebe and Tim walked behind the stall and Phoebe rushed into the arms of her dear friend and burst into tears.

Looking at Tim, who by now was clinging to her, Marj asked, 'Whatever 'as 'appened?'

'Ben's been attacked and he's in hospital!' Then he too burst into tears.

Tony, watching from a distance, saw the distressing sight and came rushing over.

'What's going on?' Marj told him what she'd heard.

'Oh, my Lord!' He took Tim into his arms. 'You all right, my boy?'

With tears streaming down his face, Tim shook his head. 'I'm the man of the house now. I shouldn't be crying!'

Tony pulled up a stool Marj kept behind the stall and sat down, taking Tim on his knee.

'Now, you listen to me, there is no shame in crying if you're a man. I've seen the bravest of men in tears. It shows you really care, Tim. Now tell me what's happened.'

While Tim was doing so, Phoebe, now somewhat recovered, was doing the same to her friend.

'There's a story going round about an attempted robbery in the docks last night, maybe that's where Ben was injured.'

'It was such a shock, Marj. Apparently, besides being very bruised, he has a broken shoulder and two broken ribs, but apart from that, he's all right. I suppose in many ways you could say he was lucky!'

'Now, try not to worry, he's in the best place, you'll just have to be brave . . . again! Honestly, Phoebe, do you really have to make your life quite so bloody hard?'

This at least made Phoebe laugh. 'Oh, Marj! Just when everything seemed so wonderful.'

'That's life love, but you'll see it will all get better in time. Now I think we all need cheering up. So you go home, lay the table, and me and Tony will shut up for the day, go and buy some grub, a couple of bottles of Guinness to build us up, and bring them round to your place. That'll cheer us all up. What do you say?'

'I think it's a marvellous idea – and thank you.'

'Don't be daft, we're mates. Now, off you go. Tony, we're shutting up shop!'

He looked surprised. 'We are?'

'We are. We're taking some grub round to Phoebe and Tim's, so come on, let's get on with it!'

Looking at Tim, he said, 'If you ever get married, be prepared to do as you're told. Off you go, son, I'll see you later.'

Chapter Thirty-Five

The following days were busy for Phoebe. She visited Ben early afternoons before picking Tim up from school, thinking it best for the boy to be kept busy. She'd had a word with the headmaster, who was most understanding and promised they would keep an eye on him.

It was now the middle of March and Ben had been in hospital for three weeks. He was waiting anxiously for the surgeon to visit him and tell him that he was well enough to be sent home to finish his recovery, wanting, of course, to be with his family.

Several of his colleagues visited him in the evenings when Phoebe was at home and that had helped pass what had seemed to be endless days, keeping him abreast of any news.

* * *

At last he was given the good news. 'You have to take things easy,' said the surgeon. 'I'll arrange for you to have some physical therapy on that shoulder and in another couple of weeks we'll X-ray your ribs.'

'I promise I'll be careful,' Ben said. He shook the man's hand. 'Thanks, I know how much I owe you and I can never thank you enough.'

The surgeon smiled. 'It's what I'm paid to do, Mr Masters, but please take care; I don't want to see you back here in a bed. I'll send you an appointment and see you in the outpatient clinic soon.'

Ben started to gather his things together, and when Phoebe arrived, he was sitting on his bed, impatient to be gone. She, of course, was delighted and they ordered a taxi to take him home.

Once home, she made him comfortable on the settee, built up the fire to keep him warm and made a cup of tea and put a hot-water bottle in the bed in case he needed to rest.

Ben sipped his tea. 'I can't tell you just how good it feels to be at home with you. There was a time when I wondered just how much longer it would be.'

'Oh Ben!' They snuggled up together, neither talking, but both needing to feel the closeness of the other.

When Tim walked in from school, he was thrilled to see Ben and rushed over to him, flinging his arms around him. 'Oh, Ben, you're home!'

'Gently!' Phoebe called out, seeing the boy's enthusiasm.

It was towards the end of April when Ben was given the all clear from the hospital and was able to return to work.

As he walked into the police station, he gave a deep sigh of relief. At last, he was back to normal. These past two weeks especially had been hard when he'd felt fit but had to wait for the doctor to sign him off, but now he could put it all behind him.

He was greeted warmly by his colleagues, who teased him unmercifully about taking time off from work, but beneath the banter, they were pleased to see him back.

His boss called him into his office and asked him to sit down.

'Glad to see you back, Ben. What have the doctors said to you?'

'That I'm fit for work, but not to do anything too strenuous too soon and to give myself time. But I feel fine and so pleased to be back.'

They chatted about various cases on the books before Ben was dismissed. He returned to his desk and was given some work to be done. He gave a sigh of relief at being back to normality and set to.

There was no such thing as normality at Wormwood Scrubs. Every day there was some incident or other, not surprising when you considered the type of inmates, who lived by their own rules – without consideration to others – and where power was the key and money talks.

Percy Stanley had neither. He who thought he was better than anyone else, found that here he was less than a nobody, nameless and unimportant. The very reason that had put him inside. He didn't have the money to buy a retinue. No one was interested in following him. If he started complaining about anything, others would just walk away. He had not one friend inside – but he did have an enemy. Harry Matthews. The murderer who had been inside for so long he was the king of the castle! He was the boss among the convicts and had been for longer than anyone could remember.

It was a recognised fact that sometimes a new inmate, full of his own importance, would try and flex his muscles. It was amusing for a while, but then Matthews would get bored and bring the game to an end in various ways, depending on how irritated he was by the offender – and Percy had really annoyed him. His refusal to do his bidding was not to be tolerated. If he let it pass it would appear to be a sign of weakness, and that was not something he suffered from at all.

Percy wasn't an idiot. He recognised that he was playing with fire, but his arrogance was such that he would not accept the situation. He was, however, careful when scrubbing the corridors after his last run-in with Matthews. He could still taste the soap stuck in his gullet whenever he thought about the incident, but the indignity of it struck in his craw and he wanted revenge. He knew that Matthews liked having fruit in his cell – it was one of his perks – and he carefully collected small iron filings and shattered glass as he cleaned the floors after some work had been done on a faulty window in his section, which had to be drilled. Then, when he was cleaning the area outside of the cell, he carefully cut small sections in an apple with a tip of a razor blade he'd acquired and inserted the sharp pieces of iron and glass, pulling the apple skin carefully into place. He expected that his adversary would just pick up the fruit and bite into it without paying attention. Then he waited.

That evening after everyone was locked up for the night and the prisoners filled their time reading or talking or making a noise, there was a sudden sound of yelling, running feet, keys rattling, doors opening and shutting, coming from the section that housed Harry Matthews. Percy lay back on his bed and chuckled.

At breakfast the following morning, Matthews was not in attendance. Percy collected his meal and sat at his usual table and looked around.

'Harry Matthews not sitting and holding court?' he said to the man beside him. 'What's going on?'

'Didn't you hear the noise last night? He was rushed to the hospital, bleeding from the mouth. Don't know more than that.'

Percy didn't answer.

A week later Harry Matthews was back in the dining room at breakfast time. Percy didn't look in his direction, but he could feel that he was being watched. Later that day, when the prisoners were allowed into the exercise yard, Percy was sitting alone, having a cigarette, when Matthews strolled over.

'That was very stupid of you,' he sneered. 'You'd best keep looking over your shoulder, because your days are numbered.'

Percy just stared at him.

Later that day, Percy was summoned to see the governor. He was marched into his office and stood in front of the large table, the governor sat staring at him.

'I like to run a tight ship here, Stanley. I'm well aware of what goes on in my prison. I know about Harry Matthews and his followers. It may surprise you to know that I don't mind his so-called exalted position because his control keeps everyone in their place and in fact it helps me and my warders to run the prison without too much hassle. That is, until we get someone like you in. A person who thinks he's important, special. Well, you are not! You're here because you committed a murder and were given life instead of the rope. But you are not satisfied to just serve your time, you want to be something you're not and never will be. I'm not having you upset my record, because if you stay here, Matthews will have to eliminate you because you're a nuisance and you won't stop making trouble – I know your kind. Now, I can't have that, so I'm transferring you today to Winchester Prison. The warder will go with you while you pack. You may go.'

Percy was marched to his cell and made to pack his belongings. As he did so, he had mixed feelings. Maybe it was for the best. There would eventually have been a settling between him and Matthews and Percy knew he would be the loser. He was content that he'd put the convict in hospital and that was enough for his inflated ego. In his own mind, he'd won.

As he walked along the corridor with the warder, Matthews stood watching him, grinning broadly. As Percy glared at him, Matthews drew his finger across his throat and then pointed at Percy. This unnerved him. Was he sending him a message?

Chapter Thirty-Six

Ben had been sent to Winchester Prison to interview a prisoner and was standing at the front desk when Percy Stanley arrived, escorted by a warder.

Ben looked at him. 'I thought they sent you to the Scrubs?'

Percy glared at him. 'Me and another prisoner didn't get on. He thought he ran the place and I didn't agree. So they moved me to keep the other bloke safe.'

The warder who'd accompanied him burst out laughing. 'My goodness, Stanley, you have a fertile imagination.'

Ben, now curious, asked, 'Who was this person?'

'A bloke called Harry Matthews, just another con.'

'You tried to take on Matthews? I can't believe even you would be that stupid!'

At that moment, the desk sergeant appeared and spoke to Ben. 'Right, Detective, your man is in interview room three.'

Ben glared at Percy. 'You're where you should be, shut away behind bars. It's your poor brother I feel sorry for. He didn't have a chance at leading a good life because of you, but at least his final few months gave him a taste of what could have been. He deserved that, at least.' He walked away, leaving Percy seething with rage.

That evening, as Phoebe was about to serve their meal, Ben said, 'I saw Percy Stanley today.'

Phoebe nearly dropped the plate she was holding as her hands started shaking.

Ben got to his feet and held her tightly. 'It's all right, darling, it was in Winchester Prison. He's safely locked away!'

'Oh my God! For one awful moment I thought he was free. The idea that we might meet terrified me.'

'You've no need to worry. He was just being transferred. Apparently, he'd been causing trouble and they moved him. If he doesn't behave here, he'll be put in solitary confinement. That would soon calm him down. Now, forget him, he's the past . . . shut away . . . out of our lives.'

But as she served the dinner, Phoebe knew it would take some time for her to forget her dealings with Percy Stanley.

During the following few weeks, Phoebe settled down to being a housewife, but she found the days long and badly missed the camaraderie of the market traders, and in particular her dear friend Marj. Having finished her housework one day, she put on her coat and headed for Kingsland Market.

As she entered the market, she could see Marj was sitting down. This was unusual because the place was busy. Marj only ever took a seat when business was quiet. When she stood in front of the stall, she was shocked to see how ill her friend appeared to be. She walked behind the stall and put her hand on her shoulder.

'What's wrong, you look awful?'

'I feels rough, girl, and no mistake.' She started coughing and holding her chest when she did so.

Phoebe put her hand on Marj's forehead. She was burning up.

'I'm packing up your stall and taking you home,' she declared. Just then, Tony came hurrying over and Phoebe told him what she was going to do.

'I've told her to stay in bed, Phoebe, but she won't listen.'

Kneeling beside Marj, Phoebe said, 'You stay here, and I'll be bringing flowers to your funeral and I'm not going to let that happen. Give me the keys to your lock-up!'

Marj only hesitated for a second, then handed the keys to her.

'Right, now you sit tight, and don't you dare move.'

Phoebe eventually managed to get her friend home. Marj was so breathless that it took a while. When they arrived, Phoebe helped her get undressed and put her to bed, then went to make a hot drink with some lemons Tony had brought over and some honey she found in the cupboard. Once she'd settled her friend and made sure she was comfortable, she went quickly to the doctor's surgery and asked for the doctor to visit, then returned and waited, having warned Marj in advance. While she waited, she bathed her forehead with a damp cloth, to try to keep her fever down.

The doctor duly arrived and examined his patient thoroughly after taking her temperature, which made him frown when he looked at the thermometer.

'You should have been in bed days ago, Mrs Jackson. You have pneumonia!'

Phoebe's heart sank. This was what her mother had died from.

'I ain't going in no 'ospital!' Marj looked rebellious as she glared at the doctor.

'But you need looking after,' he said. 'Without someone to do so, I can't be held responsible for the outcome.'

'I'll take care of her!' Phoebe said. 'Tell me what to do and I'll look after her.'

The doctor looked at Phoebe and decided she was capable. 'I'll give you a prescription for the patient's cough.' Then he gave her instructions. 'I'll pop in tomorrow and see how she is.'

At that moment, Tony arrived. 'I've shut up and come home. Is there anything I can do?'

Phoebe handed him the prescription and quickly wrote a note to Tim and Ben. 'If you could collect this prescription and leave this note on my kitchen table so Tim and Ben will know where I am and why, that would be a great help. And buy some more lemons!'

Tony rushed off to do as he was asked, thanking Phoebe for staying. When she was alone, she found some more pillows and propped Marj up higher in the bed to help her breathing and to stop her coughing so much. Then she made another drink after being told that the patient needed plenty of liquids. When Marj seemed settled, Phoebe searched the larder and made a pan of vegetable soup as

Marj had told her she'd lost her appetite. She planned to get Tony to buy some meat tomorrow to make a broth and some eggs to scramble.

Making a pot of tea for herself, Phoebe sat in a chair beside the bed and, keeping a cool cloth on Marj's forehead, watched while her friend dozed fitfully.

Early that evening Ben brought Tim to the house to see what was going on. She saw the look on Tim's face when she said that Marj had pneumonia. She knelt beside him.

'Marj isn't going to die, Tim, because the doctor and I won't allow it. I promise!' But the lad didn't look convinced.

Ben went over to him. 'Not everyone who has pneumonia dies, Tim. My mother had it one winter, and look at her now. Marj is going to be looked after by all of us, she wouldn't dare let us down now, would she?'

'I suppose not,' he said quietly. 'Can I go and see her, Phoebe?'

'Yes, come with me. She was asleep a while ago, so we'll creep in. All right?'

He nodded and followed her upstairs. As it happened, Marj had only just woken, and seeing Tim, she smiled at him. 'How's my favourite man, then?'

Tim's look of relief was so touching that Phoebe welled up inside. The poor boy had lost too many whom he'd loved, she could understand his fear.

He rushed over to the bed and gave Marj a hug.

'Best not let Tony see you 'ugging me,' she teased, ''e may get jealous!'

This made Tim chuckle and his fear subsided. Phoebe hustled him out of the room.

'How are you feeling now?' asked Phoebe.

'It was good to sleep, but I'm chilled. I can't seem to get warm.'

'I'll make you a hot-water bottle and find another couple of blankets. I've made some soup – if you could eat a little, that would help – and I'll light a fire in here.' It was only a small grate but would give out quite a heat in the room, which wasn't very big.

'Oh, Phoebe, love, you're such a good girl. I'm sorry to put you to so much trouble.' She started coughing.

Phoebe gave her another dose of cough medicine and a sip of hot lemon, and the cough subsided.

'I'll just go and do the bottle. I'll send Tony up to keep you company.'

While she had a break, she and Ben made arrangements that allowed her to stay at Marj's house. He would do the cooking at home, see to Tim and bring some food over so she could cook for Tony and herself. He and Tim would pop in every evening to see if they could help and then just wait to see how Marj was. He had been thoughtful enough to pack a bag with her nightclothes, a change of day clothes and an extra blanket to keep her warm when she sat with her friend.

'I remember Dad had to sit up many a night with Mum when she had pneumonia. Get your sleep when you can, is my advice, or you will be out on your feet and we don't want you to be ill too. I'll fill the coal scuttle before I go, so you can keep a low fire on during the night, then Tony can fill it again before he goes to work.' He gathered her in his arms and kissed her longingly. 'I do hate sleeping alone, so I'm praying for Marj's quick recovery.'

'I do know what you mean,' she told him. 'Oh Ben, do you think she's going to be all right?'

He tipped up her chin. 'We can only do what we can, but with so much care, she stands a good chance. However, it will probably get worse before it gets better. Be prepared for that.'

While they were making plans, Tony lay beside Marj on the bed, his arm around her.

'Is there anything I can do for you, love? You only have to say.'

She gave a wan smile. 'Just hold me, love, it makes me feel safe, somehow. I'm sorry to be such a nuisance.'

'What are you talking about, you daft woman? You're sick, that's not your fault. I miss you, darling, bossing me about, being with me every day and night. I feel so useless.'

'There's nothing you can do, Tony, except help Phoebe. Get any shopping and stuff like that. She's such a good girl, I don't know what I'd do without her . . . or you, but I'm so tired, darling, I want to sleep.'

He climbed off the bed, tucked her bedclothes in, kissed her softly and said, 'I'll be downstairs if you want me.'

When he walked into the living room, Ben saw the worry etched on his face. 'She's going to be all right, Tony, but it will take time.'

The man could hardly speak. 'If anything happened to her . . .'

Ben put a hand on Tony's shoulder. 'Nothing bad is going to happen to Marj, she's a strong woman, she'll get over this in time, you'll see.'

Tony just nodded. Ben poured him a cup of tea and placed the cup before him. 'Here, drink this.'

* * *

The following morning the doctor called again. Marj still had a very high temperature, which was a worry, but he was pleased with the way Phoebe was looking after his patient.

'The next two days will be crucial,' he told her. 'We have to get her temperature down, but if she's chilled, we have to keep her warm. Keep giving her liquids and try and get her to eat something to build her strength. I'll call back in a couple of days unless you're worried, then let me know and I'll come.'

It was a long day. Phoebe sponged Marj down, trying to lower her temperature. She managed to get her to eat a little porridge in the morning and some gruel at lunchtime, but she didn't want much, saying she wasn't hungry. However, in the evening she did eat a little scrambled egg and a little bread and milk. But she still had a high fever.

That night was a nightmare. Marj was restless and chilled, even a hot-water bottle didn't seem to help. Phoebe insisted Tony went and slept on the sofa to get a night's sleep, while she slept on a chair beside the bed. In time, Marj stopped shivering and eventually fell asleep.

In the morning, Phoebe woke and looked at the sleeping figure in the bed. She took a blanket and covered her, then put other blankets on top. She made another hot-water bottle and placed that under the covers. Tony had built up the fire when she went downstairs to make a pot of tea. She was weary, having only slept fitfully, checking on her friend during the night, until through sheer exhaustion she had slept for a few hours. She heard Marj call, poured a cup of weak tea and took it upstairs.

'Good morning!' she said as she walked into the bedroom. 'How are you feeling today?'

'I would love to 'ave a bath.'

'You're not strong enough for that. I'll bring up a bowl of water and give you a blanket bath, but I don't want you getting cold, so it'll be a lick and a promise for now. All right?'

'Whatever you says, nurse.'

After Phoebe had finished, she could see that the effort had tired her friend. She plumped up her pillows and went downstairs and soft-boiled two eggs, took them out of their shells and mashed them up with a little butter. This she fed to Marj with a little bread.

'Can't have you wasting away,' Phoebe teased.

Marj looked at her and spoke quietly. 'Am I going to get better, love, or is this it?'

Phoebe was shocked. 'Don't you dare say such a thing to me! Of course you're going to get better and I'll tell you why. Because you're a feisty, bossy, stubborn woman who never gives up . . . and because I'm a bloody good nurse!'

Marj smiled. 'That you are. God, girl, we've been through the mill between us, ain't we?'

'Oh, Marj, we have, but look at us. Apart from you being poorly at this moment, we've survived. We are like the phoenix who rises from the ashes, you and me. Indomitable, that's us!' She rinsed a cold cloth and placed it on Marj's forehead. 'Now, try and get some rest.' She kissed her on her cheek. 'Call me if you need me.'

Sitting in an easy chair before the fire, Phoebe thought back to when the woman upstairs had been there beside her so many times in her life when she'd needed help and a friend. Their friendship was a bond so strong that it bound them together for life and Phoebe wasn't going to let anything happen to her if she had anything to do with it. But as she sat alone, she said a silent prayer, asking for the deliverance of the woman who meant so much to her.

Chapter Thirty-Seven

When Ben arrived at Marj's house that evening, he saw just how tired his wife was. Tony was upstairs with his wife and Ben insisted that Phoebe lay on the settee. He covered her with a blanket, put cushions at her head and told her to sleep.

'But, Marj—' she began.

'I'm here, so is Tony. We're not useless, we can take care of the patient. Tim's at his friend's house and sleeping there tonight, so relax. I'll make something light for her to eat. Tony and I will take turns sitting with her through the night. You need to rest, I'm giving you the night off.'

She was so weary, she didn't argue, just shut her eyes and slept.

Ben knew how to look after Marj, having seen his

mother suffer with pneumonia. He kept a damp cloth on the patient's forehead, managed to feed her with some gruel that Phoebe had made, gave her something to drink and left Tony to sit with her and see to her other needs.

Phoebe woke just as the dawn was breaking the next morning. She stretched, and in the glow from the fire, saw Ben, covered in a blanket, asleep in an armchair. She quietly rose from her bed on the settee and crept upstairs. Tony was sleeping beside the bed in a chair and Marj was just waking up. Phoebe put a finger to her lips and pointed to Tony.

'Are you all right?' she quietly asked her friend, but she noticed how Marj's breathing was laboured and was pleased the doctor was calling later that day.

She plumped up the pillows and lifted Marj higher in the bed. She gave her a drink of water and some cough medicine, washed her face and hands and helped her onto the commode.

'I'll go and make a nice cup of tea for us,' she whispered.

She discovered that Ben, already making the tea, was holding some bread against the fire to toast. She leant over and kissed him. 'I can't tell you how good it is to wake up and see you here. How was the night?'

'Not that good. Marj's breathing was so bad, I boiled pans of water and put it near her to moisten the air. That seemed to help. It's good that the doctor will be here today. I'm going home now to take a bath and change for work. I'm not due in until lunchtime. I'll leave some food for Tim for when he gets home and I'll cook us a meal later, so I'll not be back tonight.'

She hugged him. 'Thanks for letting me sleep. I feel so much better this morning. Now, off you go.'

Later that morning the doctor called. He examined his patient. Afterwards he spoke to Phoebe downstairs.

'Mrs Jackson isn't going to improve until her fever breaks. Just keep a close eye on her during the next twenty-four hours.' He patted her arm. 'You're doing a fine job, Phoebe, you're as good as any of my nurses. You know where I am if you need me, but I'll be back tomorrow.'

During the night, Marj was sweating so much with the fever that Tony and Phoebe had to change her nightclothes and the bedding several times. Phoebe boiled pans of water, as had Ben the night before, to aid the patient's breathing, continuously wiping Marj's face with a cool cloth, sponging her arms and legs trying to stem the all-encompassing fever. She gave her sips of water and fanned her with a folded newspaper to give her a modicum of comfort. By six o'clock the next morning, their hard work was rewarded. The fever seemed to have broken and the patient lay calm and fell into a deep sleep.

'She's all right, isn't she?' asked Tony, now fearful at the stillness of his poor wife.

Phoebe felt Marj's forehead and smiled. 'She's not burning up any more, I think the fever's broken at last.' The poor man burst into tears and fled the room. Phoebe sat in the chair beside the bed and she too shed a tear. She'd been so scared during the night as she bathed Marj, wondering if her friend was going to die. The sense of relief was overwhelming, and she started to sob, burying her face into the bedclothes to muffle the sound, because she couldn't stop.

It took several weeks for Marj to recover and rebuild her strength. Eventually, she became restless and talked about going back to work. Tony had been concerned about her returning to the market, working outside again and facing the cold weather when winter came around. He shared his worries with Phoebe one day. She too had reservations about her friend's continuing health, but she had a plan and had been looking into it. Then she went to visit Marj.

Marj put the kettle on to make some tea, brought out some home-made biscuits and a cake and sat down.

'You've been baking, I see,' Phoebe said as she took a slice of cake.

'Well, I 'ad to do something. I'm going mad 'ere, love. Tony don't want me to go back in the market, so what the bloody 'ell am I going to do with meself all day?'

'That's what I came to see you about. Don't get me wrong, I love being a housewife, looking after my two men, but you can only clean a house so often. I miss the market, meeting people.'

'Don't tell me you want your stall back?' Marj asked in surprise.

'Not exactly.' She leant forward, eyes bright with excitement. 'There's an empty shop for rent on the edge of the market. It has a nice big showroom and a storage room and toilet at the back. It's in good nick, just needs a coat of paint. How about you and me opening up a shop together? We could sell anything we think would make a bob or two.

Clothes, bric-a-brac, small furniture. Anything! I've even got a name.'

Marj looked at her in astonishment. 'Well, what is the name?'

'Trash and Treasure! You know, Marj, one person's trash is another person's treasure. What do you think?'

Marj burst out laughing. 'I think it's a bloody marvellous idea! 'Ave you told Ben about this?'

'I did run it past him last night. He was a bit taken aback, thinking I was content. What do men know? Anyway, when I explained I needed to do this, he was all for it. If you're really interested, I could get the keys tomorrow and we could go take a look.'

Marj walked round the table and hugged Phoebe. 'Oh, love, of course I'm interested. You and me in business together, what could be better . . . and under cover! Blimey! That's coming up in the world, girl, ain't it?'

The following morning, the two of them inspected the empty premises together. As they walked around and began to plan the interior, thinking where to place a counter and display their goods, the two women felt the mounting excitement as, mentally, the shop began to take shape.

'We could go to auction sales and pick up a few pieces on offer. If we could buy at a good price with a little profit, we'd be fine,' Marj suggested. 'I could have a word with my friend in London where we bought your wedding dress. She'd help us out, I'm sure.'

'Oh, Marj, what a brilliant idea!' Phoebe looked round the empty space. 'We could have a counter and till here, over there we could have dress rails, a display unit for smaller bits and pieces. If we bought furniture items, we could place them around the shop, perhaps show them off as if they were in a room, you know – dress the scene. Let's face it, display is important.'

That evening at Phoebe's home, the four of them gathered, with Tim listening avidly.

'Can I still come and work for you on a Saturday?' The boy too had missed the market and his ability to make some pocket money.

'Of course you can,' Marj said. 'You're part of the team, my boy.'

This delighted him and he beamed at them.

It was decided that both couples would form a partnership and invest a certain amount of money each to cover the rent and enough items to open up a month later, which would give them time to paint the interior. Marj would go to London and see her friend and Phoebe would search for local auction sales. She would go and look at the goods on display the day before the sale and make a list of the things she thought would be suitable. Then she and Marj would attend the sale in the hope of buying items at a good price, while Tony, Tim and Ben would paint the interior of the shop. Ben insisted on drawing up a contract, making the venture a proper partnership. As he said, 'If we're going into business together, let's do it properly.'

It was a frantic four weeks! Marj had made a deal with her friend in London and had acquired some good clothes, with more to come if required. The women had been to several auction sales, which had been an education. There they realised that the dealers always got the best bargains. They managed to buy some items, but the stuff they really wanted, the dealers could afford and they couldn't. Being canny women, they advertised in the local paper for furniture items and found this to be to their advantage.

Eventually opening day arrived. Across the front of the shop was the name: TRASH AND TREASURE. Inside the bright showroom stood the counter and three dress rails full of attractive gowns for all occasions. There was also a display of long necklaces, a popular item with the ladies, and a selection of fashionable cloche hats in various colours.

Across the room they had four chairs surrounding a table with a vase of flowers, a couple of footstools on a rug and a colourful pot on a high stand with a large aspidistra in it. It looked like a corner of a cosy room. There was a rocking chair and a chest with brass handles beside it. Then a table with a collection of mixed items – odd, pretty china cups and saucers, combs for hair, a couple of ladies' fans. Opera glasses. It was like an Aladdin's cave.

Phoebe and Marj stood looking at their efforts. Marj hugged her friend. 'Well, would you ever believe this? I've stood outside this market in all kinds of weather at my stall and been 'appy in my own way, but today I can't believe 'ow thrilled I am to 'ave put that bloody stall away for good!'

'I just wish Mum and Dad could see this day,' Phoebe said wistfully.

'Oh, darlin', believe me, they'll be up there looking down on us, pleased as punch, of that I'm certain. Well, shall we open the door to the public?'

'We'd better, there's a queue already.' Phoebe walked to the door and unlocked it. 'Welcome to Trash and Treasure,' she said and stepped back.

Tony, standing at his stall, looked across the market and saw the people clamouring to enter the shop. He was thrilled for Marj's sake as well as Phoebe's. At one time he thought he was going to lose this wonderful woman he'd married, and it had nearly destroyed him, but now all he could do was smile with happiness.

Later that afternoon, Ben arrived. He looked round and saw several empty places where things had been sold. Ladies were there sorting through the gowns, being shown into the stockroom to try them on, where a curtain had been put up to give a modicum of privacy.

'How's it going?' he quietly asked Phoebe.

'You wouldn't believe it,' she said, grinning broadly. 'We've been so busy, it's just as well we have some reserve stock. We're going to have to use it already!'

'That's marvellous, darling. I think we should all go out to dinner tonight and celebrate. I'll go and make arrangements with Tony. I'll see you later. I'll come and help you when you close. Why don't you put a notice in the door asking the public if they have any goods of quality to sell, you might get lucky?'

'What a brilliant idea. I will. See you later.'

It transpired that one or two of the customers had already approached Marj about things they'd like to sell, and she had a list of goods and addresses to visit during closing hours.

* * *

That evening, they arranged for a neighbour to sit with Tim and the four of them went out to dinner. Ben ordered a bottle of champagne to celebrate. He held up his glass. 'To Trash and Treasure!' The others echoed his words.

He and Tony sat listening while their two wives gave them a detailed description of their first day. Marj was first. ''Ere! I had to rescue one gown from two ladies. Both wanted it and neither would let go. I was terrified they was going to rip it between them, so I took it off them and tossed a coin to find a winner. Really, such be'aviour!'

'There was a reporter from the local paper taking pictures of the shop! He was asking about me and Marj setting up business together. He said the article would be in tomorrow's edition,' Phoebe told them.

'I know,' said Ben. 'He's a mate of mine and I mentioned about you both starting out. He said it sounded interesting, you both being traders before. A bit of local interest, he said.'

'Ooh! We'll be in the papers, Phoebe! Local stars, love. We won't charge for autographs, they can 'ave them for free!'

'It's great publicity, Marj. We best go in early to make sure we're ready.'

'What 'appens if we're too busy to go to sales for new stock, that's my only worry?'

'We'll send the men! After all, they are part of the business, they can do some work! We'll tell them what we need and if they see something they think we can sell and they can get it at a good price, they can buy it. Ben can go when he's off duty and Tony whenever there's a sale we can't get to. A day away from the market will be a treat, won't it,

Tony?' Phoebe was grinning as she put the question to him.

He looked across the table at Ben. 'What have we done? We have created two dragons, breathing fire – and I'm no St George, they scare me to death!'

The men started laughing at the look of consternation on the women's faces.

'I'm only joking,' Tony assured them. 'Frankly, I'd enjoy the change, what about you, Ben?'

'I'm delighted to be a part of the actual business. Who knows, if the shop does well enough, you and I could retire!'

This caused much hilarity and the meal ended on a very happy note before they made their way home after such an exciting day, all ready for the morrow.

Chapter Thirty-Eight

The reporter had done a good job. On an inside page there was a picture of the shop and one of Marj and Phoebe standing outside. The man had done his homework and had written about Phoebe's father working a stall until he'd had to go to war and how she'd taken over at such an early age and carried on until her eventual marriage to the local detective. He had done the same about Marj, covering her long history in the market and her marriage to Tony, another trader, and now the ladies' latest enterprise. It was indeed a fascinating story of local interest. The women were thrilled.

During the day, some of the traders came in to congratulate them and tease them about the publicity, but it was all done with good humour. It also brought in more customers who'd read the piece. For Phoebe it was even more touching, as one or two remembered her father, which meant so much to her as they all spoke so highly of him. She told Tim all about it over dinner that night.

Although the boy was pleased, he looked a little sad. 'I don't remember that much about him, Phoebe. Only little things – and that's awful!'

'No, it isn't, Tim,' Ben assured him. 'You were only five when he went away to war. You at least have some memories of him, there are many children who were even younger than you who never knew their father, so don't feel badly about it. It's just the way things are during wartime. He would be very proud of the boy you've grown into. I know that because I'm proud of you, and so is Phoebe.'

'Don't forget you're coming to work in the shop on Saturday, Tim, because we need another pair of hands.'

This seemed to pacify him. 'I'll get to spend time with Marj, too. It'll seem strange not to see her behind a stall and with no Ben to buy fish and chips for!'

'No, and we won't have them smelling out the shop either! But you can have them at lunchtime if you eat outside, well away from the door,' Phoebe told him.

Tim hadn't seen the shop until he went with Phoebe on the Saturday. Once inside, he was more than surprised. 'Oh, Phoebe, it's so posh!'

Marj happened to walk in at that moment. 'We've come up in the world, Tim. What do you think?'

'It's lovely.' He looked around. 'It's really special. All these lovely things.' He wandered around looking at everything. 'No toys, though!'

Marj and Phoebe looked at each other. 'I never thought of that,' said Phoebe.

'Maybe we should in future. We could try a few pieces and see what happens.' Marj hugged Tim. 'Thanks, lovely boy, if you get any more ideas say so, all right?'

'All right,' he said, suddenly feeling important. He went off to find Laura and tell her all about his new job in the shop. Then he took her inside to take a look, walking her round it, showing everything on sale in detail.

'Will you look at him,' Marj said. 'He'll make an excellent salesman.'

'I'm determined he won't be working a stall,' Phoebe said.

'Quite right too!' Marj agreed.

During the next two months, business continued to thrive and Tony found himself visiting auctions and house clearances more and more. Eventually it was decided that he would give up his stall to concentrate on the buying. It seemed that he had a good eye for a bargain and was a great asset to the shop.

Gowns would arrive from Marj's friend in London when required, as the ladies that had discovered the shop were delighted with the different styles that were on offer, and many of them had special requests for gowns for special occasions, which Marj would endeavour to find with the help of her friend – at a price, of course.

Tim's suggestion about the toys had paid off and there was a corner of the shop designated to the needs of children, including a selection of children's clothes as well as toys.

The women had discussed items for men, as they were

not represented in any way, but they decided against it. 'We really don't have the room,' Phoebe said. 'I think we should stick with what we've got, but I think we could enlarge our selection of hats, they've sold well.'

Marj's friend had given them an address of a wholesaler of hats and they had acquired more stock, which was moving quickly, to their delight.

Towards the end of the summer, business was so good, the four of them met at Phoebe and Ben's home to plan for the future. It was suggested they rent the empty shop next door and move the furniture there, leaving Trash and Treasure to continue to sell all the other items. They worked out their finances against the profits they'd made and decided it would be a good idea. Ben would take over from Tony when he was off duty, to allow Tony to continue his buying, and if this didn't work they would hire someone to work in the shop so it was always covered.

'Blimey!' exclaimed Marj. 'Would you 'ave ever believed it this time last year when we stood outside selling from our stalls! Now look at us, livin' the life of Riley!'

'All because you were ill,' Phoebe reminded her.

'It was your idea, love. I'd 'ave never 'ave thought of it.'

'We have to think of a name for the new shop,' Ben said. 'Any ideas?'

'Masters and Jackson, I would suggest,' said Tony.

They all agreed it had a certain ring about it. They decided to get two men in to paint the shop as they were all too busy to do it themselves. In the meantime, Tony would spend his time buying stock for when they opened.

'We'll have more room when they take the furniture out,'

said Phoebe, 'we could build up the clothing section, which is where we make the most money.' And so it was decided.

At Christmas, the market was decorated as usual, the stalls with their lanterns and decorations, the phonograph playing carols, the two shops tastefully decorated. Extra toys were bought in to help fill the stockings of expectant children, which sold well, and on Christmas Eve the four of them gathered at Ben and Phoebe's. Marj and Tony were staying with them over the holiday so they could all celebrate together.

As they all sat down to dinner on Christmas Eve, Ben poured them all a glass of champagne, even a small one for Tim, which delighted him. Then Ben stood up.

'I want to make a toast. Little did I know when I was posted to the market as an undercover policeman that I would have been so lucky to not only meet the woman who would become my wife and a young boy who would become my son, but also Marj and Tony, my two great friends. Look at us now! Business partners into the bargain.'

Everybody cheered.

'I just want to thank you all for being in my life. But there is one more thing, which makes it complete: my darling wife is pregnant! Our baby is due in June.'

Everyone spoke at once. Marj got up and hugged Phoebe and planted a kiss on Ben's cheek, Tony shook Ben's hand and kissed Phoebe. Tim, who had been told the good news earlier, was looking delighted.

'So, my dear friends, a toast to friendship and a new arrival!'

They all repeated the toast and drank. Tim wrinkled his nose from the champagne bubbles, which made him sneeze to everyone's great amusement.

Marj put an arm around the boy. 'So darlin', you'll 'ave a brother or a sister, but whichever it is, you'll always be my favourite boy!'

He flung his arms around her. 'Oh, Marj, I do love you!'

Blinking away the tears that threatened to flow, she looked at him. 'And I love you too and don't you ever forget it!'

That night as they lay snuggled up together, Ben looked at Phoebe. 'Thank you for making me so happy. Imagine it all began when you sent Tim over to me on my first day in the market to ask if I wanted some fish and chips!'

She started laughing. 'My mum always used to say a way to a man's heart is through his stomach!'

'There! There's me sure it was because of my good looks.'

'Oh, that was part of it. Had you been a shabby, ordinary-looking soul I'd have let you starve.'

He chuckled softly. 'No, you wouldn't, you've too soft a heart for that.'

Sighing she said, 'We've been through so much when you think of it. You helped me when Mum died, when I had trouble with Percy Stanley, when Marj was so ill. Those were dire days.'

'But we came through them, darling, and now we've the businesses, both making money, two great partners and a baby coming. How lucky we are. Now, you know that Tim will get us up early, so I suggest you get some sleep, because tomorrow is going to be a busy day.' He kissed her. 'I love you, Mrs Masters.'

'I love you too, now go to sleep.' But as she closed her eyes, she thought back to the early days and how Ben had been at her side helping her through so much. He'd been like a rock when she was really struggling and before she knew him well. She and Tim were so lucky to have found him and now he'd have another child to raise. Their life was complete, and it would be good for Tim to have a brother or sister of his own. She let out a sigh of contentment. Ever since she'd opened the shop, she'd been so busy that finally she'd laid to rest the ghost of Percy Stanley. No longer did she have bad dreams about him, she never even thought about him any more. He was now very much buried in the past. She had so much more to think about. Especially now. Tomorrow was Christmas Day, peace on earth and goodwill to all men, as the saying goes. *That's exactly how I feel*, she thought. 'Merry Christmas, everybody,' she whispered as she snuggled down next to the man she loved.

There was little goodwill inside Winchester Prison on Christmas Day. Percy Stanley was found dead in one of the toilets with his throat cut and a note pinned to his top. I WARNED YOU, it read.

Acknowledgements

I don't know who to thank for giving me the ability to write which allows me to do the work that I love. I am so blessed. Thank you, Judith Murdoch, my agent of over twenty years, who saw something in my first manuscript.

All the editors I've worked with who have helped me along the way, I thank you and also my two daughters, Beverley and Maxine, who have loved and encouraged me.

JUNE TATE was born in Southampton and spent the early years of her childhood in the Cotswolds. After leaving school she became a hairdresser on cruise ships the *Queen Mary* and the *Mauretania*, meeting many Hollywood film stars and VIPs on her travels. After her marriage to an airline pilot, she lived in Sussex and Hampshire before moving to Estoril in Portugal. June, who has two adult daughters, now lives in Sussex.

junetate.info